W9-CLG-581

And
New Stars
Burn

WITHDRAWN
FROM THE RODMAN PUBLIC LIBRARY

Faith Baldwin 1893-

And New Stars Burn

Thorndike Press • Thorndike, Maine

RODMAN PUBLIC LIBRARY

Library of Congress Cataloging in Publication Data:

Baldwin, Faith, 1893-
    And new stars burn / Faith Baldwin.
    p.   cm.
    ISBN 0-89621-901-1 (alk. paper : lg. print)
    1. Large type books. I. Title.
    [PS3505.U97A74   1989]   89-4439
    813'.52--dc20   CIP

Copyright 1940, 1941, © renewed 1968, 1969 by Faith
Baldwin Cuthrell.
All rights reserved.

Large Print edition available in North America by
arrangement with Henry Holt and Company.

Large Print edition available in the British Commonwealth
by arrangement with Harold Ober Associates.

Cover design by James B. Murray.

Dedication

This book is dedicated to places and through these to the people who made them memorable. It began in, and therefore belongs to, a house in Ross, Marin County, California, which we have never seen. It belongs to Ewa, on the Island of Oahu. And to many places in Honolulu — Puiwa Road and Kalakaua Avenue; Malakai Heights and Mott-Smith Drive; Diamond Head Road and Waikiki; to Kahala Avenue, Judd, Nuuana. It belongs, over on the Big Island, to Kailua in the Kona district, to a ranch in Kohala, a beach house at Weli-Weli and a sugar plantation at Ookala. It belongs on Kauai, to a place called Kilauea, and by the same token over on Maui, on which we have never set foot, to a place named Wailuka. Our friends will understand.

Most of all it belongs to Hawaii Nei, to all the magical Islands and their people, and, very nostalgically, to the brooding shape of Diamond Head herself, dreaming upward from the incredible, unforgettable sea.

So, to all who have made this inadequate

story possible our gratitude and affection . . .
Mahalo, Hoalohas, ame aloha nui.

We very much doubt the accuracy of our Hawaiian but if the meaning shines through perhaps the errors will be forgiven.

Foreword

It is always difficult to write about an actual place, unless it be as indifferent and, in a sense, as anonymous as a great city. My knowledge of the Hawaiian Islands derives from two visits and a deep affection. I speak with no authority, I have not the impertinence; I would not presume to write a see-all, hear-all and tell-all book. Some may complain that, like the sundial, I count only the sunny hours. If so, I err on the side of the angels, and if there are flaws in Paradise only a citizen of that delectable community has the right to point them out to others.

In justice to my friends in the Islands, I must also explain that I have taken liberties. I have borrowed place names and I have created them. Certain settings, sugar plantations and cattle ranches, are merely composite pictures. Now and then I have stolen an actual location, given it a new name and furnished it with imaginary people. I hope to be forgiven. Also I have caused an eruption of Kilauea. At the time of writing there hadn't been one since 1934.

For the rest I ask tolerance toward any errors and remind my readers that my title is taken from the sonnet by Rupert Brooke called "Waikiki." The line reads "And new stars burn into the ancient skies."

Chapter 1

It was not likely that she would ever forget her twenty-third birthday because it was on that day that she first became aware of Dexter Warren's existence and so, in a manner of speaking, was born all over again.

She hadn't wanted to go to Ellie Underwood's party. Ellie was famous for her parties, even in Washington, but parties were pretty much alike. You went, you had something to eat and drink, you talked to a thousand people, some of whom you knew pretty well, and met a thousand strangers. Ellie's vast drawing room would be filled with smoke, chatter, pretty women, clever women, and men who were on the way up. You rarely met a man who was on the way out at Ellie's, which was something of a triumph for the widowed Mrs. Underwood, when you stopped to think how soon those on their way up might be on their way out, all things considered. And at Ellie's you were assured of the attention, graceful and mannered, of the youngest, best looking embassy attachés, the youngest, most socially possible congressmen, and of course the most distinguished visiting firemen. You met all the debutantes, all the bachelors, the smartest ladies and gentlemen of the Fourth Estate and, as a leaven, the really influential dowagers.

Administrations came and went, and with them their following, the job holders, the hangers-on, the advisers, the men behind the throne. But Ellie had survived a great many Administrations. Back in the early nineteen hundreds her husband had been Speaker of the House. A good sound man, as even his many enemies admitted. But he was dead and gone these many years and Ellie survived, possibly in order to function as a hostess. She was childless; she had, and thanked God for it, few relatives. She lived in her enormous old house, attended by ancient, capable servants and by an efficient secretary with whom she had once gone to school — if you could imagine Ellie going to school.

The girl who was having her twenty-third birthday stood in a corner by the big windows and talked to the young South American who had brought her a cup of tea. The last rays of warm October sunlight slanted in and glimmered on the polished floor. The Embassy youngster was new to Washington and greatly impressed. He waved a pâté sandwich and spoke glowingly of the Lincoln Memorial. But the admiration in his eyes was more personal.

Dexter Warren came in, to stand in the archway between drawing room and library. He had been in the library for over an hour talking to a man who might be useful to him. That was, he reflected, the trouble with Washington, fabulous city . . . so many men might be useful to you, so few were when it came to cases.

His hostess tottered up to him on her tiny feet. She was a colossal woman, and in the astonishingly spreading environs of her face her eyes were bright and black and watchful. Dexter, from his great height, looked down at her. He had known her for years and she never failed to amuse him. Her pretense of amiable idiocy was as transparent as cellophane. She claimed never to lift a hand to further anyone's ambitions. Indeed, it was an effort for her to lift a hand at all. She was fond of saying that at her age — she was over sixty — nothing interested her except good food and parties. Dexter Warren knew better.

She asked:

"Well?"

He nodded, smiling. He said, "Very well, I think . . . thank you, Ellie."

How she loved having her fat stubby finger in every pie, plum or mince, he reflected. If Underwood had lived . . . but he hadn't . . . and Ellie hadn't become First Lady of the Land as she had hoped once upon a time. She was resigned, now. She liked this better. First Ladies came, created their furor, and departed. Ellie remained, Ellie to all Washington, to Paris and London, to New York and Boston, to Newport and Palm Beach, Ellie who had inherited a copper fortune and who spent it lavishly, on such entertainments as today's.

She said, with her funny little smirk, her small mouth almost obscured in the vast reaches of her face:

"Handled properly, our friend in there" — she jerked a shoulder and her chins rippled — "may be worth your while."

Dexter Warren said gravely:

"At the moment he's had too much to drink."

"Jenkins will attend to that," said Ellie serenely. Jenkins who saw all, said nothing, but acted. He was entrusted with the responsibility to see that no party of Ellie's ever approximated a brawl.

Dexter Warren looked across the room. He saw, at the far windows, a girl who was not too tall and not too short. Her figure was superb.

She stood with a teacup in her hand, her small head bent a little, quietly listening to the man who stood beside her, talking rapidly, gesticulating.

"Who's the girl by the window?" he inquired.

Ellie turned. She answered, "Lani Aldrich. Why?"

"I'd like to meet her."

Ellie made a curious sound, half snort, half sigh. She said, leading the way, "If I don't present you someone else will, and may God help her."

"You do me too much honor," said Dexter, following.

They were halted a dozen times but Ellie pushed through the crowd with the tenacity of an armored tank. When she reached the windows the girl set her teacup on a small table and turned, smiling. Ellie didn't smile. She said, "Lani, this is Dexter Warren, and don't say I didn't warn you." She murmured the Brazilian's redundant name, and vanished, if anything as solid could be said to vanish.

The Brazilian vanished too. He never knew how that came about. One minute he was talking to a charming girl about the Lincoln Memorial and the next he was somewhere else surrounded by debutantes and Miss Aldrich was nowhere to be seen. It was remarkable.

As a matter of fact it wasn't. Dexter said briskly:

"I've been waiting to talk to you all afternoon, Miss Aldrich — I've a message for you from mutual friends. I wonder if we could find a place . . . "

She hadn't time to answer. He'd smiled at the Brazilian, murmured, "If you'll excuse us?" put his hand under her arm, and presently she found herself out of the big drawing room, in a smaller, more intimate setting. There weren't many people about, and the noise of voices and the determined playing of the orchestra were muted.

"Here," he said firmly, and indicated a couch against the wall directly under a very nice Goya. "How's this?"

She sat down and looked at him. She asked: "What mutual friends?"

"I haven't the least idea," he told her, "but a brief conversation will certainly disclose some . . . and they would have sent messages had they known I was going to see you."

He certainly was not good looking. His chin was too square, his nose too prominent. His eyes were indeterminate in color, his hair pepper and salt. There was nothing unusual about him except his height, and his voice. His mouth was almost ugly, but when he

14

smiled you forgot that.

She asked:

"You're not — Washington?"

"New York. Here on business. You don't hold that against me?" he asked anxiously, offering her a cigarette. "By the way, how about a drink?"

She shook her head, smiling.

"Lani," he said, after a moment. "That's an odd name and very pretty. Is it a nickname?"

"It's short for Iolani," she answered — "which is too much for most people."

He repeated it after her, reflectively. She said, smiling, "And you spell it with an I — " she spelled it for him — "only you don't pronounce it that way. The I becomes an E . . . it's Hawaiian."

"Hawaiian?" He lifted a heavy eyebrow. "How come?"

She had had to explain for all but seven of her twenty-three years. She settled back in her corner of the couch, began again, obediently.

"I was born in the Islands," she said, "but left when I was seven, shortly after my father's death. My mother's home originally was Washington, we eventually settled here."

"Eventually? What happened in the interim?"

"Europe, New York, Connecticut — Cali-

15

fornia. We've traveled," Lani said, "for most of those years. We came here to stay, just a month ago. Of course, we've been back on visits."

"I see." His eyes were on her appraisingly. She was, he decided, very nearly beautiful, the structure of her face, the setting of her eyes, her skin pale and smooth as cream. Under her little hat her hair was very dark.

He said lightly:

"I can never imagine anyone settling in Washington. It's always seemed a state of mind to me."

"It's a lovely city," Lani reminded him. "I'm growing fond of it, rather."

"But you couldn't strike roots," he persisted.

"How did you know that?" she demanded. "No, but then I've never been anywhere long enough to strike roots, really."

"School?" he suggested. "College?"

She shook her head, smiling.

"Governesses," she answered. "You see, my mother's a semi-invalid. She's never wanted me to be away from her for any length of time. When she's — better, we travel. When she tires, or is not so well, we stay somewhere for a time. And then we move on."

A waiter went by and Dexter Warren looked at the girl. He asked:

16

"Food . . . drink?"

"I've had tea, thank you." She glanced at the watch on her wrist. "I'm sorry," she told him, "but I'm afraid I must go. My mother will be expecting me and we are having a few people for dinner . . . and — "

A girl came into the room, saw them, came over. She put her arm around Lani as the introductions were made. She was a pretty, friendly girl, the daughter of a Cabinet member. She said, "I've been looking for you, Lani — many happy returns. I'll see you tonight, do tell your mother that this once I promise to be on time."

She dashed off again, sables looped over her arm, long blond hair cascading to her shoulders.

"Cherry," explained Lani, "is always late."

Dexter asked:

"Is it really your birthday?"

"I'm afraid so."

"How many does this make? You don't have to answer, and remember that anything you say will be held against you."

"Twenty-three," she said, laughing.

"Twenty-three." He was silent a moment, remembering. At twenty-three, Dexter Warren had been a year out of his university, a long lean boy with an ugly arresting face, no money, and boundless ambition. At twenty-

17

three he had had a job in a private banking house. At twenty-four he had married the daughter of the senior partner. Fourteen years ago.

He asked:

"Are you having a birthday cake?"

"Of course," she said, a little startled.

"And do you wish on the candles?"

She nodded, smiling faintly. "Does that seem very childish to you?" she inquired.

"No," he said, "it seems as sensible as any other form of wishing. What will you wish for, tonight?"

"If I tell you," she reminded him, "it may not come true."

Dexter laughed. He said:

"You may change your mind between now and tonight."

She said slowly:

"For a great many birthdays I have wished that someday I might go back to the Islands."

"To Hawaii? You've never been back?"

"No, never."

"Do you remember it at all?"

"In snatches," she told him. "I remember the color of the water, and the light on the mountains. When I hear Hawaiian music I remember a room in our house, I remember the *lanai*, overlooking the sea. When I smell gardenias — " She broke off. "You'll think me — "

"I cannot tell you what I think you," he said quickly, "not here, not now."

She looked at his intent face and her heart quickened. She said hurriedly, "But I really must go, Mr. Warren."

"I'll wish for you too," he said, "tonight. Perhaps I'll even find and buy a birthday candle, light it and blow it out. I'll wish that you may attain your heart's desire. And perhaps I'll wish something for myself . . . or wouldn't that come true, on your birthday?"

"Why not?" she asked casually, but her head went on hammering and she remembered Ellie saying in her soft small voice, "Don't say I didn't warn you."

Ellie came into the room now in her deliberate, direct way. She couldn't be anything but direct. She said:

"Dexter, I've been looking for you. Richardson has turned up and wants to see you." She patted Lani's arm. She said, "Lani can't monopolize you longer."

"I'm going," Lani assured her and bent to touch her lips to the older woman's cheek. She smiled at Dexter and before he could move she'd gone through the archway into the drawing room.

"Well, come along," said Ellie impatiently, as he stood there, looking after the girl, a cigarette smoldering between his fingers.

19

"Wait a moment." He turned to put the cigarette in an ash tray. "Tell me about that girl."

The small, obscure mouth tightened. Ellie asked, "Why should I? Don't you have fun enough in New York? That's a nice girl, Dexter, a very nice girl."

"I don't doubt it. Tell me about her."

Ellie shrugged. She was fond of Dexter Warren, and the fact that she disapproved of him did not make her less so. Also, she disliked his wife.

"There isn't much to tell," she said, "but — "

"Sit down, tell it in comfort. Your rabble can miss you for a moment and I would be delighted if Richardson didn't think me too anxious," he said.

Ellie sank on the couch, with mutterings and heavings. She complained:

"The damned thing's too soft, I shall never get up, without a block and tackle. I suppose you're right about Richardson. But if I were you I wouldn't be too sure of myself. He's shrewd. Tell me, Dexter, why do you go on making more and more money for Muriel to spend?"

"God knows. Tell me about Lani Aldrich."

"Why?" asked Ellie.

"She interests me. Twenty-three, and the

poise of thirty-five. Yet she looks eighteen and untouched," he said. "It's an interesting combination. Also, she's lovely."

"She may not be the prettiest girl in Washington," said Ellie with vigor, "but she has more character, more real charm. Her mother was a beauty in a different way. I remember her as a debutante, a red head with tremendous vitality and the most marvelous skin. Lani's inherited that, but for the rest she's like Aldrich. I remember him, although I saw him only once, when he came to Washington to marry Mary Carrington . . . and take her back to Hawaii with him."

"Carrington?" asked Dexter. "The Virginia family?"

"Exactly. Mary Carrington was the most popular girl of her year. She could have had anybody in Washington. Her father was senator from Virginia, and she made her debut here. There were, literally, dozens of men who wanted to marry her . . . and not, may I add, for the Carrington money although in one or two instances it may have had some influence. When she left Washington that spring to go to Hawaii on a holiday she was assumed to be engaged to young Norval — you wouldn't know him, he was attached to the British Embassy, and afterwards became Lord Lessingford. But she came home engaged to Aldrich."

"Who was he?" asked Dexter curiously.

Ellie tried to shrug. It was always an effort.

"I wouldn't know. Missionary stock on his mother's side. Sugar plantations and what not. Anyway she married him, went off and was, from all one heard, excessively happy. He was killed in a accident when Lani was a child and then they came home. Or rather they traveled, here, there, everywhere. Last month they came to Washington and took an apartment. Mary does not go out, she has a bad heart. People go to her — I went, shortly after their arrival. She can see just a few people at a time, as she tires easily. Lani never leaves her for long, they are devoted, and I have an impression that the child is frightened when she's away from her."

"Frightened?"

"That something will happen. Mary isn't the maternal monster type who'd keep the child cooped up in a sickroom. She makes her go out — but I've often seen Lani leave a party to telephone."

Dexter nodded and rose. He offered his hands to Ellie and pulled her to her feet. "Thanks," he said. "Now I'll go see Richardson and, as you suggested, make a little more money for Muriel, which she doesn't need."

Ellie walked with him back into the

crowded room. She said:

"I wish I knew why you were so interested in the Aldrich history."

"Perhaps," he answered, "because if I were ten years younger — and free . . . "

"I've heard you say that before," Ellie said, panting with the effort to keep up with him. "The last time was in New York. The girl was Agnes Palmer. I saw, by the way, that she had gone to England for what is euphoniously called an extended visit."

He said, smiling, "You see too much, Ellie."

"One thing," said Ellie, "that I wouldn't like to see would be business bringing you to Washington too often."

Chapter 2

Lani walked the short distance to the apartment. The sun had set and the soft October dusk was a dreaming blue. She walked quickly with a long, beautiful stride and people turned to watch her, a slender girl in a tailored suit, dark furs cascading about her shoulders, and a bright, tiny hat. She was smiling, even in the dusk you could see that.

The elderly colored manservant who opened the door to her smiled too. He had every reason for rejoicing. His father had served the Carrington family and Joseph, the son, had grown up with Miss Mary. He remembered her at her coming-out party, he remembered her at her wedding. Now Miss Mary had come home, and before her return had sent word to Joseph that if he was free she would like to have him with her. He was free, as was Rheba, his wife, so here he was back again after the long years of odd jobs in inferior people's houses, of, even, carrying luggage at the station.

He asked softly, "Was it a nice party, Miss Lani?"

"A lovely party, Joseph," she told him. "Where's Mother?"

"In the drawing room, Miss Lani, lying down . . . some ladies come to tea but they've been gone a good while, now."

Lani took off her hat and shook her head. She hated hats and their restriction. Her uncompromisingly black hair was thick and soft with a deep natural wave, and she wore it cut close to her small head. She dropped her furs and her jacket, went into the drawing room and announced, "I'm home . . . are you tired, darling?"

Mary Carrington lay on a long couch. Her face was small, very still and pale under the masses of coppery hair which she had never cut and which had not turned gray. She wore her lipstick bravely, brightly, as if in defiance. Her eyes were blue and her features were very lovely. But the vitality which Ellie Underwood remembered, which had distinguished and informed her, was gone.

"Not very. Meta dropped in and, later, Thelma. They were full of Administration gossip," she said, smiling. "Was Ellie's very dull, dear?"

"No. I met such an attractive man . . . "

Lani sat down on a big footstool and took

her mother's hand. The pleasant room was quietly lighted, charmingly, impersonally furnished. Lani holding her mother's hand to her cheek thought suddenly, It would be fun to have a place of your own, every stick of furniture in it. She had the haziest memories of the house in Hawaii, the last house she had lived in in which she had belonged. After that, hotels and apartments, all furnished with other people's belongings.

"Washington?" asked Mary. Her heart pained her, not a real pain, not a physical pain. But she dreaded this always, the day when Lani would say, "I met such an attractive man." Yet she had said it many times and it hadn't come to anything. Selfish, horrible. I'm not like that really, Mary told herself angrily. I want her to have the best, to be as happy as I was . . . no, not quite as happy. I should have been warned, no one should be as happy as that.

Lani wouldn't leave her, she knew, not ever. But Lani would fall in love one day, seriously in love . . .

"New York," Lani was saying, "his name's Dexter Warren."

Mary's slender brows drew together. She said, "I've heard that name somewhere, seen it, too — newspapers, hotel registers? What was he like?"

"Oh, ugly-good looking," Lani answered, smiling, "and terribly tall. About thirty-eight or forty, I think. Lots of charm. He seems to know Ellie well."

"What does he do?" her mother asked her.

"I wouldn't know," said Lani. She clasped her hands around her knees, her gray eyes dreaming. She added, "He's — nice."

Her mother said, with an effort:

"One of these days there'll be a man who — "

"Nonsense," said Lani stoutly, "I'm a born old maid."

"Anything but that," her mother told her, "heaven forfend."

"Trying to get rid of me, Miss Mary?"

"Naturally. How do you suppose I feel with a spinster on my hands?" her mother asked. "At your age I had had a dozen proposals, I had broken two engagements and I had been married to your father for two years . . . and you, my darling, had been born."

She thought, If she meets a man who would be impatient with an invalid mother-in-law, who would be jealous of the close tie between us? Or if she falls in love with one whom she must follow to the ends of the earth as I would have followed Alan?

Lani asked gently:

"Sure you're not too tired to see people tonight?"

"Of course not . . . I'm not coming out to dinner, I'll appear afterwards for a little while. Oh, I forgot, there's mail and packages in your room, Lani."

"Golly!" Lani jumped to her feet and stretched her arms above her head. Her waist was very slender and the soft, short-sleeved sweater, flecked with gold thread, was molded to the fine carriage of her broad shoulders and the small high breasts. "Packages," she said, like a child. "I love them!"

She disappeared and returned presently with the packages piled in her arms. She had friends, all over the world. She did not see them for months on end, for years perhaps, but they did not forget her. Perfume from the English girl she'd known in London, who was now in New York, a cigarette case from her mother's cousin who lived in Greenwich, books from the man who had been so attentive to her last summer in Maine . . . and a dozen cards.

She said, displaying them:

"People are wonderful . . . the way they remember . . ." She held the fragile bottle of scent to her nose and sniffed. "Gardenia," she said, her eyes closed. When she opened them she added, "I wish we could see Maurine again. Perhaps we could coax her to come here for a visit if it wouldn't tire you."

"I'd enjoy it," her mother said.

Lani said, after a moment:

"I'm glad we're going to stay put for a time."

Mary Aldrich sighed. She said:

"It hasn't been easy for you, deprived of so much that other girls have, boarding school, college, a settled place to call home . . . spending your time cooped up in hotel suites with me, or in a room beside mine in a nursing home or hospital. I feel as if I had cheated you. Girls should have roots," she said anxiously, "and you haven't. For as soon as you make friends I take you away again."

"Nonsense," said Lani, "we've been all over this a hundred times. I have a marvelous life. And my roots are wherever you are. You know that."

Her mother did not appear to listen. She was saying, in a small voice:

"I can't help it. It's as if I'm driven. Each place I think, This will be the one place in which I can remain . . . but it never is. I grow restless and have to go on. You see, Lani, I'm always looking for something I'll never have again, peace, perhaps, contentment."

Lani dropped to her knees beside the couch.

"Darling, don't distress yourself," she said, "don't, please. I know, I understand."

29

"Sometimes," her mother said in a whisper, "I feel as if the finest thing I could wish for you would be to feel toward some man as I did toward your father — as I still do. Sometimes I think it would be the worst thing that could happen to you. The best, the worst? I don't know, Lani, I don't know."

Parker, the maid who had been with them ever since they went to England, following Alan Aldrich's tragic death, appeared in the doorway. She was a spare woman with a grave, self-contained face . . . a trained masseuse, a more than competent personal maid. Lani's mother relied on her for everything. There were times when there were trained nurses in the menage but no one could quiet Mary Aldrich as Parker could, Parker who would sit for hours beside her, reading her to sleep or massaging her still beautiful body, relaxing the taut nerves.

She said, now:

"It's time you dressed, Miss Lani, and for Mrs. Aldrich to rest if she's to see people later."

"She's like Nemesis, unescapable," said Mary Aldrich. Lani gave her both her hands and she stood up, a little shorter than her daughter, and despite her ill-health looking less than her forty-five years, except when you saw her eyes, which were unsmiling even when she smiled.

Lani took her packages back to her room. She had a new frock; it was very becoming. Yet she regarded herself in some dissatisfaction after she had dressed. Parker came in to see if she could help and commented, "It's lovely, Miss Lani, and so becoming."

A simple frock, beautifully draped, the color dusty pink. With it she wore the aquamarines her mother had given her this morning. They were the color of water she vaguely remembered, sea water in the shallows, clear pale green, clear pale blue. She put her hand to the necklace, she turned her wrist, to admire the luminous quality, and noticed almost indifferently that the two square stones clipped to her ear lobes made her eyes less gray than green, less green than blue.

She had such a stupid thought standing there looking in the mirror . . . thinking, No one will see me tonight, no one who matters.

Her guests arrived presently, the daughter of the Cabinet member, a daughter of the senator from North Carolina, and Ellie Underwood's attractive niece, Marcia . . . and four men, a lawyer, a doctor, an attaché from the Swedish Embassy, and Gordon Herold, whose father was mysteriously influential in the Administration and whom Lani had met during the summer. He was very much in love with her, he had asked her to marry him.

He was attractive. She liked Gordon.

It was during dinner that the flowers came, a great square box, extravagantly bound with white satin ribbon. Joseph, grinning happily, brought it to the table and Lani untied it. Gardenias, dozens of them, creamy, perfect as a carving in ivory, the flawless petals heavy with fragrance.

The girls exclaimed and Gordon Herold, seeing her face, said ruefully, "Why didn't I think of those?" But he smiled, glancing at the pale pink orchids, pinned to her shoulder, which he had sent.

Lani was reading the card. Her short thick eyelashes, straight and very black, veiled her eyes. But her mouth curved.

"How's for seeing the card?" someone suggested.

Lani shook her head. She gave the box back to Joseph . . . "The silver bowls," she said, "the shallow pair. Ask Parker if she'll fix them for me, Joseph."

One of the girls, the senator's sharp-eyed little daughter, noticed that she slipped the card down the front of her frock . . . Good news, thought the senator's daughter happily, turning her large blue regard on Gordon Herold whom she had coveted for two years.

The birthday cake came next. Twenty-three candles and another to grow on. Rheba had outdone herself.

Lani leaned over the cake. Candlelight flickered in her eyes, glowed on her face. She was thinking of the card.

"Blow out a candle for me," it ordered, in stubby black writing, "and wish that I may see you again soon . . . Dexter Warren."

They drank their coffee in the drawing room and Mary Aldrich joined them later, to lie on the couch and hold court. She wore a hostess gown which Lani loved, sapphire-blue velvet, furred at the hem. Parker, helping her with her heavy hair, had said, "It becomes you, Mrs. Aldrich," and Mary Aldrich had thought, glancing in the mirror, Alan always liked me in blue.

What was the use of wearing blue now, to match your eyes, eyes which had been blind so long, with weeping, with not seeing the one person on earth whom you longed to see?

Unfair to Lani, she had thought, going out into the drawing room with the careful step of one who carries death in the palm of her hand, and fears to stumble. For she loved Alan's child, completely. That was how she thought of her . . . *Alan's* child. That was why she had made the only possible sacrifice, willed herself to live, let herself be wrapped around with the cotton wool of care, did nothing voluntarily to hasten by a day, by an hour, the eventual release.

Talking to the youngsters, solicitious and charming, Mary's glance was drawn to the bowls of gardenias set, one at each end of a long polished table. She cried, "How lovely! Have they just come?"

Lani nodded but when Gordon Herold moved to pick up a bowl and bring it to the couch, she stopped him. She explained, "Mother finds the scent too strong if it's near her," and Mary looked at her gratefully. She couldn't bear gardenias, she couldn't endure fragrances which made her remember.

Lani came to the head of the couch, looked down and spoke softly. "I'll have them taken out . . . and put in my room for tonight. Tommorrow they can be thrown away."

"Who sent them?" asked Mary.

Lani bent close. She whispered, "Dexter Warren," and moved away as the young Scandinavian came up to talk to her mother. Presently they were going on to a place where there would be good music, and dancing and supper, a new place, very popular.

At three the next morning Lani let herself in with her key. She took off the short sable cape which had been her mother's last Christmas present and put it over her arm. She went softly into the drawing room and through to

34

the small library. Their landlord, now in Europe at an important post, had a good and catholic taste in books. Fine bindings, first editions. But somewhere there was a book —

She found it, on a lower shelf, the fat red copy of Who's Who, and sitting on the floor, careless of her frock, she unpinned her orchids and tossed them aside. She opened the book and bent to the page under the one light she had switched on. Warren — Warren. There it was, Dexter Warren . . . and the date . . . She had been right, she thought, he was thirty-eight. His birthplace, New York City . . . schools, college, and then . . .

m. Muriel Davenport . . . m. for "married."

The rest couldn't interest her, president of this, director of that, office such-and-such place, homes, New York, Palm Beach, Long Island . . . clubs —

m. *Muriel Davenport*. Fourteen years ago.

She replaced the book and rose. She was chilly, let down, all the excitement, the bubble and glitter gone from her evening. She had had such a good time. Even Gordon's second, stammered proposal hadn't bothered her much . . . nothing had. Dancing, she had felt the sharp edges of the little card cutting her soft flesh. She had liked it.

She picked up her wrap, switched off the light in the library, the drawing room lights, and went to her bedroom. On her dressing table and on a low table by the chaise longue, she saw the gardenias. She had smelled them before she entered the room. Waxen and perfect, they dreamed in the water, set in silver.

She could not sleep in the room with so strong, so hurting a fragrance. She took the bowls, carried them into the bathroom and set them on the dressing table there. Much later when she was in bed and the cold October air blew through the room she imagined that she could no longer smell them.

Her eyelids were heavy, her throat ached, there was the sting of tears, sudden and uncomforting.

What was the matter with her? she asked herself angrily. Behaving like a schoolgirl . . .

Dexter Warren was nothing to her, merely a man whom she had met at a big party, with whom she had had a brief conversation. She had met hundreds of attractive men.

Why hadn't it occurred to her that he was married? Of course he would be, such a man didn't live to be thirty-eight and remain a bachelor. Yet it hadn't occurred to her.

He had been pleasant, he had admired her, he had all but said so. He had sent her flowers because it was her birthday. A dozen men had been pleasant, admired her audibly, sent flowers.

Tomorrow she would write a note to his hotel — the name was on the card — and thank him. And she would probably never see him again. And in a day or a week she would forget that she had ever seen him. Her fantastic excitement, her secret exhilaration, the sense of expectancy, of doors opening on gardens — had all been part of her birthday, light and heady as a glass of champagne. But now the wine was flat in the glass, and the effect had worn off, fleeting and unreal.

Chapter 3

In December, she sat facing Dexter Warren over a corner table in an obscure little hotel in an obscure little town in Virginia not very far from the city. No snow had fallen, the trees were bare and black against a somber gray sky and the dining room was cold. Lani shivered and pulled her furs about her.

There were a few people in the room, mostly men who looked like traveling salesmen. The waitress was blowsy, careless and indifferent. Luncheon was indifferent too, but neither Lani nor Dexter cared.

He said:

"It's getting harder, Lani — being with you, in these out-of-the-way places. I hate it for you, darling."

"I don't mind," she said.

He sighed and put his cigarette in the ash tray.

"I mind, for you. We should meet — in the happy places . . . laughter, music, gaiety, charm. Or else in some quiet place utterly lovely, where we could be alone."

"Dexter, please."

He said, staring at her:

"How did this all happen? Why did it happen to us?"

How had it happened? She could tell him, tracing it, step by step. The formal pleasant note, sent to his hotel, which was to end something which hadn't really begun. Then the next night, meeting him at the dance, feeling his arms around her, watching his face change when he saw her come into the room . . . So it had begun, a lifetime ago, it had never ended, it would never end. Not for her. But she was on her guard, she had been hot with shame, fearing that perhaps he would guess . . .

Dancing, talking of the gardenias, and of her birthday. And then his face dark with gravity, and his voice saying, "I have to see you again, I must. Tell me I can't, Lani, because it isn't fair to you, and I'm not strong enough to tell myself that and mean it."

He'd taken her out of the crowded room and found a corner in the big house where, for a moment, they could be comparatively alone. He'd said, standing there with his hands in his pockets . . . not touching her, and yet she felt as if she were in his arms:

"I'm married. Do you know that?"

"Yes."

"Ellie, I suppose?"

She looked at him soberly, with the appeal of a child.

"I — I looked you up," she said, "in Who's Who, early in the morning, when I came back from my birthday party."

He said:

"I'm in love with you. I've no right. But that hasn't anything to do with it. Rights!"

Lani nodded. After a moment she said:

"We won't see each other again."

"You have said it," he told her, "as I asked you to, but I haven't heard. Not a word."

She asked, "How can we?"

He made a curious little gesture with his shoulders. He said:

"Talk to Ellie, if you like. She'll tell you that Muriel and I haven't lived together for a number of years . . . but she won't let me go."

"Why not?" asked Lani gravely, leaning against a tall chair. Tonight she wore the aquamarines again and a black velvet frock, low, off her shoulders. She had never liked the dress until tonight.

"I'm useful to her," said Dexter.

Gordon Herold had come in then. He was the son of their host. And this was his dance. He spoke deferentially to Warren, as a young man to one considerably his senior, and took Lani away. Dexter remained where he was, looking after them. When he went back to the ballroom, Lani had gone.

The next time he was in Washington he came to call. He had a letter to Mary Aldrich from an old friend, a Philadelphia woman who had known Mary and Lani in Europe. Lani was not in when he presented himself and his letter. When she came she halted in the doorway as if frozen, incredulous of her eyesight . . . Dexter Warren sitting there, in the low chair by her mother's couch, and Joseph following Lani in, to bring fresh tea.

Her mother said brightly:

"Lani, you didn't tell me that Mr. Warren knew Doris Kimberley."

"I didn't know it myself," said Lani, coming slowly into the room.

Afterward she spoke to him, for a moment, in the hall.

"Why did you do this?" she asked him directly.

He said:

"You would not have let me come to see you. This seemed the only way."

When she returned Mary smiled at her.

"You were right," she said, "a very attractive man. Doris says — but, here's her letter."

Lani read it. That is, she looked at the words, none of which made sense to her. Mary was going on:

41

" — many mutual friends," she was saying, "of his and his wife's."

Lani smiled, and it seemed, without effort. She said lightly:

"Isn't it a pity he's married? But then, most nice men are."

Mary turned her head away. She thought, It wasn't anything then, the way she spoke the day of her birthday, the way she looked when she told me who had sent the flowers. That was just birthday and being young . . . and in love with all the world.

She said sincerely, "I hope he'll come again."

He did. He came to see her, Mary, and to dinner, now and then. He was in Washington very often, flying down for a day, for two days. So it began. Riding while the weather held, finding him waiting for her, the first time he borrowed a riding kit from a friend in town, the next time he brought his own. He could always borrow a horse. And then, lunch here or tea there. Until Ellie raised an eyebrow and spoke to Lani one day privately.

"Hadn't you better be careful?"

"Of what, Ellie?"

"Of Dexter Warren. I've known him a good many years. You know he's married?"

"Of course," said Lani, "he comes to see us — Mother and me — when he's in town. He's

42

a great friend of Mrs. Kimberley's, you know
. . . Mother adores Aunt Kim."

"You've been seen with him alone," said
Ellie; "people are beginning to talk."

"Let them," Lani laughed, and her eyes
were very dark, "as long as Mother doesn't
mind. Honestly, Ellie, I'd never suspect you
of antediluvian ideas."

"Nor have I any," said Ellie. Her several
chins quivered. "But I'm very fond of you . . .
and Muriel Warren's a rather unpleasant
woman."

A beautiful woman, however. Lani saw her
picture in a current Vogue and stared at it incredulously. Somehow she had thought of
Dexter's wife as dumpy, uninteresting, with a
shrewish face and mean small eyes. Wish fulfillment. But the Muriel Warren who looked
back at her from the shiny page was tall and
slim, her fair hair tossed to the top of her
head, pinned there with diamond stars. Er-
mine slipped arrogantly from her shoulders,
her black frock was draped to disclose her figure. Her hand held a cigarette in a long
holder.

This was the picture Lani saw as she sat under the drier and glanced idly at the magazine
in her lap. The beauty salon was vocal with
the light voices of women. The noise of the
drier was suddenly unbearable, and the heat.

She shrank under it, she winced back from the picture as if Muriel Warren had raised that hand and struck her.

People were talking, she thought. She told herself over and over again that she didn't care, not for herself, only for her mother. For her mother's sake people mustn't be given occasion for teacup, cocktail-glass gossip.

After that, the obscure hotels, the little frequented places, daytimes. At night, he usually managed to appear where she would be. He knew the people whom she knew, he could telephone them casually, say, "Look, I'm in town," and the invitation would be forthcoming. An extra man was always acceptable, manna from heaven in most cases.

Now they sat here this December day, ate next to nothing and didn't know what they ate. Dexter had a highball in front of him, Lani had coffee, strong, black, bitter . . . it was worse if you attempted what passed for cream.

She said slowly, "I can tell you how it happened. It doesn't matter, does it, now that it has happened?"

She looked at her watch. She mustn't be gone too long. Presently they would drive back to Washington, she would drop him long before they reached the section in which she lived, he would take a taxi and be gone from her.

He was saying now, not looking at her but tracing an intricate pattern with the bent tine of his fork on the threadbare cloth:

"Lani, if you could come to New York . . . for a visit, say a week, two weeks? There are so many quiet places, and — "

She said soberly:

"And Mrs. Warren has left for Palm Beach to open the house. You're expected there for Christmas." She looked at him miserably. "I know, I picked up a New York paper somewhere the other day, and read that."

He said, "It's just — appearances. She'll have a houseful of people who don't care whether it's Christmas or Fourth of July. I'll go down for perhaps three days. I wouldn't go at all if you were to be in New York. But you can't be, of course."

"No."

"After Christmas, then," he urged her, "for a little while? We could be together, we could — "

She interrupted again.

"I can't leave Mother, I have never left her."

"This once. She'd be all right, Lani, you'd be so near, you can fly . . . surely if you said you wanted to go to town, to see that English girl of whom you told me?"

She said, "Mother would want me to go.

45

But I couldn't, Dexter."

"I suppose not," he said.

"We must go now," she told him, and he beckoned the waitress and asked for the check.

Driving back there would be a road, off the highway, and he'd say, take that, for just a minute . . . and off that, another road, possibly not more than a lane, muddy with recent rains or rutted hard with recent frosts, as the case might be. There she would pull off and stop the engine, and he would take her in his arms and kiss her. Each time she swore she would not, she would not leave the highway. Each time she did, helpless under his hands, and the urgency of his lips and the desire in his eyes . . . and hers.

When she left him, he had promised to return, before Christmas if possible.

He did not, but his letters came faithfully. Joseph used to give them to her, smiling. He didn't know from whom they were but he knew they made her happy. When the letters came she went about with shining eyes, and her low voice had a newer music. Happiness shone from her. Reading his letters she could forget the hopeless things, spoken and unspoken, between them.

"I've asked her for my freedom before, Lani. She won't give it to me. Don't you understand? I've an unfortunate flair for business. I've kept the old firm on its feet through the bad years, I've made money for her. She trusts no one, when money's in question, except myself. And I can't divorce her."

"But you told me," Lani had said, humiliated, sick that this thing must be discussed between them, "that there were other men, that you were sure."

"I am sure. I have no proof."

The gardenias came again at Christmas and a great box of red roses for Mary. And a package, sent by mail. He had written, saying it would be there, a small package unnoticed in the heap of brightly wrapped shapes, square and round and oval, tied with ribbons and gay with holly. Lani put it away in the bottom of her bureau drawer and early Christmas morning, before she went to her mother's room, she crept out of bed, barefooted on the cold floor, took it from its hiding place and back to bed with her, to open it with the unsteady fingers of impatience.

Little packages in the bigger one, a silver bracelet set round with silver hearts; a silver bracelet chiming with silver bells; a Christmas angel carved from wood, with a sweet, silly face and gilded hair; something that looked like wooden roses, and a wooden bottle, carved with flowers, the top set with olivines and perfume in a glass tube within. Fern lei, the label read.

On the card he had written, "I want to give you the world, the stars out of the skies . . . I can send you only these foolish gifts . . . and my heart."

Silver bangles would go unnoticed, the angel might be from anywhere, not straight out of heaven, the wooden roses and the perfume were unspectacular. Anyone might have sent them.

Later in the day Mary, looking over the Christmas things, spoke softly, as if to speak hurt her.

"That's Hawaiian perfume, in the bottle, isn't it? I don't know it . . . but the wood is monkeypod. Who sent it, dear?"

She would not lie more than she must. She had lied, she had become proficient in lying when she took the little car and went to meet Dexter. She said steadily:

"Dexter Warren sent them, and the wooden roses, he knew I was born in the Islands."

"They aren't wooden roses," said her mother, "although they look as if they were." She lay back with her eyes closed. After a while she said she didn't want to look at anything more just now.

Lani crept close to her, sat on the edge of the couch. She was frightened, but she had to know.

She asked, "You don't mind Dexter's sending me these?"

Mary opened her drowned blue eyes. She said, "Idiot! Of course not, it was charming of him." She closed her eyes again, and Lani's heart raced and steadied. She said, "I'll put them away, dear. I've given Parker the gardenias, she can take them with her when she goes out — wherever it is she is going."

"You won't mind putting me to bed?" asked Mary. "Parker's been so good, she never goes out and now she has a chance to see an old friend. The husband is employed by someone at the British Embassy."

"I'd love putting you to bed."

"You should have gone out too, on a party."

"Christmas night? But I never do."

She didn't want to go out. After she had tucked Mary in, after she had given her her sleeping medicine, the kind that relaxed her but did not harm her heart, after she had kissed her and opened the windows, she wanted to go to her own room and ring the bells on one bangle and count the hearts on the other. She wanted to put the gardenia she had saved under her pillow, the angel on her night table, and to open the monkeypod bottle and touch the thin glass tube to her wrist.

She thought, after she turned out the lights,

that life was simple for her mother because living it was so hard. Life, Lani thought, more sensitive to her mother's grief now that she, too, was in love, was so unendurable for Mary Aldrich that she saw everything, save her sorrow, in the simplest colors, the simplest lines. She might have been faintly anxious when Lani came home that October day to tell her, "I met such an attractive man . . ." But when she learned that the man was married, when she met him herself, pleasant, courteous and charming to her and to her daughter, anxiety vanished. It would never occur to her, Lani reflected, that I'd fall in love with a married man. When he sends me flowers, or little gifts at Christmas, she sees it as a friendly gesture, from an acquaintance who has been entertained in our home.

She thought, hardly daring to think, If she knew, it would kill her.

Knew what? That her daughter was in love where she had no right to love, that she had been meeting Warren in secrecy, or in as much secrecy as she could manage, that locked away in a small steel strongbox were the letters which every day she took from hiding to read, and that he had held her in his arms and kissed her.

No, it would not kill her, thought Lani, but she would be so desperately sorry for me . . .

and we would go away again, away from Washington, away even from the United States, perhaps. And I couldn't bear that.

He stayed in Palm Beach longer than he had said. It was the middle of January when he came back. She saw him again at the house of a Cabinet member, at a tea. Everyone was there, everyone who mattered in Washington and he who most mattered to her. It was growing increasingly difficult to meet him casually under the eyes, within the hearing of two hundred people . . . To say, "When did you get in?" and "Where have you been?" "How brown you are," and "Is Palm Beach fun this season?"

There was a moment when they were alone, people eddying about them, voices shattering their eardrums, yet in a way alone, standing together . . . the untouched cocktail glass in her hand.

"I was writing you tonight. I'm coming to town next week."

"Lani!"

"Don't look at me like that, don't say my name. Look away," she said desperately, "laugh, do anything. I can't bear it . . . Yes, I'm coming. Maurine is sailing suddenly, she can't come to Washington, she has so much to do before she leaves. I'm going to her instead, for . . . two days," she explained slowly, "but

51

I'll stay . . . three. That will give us a day. I'll stop at her hotel, and see her off, and then come back to the hotel."

He said, "We'll just have a day, then."

"That's all."

"And your mother?"

"She wants me to go. Her cousin, Wilma Carrington, is coming here from Richmond, she'll stay with her. Mother hasn't seen Wilma for several years. She's been away since we returned to Washington. It's all arranged, Dexter."

He said, "I don't know whether I'm crazy with happiness or whether I'm sorry."

"Sorry!"

"One day!" he reminded her.

When she left Washington Parker promised to telephone if her mother seemed at all ill, even over-tired. She would return at once. Cousin Wilma said, "Nonsense," and pinched her cheek. Cousin Wilma was lean, hard, somewhat bowlegged, born, apparently, on a horse. She looked like one, she smelled faintly of her stables and she was a riding fool, and a darling. "Stuff!" said Cousin Wilma. "I'll look after Mary. You go off on your holiday."

At any other time it would have been fun to be with Maurine . . . round, fair, friendly as a kitten, and as glad to see her as if she had never been going to see her again. But, much as Lani liked her, there were the two days to get through, a whirl of last-minute shopping, of meeting dozens of people all of whom adored Maurine, of helping pack, finding mislaid passport and tickets, of listening to the London gossip.

"And of course you remember Hal? You know he was mad for you, darling — well, he married a girl from Birmingham, of all places! Did I write you? I meant to . . . I understood when I saw her. She's like you, rather."

The third day came and Maurine had sailed.

Dexter was waiting for her when Lani returned from the pier. They couldn't do more than smile at each other, in the hotel lobby.

He said:

"Car's outside. Ready to go?"

She was ready, and they went out and drove beyond the snow-choked city, to the cleared highways and into the country. There was an inn there by a little river, too swift to be more than bound with ice at the edges, there were bare trees, leaning, a big quiet room and a fire . . .

After luncheon, they sat by the fire, on a couch. There was no one about, the waiters had departed, only an old red setter came and sat beside them, thumping his tail on the wide floor boards.

He said, "I couldn't tell you, the other night . . . the reason I stayed away so long, I was trying to persuade Muriel . . . "

"And you couldn't," she said, knowing the answer.

"I couldn't. She said, 'You're in love, you want to marry,' and I said, 'Yes — ' "

Lani was very white. She asked, "And then?"

"I wouldn't tell her more . . . she said she'd find out — not that it mattered. We quarreled, badly. I threatened her, I suppose. She said, coolly enough, that I had no proof and that she could find out who the girl was and if she was a nice girl she might take steps, if I attempted anything. You understand," he said angrily, "just what she meant?"

"I'm afraid so. Please," said Lani, "let's not talk about it now, let's just take what we can now, Dexter, this little while."

They stayed there talking, sometimes silent. Tea came for Lani after a while, cocktails for Dexter. And now and then he rose to put another set of records on the phonograph which played twelve records without changing.

"We'll pretend," said Lani, "that nothing is the way it is — except ourselves loving each other. We're going away on a trip, tomorrow."

"Darling, where?"

"Back to the Islands," she told him . . . "green as I remember them. I look for them in the magazines. None so lovely as my memory, only it isn't a memory, it's a dream . . . There'll be white beaches and the surf coming in and mountains in mist, or silver rain slanting down and then the rainbows . . . I've bought all the books about Hawaii, Dexter, travel books and novels and the legends. I hide them from my mother and I read them. I've done it since I was twelve. Am I crazy to remember so well a place that I've forgotten?"

He said, "Funny, I've never been there. Perhaps it was because we were to go together."

"Tomorrow," she said, "we'll fly to the Coast, board a ship, and go. No past, no future . . . just the present. And I'll take you to places I knew as a child and I'll remember again . . . forever."

A few people came in, and then it was dinnertime and they had eaten where they could look out and sense the dark icy flowing of the river near them, and a long time afterwards they started back to town.

Lani did not talk much, as they drove in slowly, because when they reached the city the streets were treacherous with ice. She said finally:

"The loveliest day. Tomorrow, I fly back."

Dexter said quietly:

"The apartment is closed. I'm living at the club. The servants are in Palm Beach. There's a small apartment in town which belongs to a friend, now in Central America. I have a key. He left just before Christmas. We know each other very well. When I asked him for the key, he asked no questions. He never will. Must I take you back to your hotel, Lani?"

He had not meant, he had not planned . . . As a matter of fact, he had had the keys of that particular *pied-à-terre* for some time. It belonged to him, he paid the rent. He had not planned anything, he hadn't planned the Agnes Palmer interlude. He had drifted into that, as he had drifted into this. But Agnes was a different, wiser, more knowledgeable girl. And she had no ties, except a guardian uncle who didn't care as long as he drew the income from the estate. Muriel had laughed a good deal about Agnes. But Lani had ties and Lani wouldn't make scenes; whatever happened she would go back to the pretty invalid mother and . . .

It wasn't like the Agnes Palmer business; the hell of it was that it was always like the first time, every time. And he had had just one too many highballs although to all intents and purposes he seemed sober enough; he drove even more carefully than usual. But they had been together all that afternoon in the drowsy, quiet place, with the fire burning . . .

"Must I take you back, Lani?"

He couldn't pull off the road here, couldn't stop and kiss her into mindless acquiescence. But she could feel his desire, as if it were hands laid upon her body and a mouth over her own. She said, after a long while:

"Yes, you must."

"Darling, we've had so little . . . you said yourself to take what we could now. Are you afraid, Lani?"

"I'm not afraid," she said. She loved him so much that she thought she could die of it. But this wasn't what she wanted. It wasn't good enough for her love, for Mary's daughter.

"Then why . . . *why?*"

"I can't," she said miserably. "Don't hate me for it, Dexter. It's just that I can't. Forget that you asked me, forget that I refused. Remember just that we had today. Perhaps," she added, and the tears rolled steadily down her cheeks, wet and cold, "perhaps it should be the last day."

He thought, I'll let her believe that, and then, after a while — I can wait, he thought. Aloud, he said:

"Perhaps . . ."

He left her at her hotel and she went in hurriedly, hoping no one would notice that she had been crying. And the next day she flew back to Washington.

Chapter 4

Joseph met her, his black face shining with pleasure. Driving her little car skillfully through the heavy traffic, he answered her questions. Everything was fine, they'd had one day of rain and sleet, then it had faired. Miss Mary was fine too, she and Miss Wilma had been out for a drive in the big car. Rheba's cold, begun before Lani's departure, was well. Say what you wanted about them doctor's medicines, Rheba always held with goose grease and it worked, for sure.

Lani thought, I might never have been away. Nothing had changed, Joseph was the same, the city was the same, the apartment, when she entered it, was the same. Her mother greeted her, held her close. She asked, "Do you realize that this was the first time — ?"

Cousin Wilma snorted; with a little imagination one would have said she pawed the ground as well. She said:

"Does your mother good to get away from you. Can't say as much for you, Lani, honey.

You look tired."

"Maurine," Lani told them, "is a strenuous hostess. Yes, she sailed ... in a riot of orchids. She had half the eligible bachelors in New York at her feet, but she sailed."

Her mother said, with a long sigh:

"I'm glad you're back."

Nothing had changed, not even herself. In her room she looked in the mirror for a long time. She looked just the same, a little white perhaps, her eyes shadowed. But she'd looked like that often during the days when Mary Aldrich was less well than usual and her daughter slept lightly, anxiously, and woke to fear.

Eyes just the same, gray eyes, looking back at her.

She thought soberly, It can't be I — it's another girl, a girl who's in love with a man who isn't free to marry her, who spent most of yesterday with that man and listened without shock to his suggestion that she spend the night as well as the day with him ...

Perhaps this generation wasn't easily shocked.

She thought, If I could be sure we'd harm no one but ourselves? But she couldn't be sure. She thought, Was I right, must we take what we can ... even if we regret it afterwards? Life's so short, she thought bitterly, just past her twenty-third birthday.

His flowers came that afternoon. There was no card but no one else sent her gardenias.

In the morning she had the letter. He wrote:

"I wanted word to come with the flowers. But one can't wire what I want to say. The hours since I saw you I've spent cursing your wisdom, your common sense. I hate your wisdom and your common sense, Lani.

"I won't be coming to Washington for a while. It's too difficult. And we can't just mark time. Things stop — altogether, or they progress. Nothing else is feasible. No compromise.

"You're better off than I. You're very young, there will be other men . . . this won't mean anything, soon. But I'm so much older than you, there won't be anyone else. You see, I love you very much.

"Before you change your heart, Lani, perhaps you'll change your mind. Perhaps I'm counting on that."

She gave the gardenias to Cousin Wilma to take with her to Baltimore where she was going on another round of visits. She tore the letter into very fine pieces. But not until she had it by heart. The heart which wouldn't change. How could you say that, she demanded mutely, how *could* you?

She did not answer the letter. There was so much to say and so little, all of it futile.

A day or so later it snowed. The curtains were drawn against the early dusk and the falling flakes slurred against the pane. In the living room a fire burned on the hearth and Mary's couch was drawn close to it. Lani sat in a big chair beside her, and Joseph had just brought tea when the doorbell rang.

He went, with his unhurried air of patience and portent, and returned with a letter for Mrs. Aldrich. "It came by messenger, Miss Mary," he said, "he didn't wait for no answer."

Mary took the envelope with the imprint of a Washington hotel in the upper left-hand corner. She frowned at the writing, square and masculine, tore it open. Lani, looking up from the fire, came back to the quiet room with the feeling that she had been leagues away, sitting there, dreaming, watching the flames, happy in her unhappiness, perhaps, as only first love can be.

"Darling, what is it?" she asked sharply, for her mother was very white and her hands shook.

"I'm all right," Mary said, "only I can't see him . . . I *can't*. You'll have to telephone him, Lani."

The letter fell from her relaxing fingers and

62

Lani stooped to pick it up. She asked, "Am I to read it?"

She read it, while her mother waited.

"Dear Mary," it read, "I am here on business with my nephew, Jim. We return to the Islands the day after tomorrow, flying to the Coast and catching the clipper. I have just learned that you are here. Would you see me, or would it be too painful for you? I want so much to see you, my dear, I have so much to tell you, so many messages to bring you . . . No one has forgotten you, all send you their aloha . . . "

It was signed "Frederick."

"Frederick?" asked Lani, wondering.

"Frederick Bruce, your father's closest friend. They grew up together." Mary spoke with an effort. "Lani, do you remember him at all? You used to call him Uncle Fred."

Lani thought a moment, then shook her head. "I'm afraid not," she said. "Angel, of course you needn't see him. Don't talk about it now if it upsets you."

"Frederick Bruce," repeated her mother. "Do you remember the day your father died . . . and how he died? I've never spoken of it to you."

Lani said:

"I don't remember anything. Except someone coming to take me to her house. A woman

. . . There was a garden and a big boy."

"Jim Bruce," said her mother; "he is five or six years older than you. The woman was his mother." She drew a deep, broken breath. "Your father and Fred were over on Hawaii, the Big Island, shooting . . . there was an accident . . . Fred Bruce stumbled, the safety catch wasn't . . . the gun went off — Your father was killed."

"Please," cried Lani. She knelt by her mother, put her arms around her. "Please . . . "

"I was fond of Fred," said her mother, "and your father loved him. I didn't blame him, even then. He was just the instrument. But I never wanted to see him again. Seeing him, I'd remember that the last time I saw Alan — alive . . . "

Lani rose. Her mother asked faintly:

"What are you going to do?"

"Ring for Parker."

"Wait. Telephone Fred, Lani, explain, if you can. No, meet him, that will be better. Ask him if he will meet you — tonight perhaps, for dinner." She added, "Everyone thinks me morbid. Perhaps I am. They don't understand."

"Of course not," said Lani gently. She thought, I could understand. I never have, really, until now.

Mary said:

"Fred never married. This boy with him is his brother's son. His brother is dead now. Your father's cousin, Helen Aldrich, who married William Gaines writes to me ... sometimes once a year, sometimes oftener. When I feel that I can, I answer. She tells me these things, she urges me to return, with you." She added, low, "There's no return to Eden, Lani."

Lani rang for Parker, who came, looked at Mrs. Aldrich, took her back to her room, made her lie down. Outside the closed door she spoke severely to Lani.

"Did something upset her, Miss Lani?"

"I'm afraid so."

Parker said, "The doctor was here while you were in New York. Mrs. Aldrich didn't want me to tell you. He just came in to see how she was and — "

"She's better," said Lani fiercely, "she looks better. This is just a temporary shock."

Parker said quietly, "She's no better, Miss Lani."

Lani went back to the living room. Her hands shook and her knees. She called the hotel at which Frederick Bruce was staying, and found him in. When he spoke his voice stirred a blurred memory, the memory of a big man with black hair, a man who laughed a good deal. She said:

"This is Lani — "

"*Iolani!*" said Frederick Bruce. He cleared his throat. He said, "Your mother has had my letter?"

"Yes," said Lani. "This is going to be hard to say, Mr. Bruce — "

Frederick Bruce was silent for so long that she thought they had been disconnected. She asked, "Mr. Bruce?" and he answered:

"I'm here. She won't see me, I suppose. I expected it — yet I hoped . . . I wanted to see her — and you."

Lani said:

"Mother wants me to see you. She thought, perhaps, that if you were free tonight — or sometime tomorrow?"

"Tonight," said Bruce. "Would you dine with me and Jim? . . . Good. At seven-thirty."

Later she went to her mother's room and stood looking down at her.

"I telephoned Mr. Bruce," she said gently; "I'm dining with him tonight. He understands, darling. He sent you his love."

"Give him mine," said Mary Aldrich. She raised herself on her elbow, her long hair, scarcely dulled, fell about her thin shoulders. "Make him understand. It isn't that I'm bitter or that I'm not fond of him. It's just that I can't endure . . . Especially not now," she said oddly, "when everything's worn so thin."

Lani dined with Frederick Bruce and his nephew in their pleasant suite. The moment the older man took her hand, she remembered him, although the black hair was very gray, the lean face lined, and the tall shoulders stooped. She did not remember James Bruce at all . . . not this stocky young man whose shoulders seemed wide for the rest of him, and whose bright blue eyes regarded her, smiling, from under a shock of what looked like constitutionally untidy hair, burned with the sun, and very fair in contrast with his brown face.

He said:

"But I remember you, Iolani — not that I had much use for you, because of my superior years. But we played together now and then . . . once we all went off on a vacation on Kauai . . . up at Kokee . . . You wouldn't remember that. You fell off your horse . . . and once you tumbled into a pool — you don't remember?"

She shook her head.

"Not at all," she told him. "I'm sorry."

She liked him, he was amusing, he was different. But her interest was centered in his uncle. After dinner, over their coffee, she tried to make him understand.

"It's taken me a long time to understand, myself," she said. "You see, she was so much in love with my father . . . they were ideally happy and the shock — "

"He was the finest man I ever knew," said Frederick Bruce. His face was set in unhappy lines. He asked with an effort, "You know, of course, how he died?"

"I didn't," said Lani, "until this afternoon."

"My dear," he said, and turned his haggard eyes on her, "there's nothing I can say . . . except that I would give my own life at any time to restore his."

Jim Bruce said loyally:

"It was an accident. I'm sure that Iolani's mother — "

"She said," Lani said swiftly, "that she'd never blamed you, Mr. Bruce."

"Mr. Bruce?"

"Uncle Fred," Lani corrected herself, "never. Not even at first."

"I know. She's a wonderful person. I remember her when she first came to the Islands, on the cruise. And then, when Alan brought her home. No one who ever knew her has forgotten her. Each year we hope she'll return."

"She won't," said Lani; "she couldn't. And she's not well, Uncle Fred."

"I know. Your cousin, Helen Gaines, told me. It is her heart, isn't it?" he asked.

Lani nodded. She said:

"People have tried for years to make her return, to face things . . . that's how they put it. But she isn't capable . . . you mustn't think she's weak or morbid, Uncle Fred. It's just that she hasn't much strength . . . not more than enough to last her through each day. As if it were measured out, so much for each twenty-four hours. And she can't take on anything more, any extra emotional strain."

He said gently:

"We knew about that heart, after you were born. Your father was very careful of her, he carried her on his hands. He loved her so much."

Lani's eyes were dark with tears. She said, "Tell me all you want her to hear."

There were messages, dozens of them. There was friendly gossip. There was the business that had brought the Bruces to Washington.

"Sugar," said Frederick. "You wouldn't be interested but we're fighting for our lives. Jim here, is head *luna* at Waipuhia."

"You'll have to translate," Lani warned him, smiling.

"I forgot. You seem one of us. You are one of us," he added gravely. "I fancied perhaps your mother had talked to you about . . . No, I suppose not. Well, Waipuhia is a sugar plantation on Hawaii. The near-by town is Mana. Bill Gaines, who married your father's cousin, Helen Aldrich, is manager there and Jim's head overseer, if you like the term better than *luna*. Bill's incapacitated . . . thrown from his horse; he has a badly fractured leg. The assistant manager, Davidson, had to take over. So they let Jim come with me because he has a fabulous head for figures, spent more than the usual apprenticeship on our experimental station, and also is equipped to act as my secretary. We've been here two days and we leave day after tomorrow. Jim has to get back to work and so do I."

Jim said, smiling:

"He hasn't told you what a swell head *luna* I am, Iolani. Or that he's a big shot: Bruce, Remwick, Anderson — Sugar Factors."

She shook her head, and said:

"I don't understand a word. It seems odd to hear myself called Iolani. No one does, not even Mother."

"What do they call you?" asked Jim.

"Lani. It sounds like Lanny, the way they say it, the way I think of it myself . . . short, snappy. As for Iolani, they can't pronounce it."

Jim smiled at her. He said, "Come back to the Islands. We'll have you a *kamaaina* in no time."

70

"Do I want to be one?" asked Lani cautiously.

Frederick Bruce laughed. He said:

"It means old-timer, child of the land. Sometimes a person who has lived for years in the Islands but who has not caught their spirit, never becomes one, but remains a *malihini*, or stranger, all his life. On the other hand, I think you'd become a *kamaaina* within a few hours."

She said slowly:

"No one knows how much I want to return. Least of all my mother. You understand why I can't?"

"I understand," said Frederick gravely.

Joseph called for her, a little later, and the two men went down and out to the car with her. Frederick held her hand a long time. He said, "You look very like your father, Iolani." And stooped, swiftly, to kiss her cheek. "Thank you for coming," he told her, "and give your mother my love . . . if she will accept it."

"She sent you hers," said Lani.

Jim Bruce stood bareheaded in the frosty night and took her free hand in his. He said:

"You'll come back, you'll fall off your horse again, I'll pull you out of a pool. It's a promise. We'll see you at Hale-O-Ka-Moana, one day."

71

"What's that?" she asked, laughing.

"That's the manager's house," he told her, "at Waipuhia . . . the name means House of the Sea."

Mary Aldrich was awake when Lani came home, for Parker opened the door when Lana rang and said, "Your mother wants to see you, Miss Lani."

"She isn't worse!"

"No. But she's restless, I can't get her to sleep till she's seen you."

When Lani went in to sit beside the big bed and hold the thin hand, Mary wanted to know everything, how Fred looked and the boy Jim, and what they had said, every word.

Lani told her as well as she could remember, except for words about her father which she remembered best of all. The Hawaiian names were difficult but her mother said them for her, dreamily. She asked, "He didn't speak of Alan?"

"He said he was the finest man he ever knew."

Mary's eyes closed. She said, "I suppose I am a coward . . . don't blame me too much. Perhaps, next time he comes."

"He said," Lani told her, "that he might be back, in the late spring."

"Then," said her mother with sudden energy, "I will . . . I *will* see him, Lani, I promise."

She smiled and presently fell asleep, and Lani went softly from the room thinking, She is better; Parker's wrong and the doctor; if she hadn't been she wouldn't have promised. She always keeps her promises.

She could not keep this one, for less than a week later Mary Aldrich died, quietly, in her sleep.

Chapter 5

Everyone was very kind . . . all their friends,
the lawyers, Cousin Wilma, Ellie Underwood.
There were flowers and a cable from Dexter.
She had not heard from him again since the
letter which reached her the day after her
return from New York. This cable came from
South America. It said among other things,
"all my love . . . " and she put it aside to read
again when the curious, numbing shock had
passed.

There were cables from Hawaii, dozens of
them, and letters . . . from Frederick Bruce,
Jim, from Jim's mother, from Helen Gaines,
from people whose names Lani had never
heard or had forgotten. There were flowers,
carloads of them.

The legal matters were simple. Mary
Aldrich had left everything of which she was
possessed to her daughter. Her fortune, which
was considerable, her inheritance from the
Carringtons, dead prior to Lani's birth, was
safely invested in solid, unexciting bonds.

And there was a block of sugar stock, which Alan Aldrich had left his wife.

Ellie Underwood asked:

"What are you going to do now?"

Lani looked at the enormous, concerned woman and shook her head. She said, after a minute:

"I've had invitations — to go to Hawaii to my father's people, to go to England and stay with Maurine, to go live with Cousin Wilma. But I don't want to do anything yet except get away from here for a little while."

"Gordon Herold has asked you to marry him, hasn't he?" asked Ellie.

"How did you know?"

"He told me. You could do worse, Lani; he's a good boy and his father would give him the moon."

"We don't want the same moon," Lani said. She looked tired and quite lovely. She was not wearing black. Her mother had hated it.

After a moment she said, looking around Ellie's great drawing room, the room in which she had met Dexter Warren, and which was now empty except for herself and her hostess:

"I am going to New York for a time. It was good of you to take Joseph and Rheba, Ellie."

"Nonsense. I could use them. My two are due to retire. Jenkins has been at me about them. What about Parker?"

"She's going back to England. I asked her to stay with me but she wants to go home. She's saved, all these years. I don't blame her. As a matter of fact, I am a little relieved," Lani admitted; "Parker's almost too good to be true and I don't want or need a maid, Ellie."

Ellie said, "Let me know what you plan to do after you return from New York . . . or won't you return?"

"I don't know. Why should I? I have no roots, anywhere, now. I couldn't go back to the apartment in any case. I'll always be grateful to you for insisting that I come here. The agents say that it can be rented very easily . . . they have someone, in fact, who wants it. We hadn't much, you know, just a few personal things. I'll take them to New York with me and live in a hotel for a time until I decide what to do."

Ellie thought, If Dexter Warren has any hand in your decision . . . but she couldn't say it. Not to this pale girl, with the tired, grieving eyes. All she said was, "Well, when you make up your mind, let me know."

Lani went to New York, with her trunks, her hand luggage, in which the little strongbox was packed, and the bundle of letters from her mother's friends all over the world.

Someday she would really answer them; they deserved more than the brief notes of gratitude she had been able to manage.

She had been settled in her hotel for several days when Dexter called her.

"I just got into town," he said. "I flew. I heard you were here. When may I see you?"

"Any time. I've been waiting," she said.

He came that afternoon and sat by the fire in her little suite and looked at her. He said:

"Lovelier than I remembered. Lani, there's no use my trying to tell you how sorry I am."

"Don't try."

"What are you going to do, darling?"

"For a time, nothing," she told him. "I have friends here, they are very kind to me and — "

He said, "You have me." He went over to sit by her on the couch and pulled her into his arms. At the touch of his cheek against hers she began to cry. She had not been able to cry, not really, for so long.

He held her, smoothed back her hair. He was terrified of crying women, they disturbed him, but this was a child sobbing in his arms and he knew it was not because of him that she wept.

After a while, "I'm sorry," she said; "I haven't cried much." She dried her eyes, steadied her voice.

He asked, "You'll let me come, often?"

She looked at him unhappily.

"I don't know, Dexter," she said. "I don't know what to do."

He came. For tea, for dinner, he took her to quiet little places, he took her to the movies where they sat and watched the screen like children, hand in hand. He took her to the theater. "You don't mind?" he said; and she replied gravely, "No, I like to go . . . that hasn't anything to do with the way you mourn in your heart."

They went alone always, and sat in the balcony, and did not dress. But the theater, good as the season was that year, did not interest her. She read a good deal, saw her various friends when she was not with Dexter. Drifted, marked time. Slowly the numbing shock passed, she became fully aware of her loss and tried to adjust herself to it.

Dexter told himself that he was a patient man, that he could wait. He told himself that he was as much in love as ever. Despite the fact that the girl he'd met in South America had returned from her cruise, a very entertaining girl, a fashion designer, chic, clever, and exceptionally good looking. She had been married and divorced, she knew all the answers. She was not interested in marriage, not even in romance. She had a franker word for it. She had caught lightly at Dexter's imagination the few days they had known each other in the hotel in Rio . . .

Ellie Underwood was in New York on a shopping expedition. She came to the hotel and had luncheon with Lani. "You look better," she told her; "you've regained the weight you lost, and the color." Then she leaned across the table or as nearly as her structure would permit.

"You've been seeing Dexter Warren," she said.

Lani nodded.

"You know everything, Ellie," she said serenely.

"I'd like to . . . one does hear things. I warned you, Lani. About Muriel Warren. You know that she'll never let him go."

Lani's mouth tightened and she said nothing.

"My God," said Ellie furiously, "I believe you're really in love with him!"

She was aghast and looked it.

Lani asked steadily:

"And if I am?"

"You're telling me you're of age, that you have your own income and no guardians, and that I'm to mind my own business. Granted. But I won't. But Dexter Warren plays the field. He doesn't want to be free, my dear. If

Muriel divorced him, he'd be furious. She's his protection as well as his bread and butter. How long do you think he'd keep his various high-sounding jobs without her? Oh, I know he's made money for her, and plenty of it, but he had to have her capital to begin with. I tell you, Lani, you're wasting your time."

Lani was scarlet. She said furiously, "I don't believe you."

"All right," said Ellie. "Forget it. I'm a fat old woman who likes to meddle. We'll talk about something else. But you know I'm fond of you."

Lani said, "I'm not angry. Perhaps you believe what you say. I can't."

"But you can't go on like this," cried Ellie, "it isn't within reason." She put it bluntly. "You can't be his wife," she said, "and I don't think you'd be content with being his mistress."

"I'm my own mistress," Lani reminded her somberly.

Ellie sighed. "All right," she said, "I've had my say and that's that — but — God help you, Lani. I'm not going to try and drag in the usual appeals. That's hokum. As you say, you're free, you've no one to whom you need answer, least of all to me."

After a moment Lani said, "Thank you, Ellie, I'm sorry if I — "

"Forget it," interrupted Ellie shortly.

The next time she saw Dexter they lunched together in a French place, the bar taking up half the space, the ceiling low and smoky, the menu written in chalk on a big slate, and the food excellent. The room was crowded, and they knew no one there, which was why Dexter had selected it. The fashion designer, Susan Tait, had mentioned it to him. He hoped she wouldn't be here today. She wasn't.

Lani said:

"I'm leaving the hotel as soon as I can find an apartment. You see, as long as my mother lived I had a home, wherever she was, whether it was a hotel or a furnished flat or a hospital." Her voice caught, she was silent. She felt the hard warm pressure of his hand over hers and she tried to smile at him. "Now," she concluded, "I have to make a home — alone."

"Never alone," he assured her at once. His heart pounded with the old triumph which was always, in its first inception, new.

Lani's eyes widened, the color came swiftly into her cheeks. She asked, low, dazed with hope:

"You — you've spoken to your wife, again . . . and this time . . . she'll free you, Dexter?"

He shook his head and her heart leaped and

then steadied, after that first wild tumultuous hope. He said gently:

"Yes, I've spoken to her again, Lani. It's no use. And my hands are tied, for if I tried to force her, she'd manage to learn who you are and drag you through the most humiliating — "

He broke off. They had been over this ground before. After a moment Lani said unhappily:

"There's nothing she could say, really. We've done nothing."

She was silent, thinking back over their relationship, the stolen, secret hours together, kisses, pledges. She went on with sudden defiance:

"Nothing wrong. It isn't as though you were living together, or as though you were — she were still in love with you and wanted you — "

His face was dark suddenly, and still, shut away from her, his eyes veiled. She wondered forlornly what she had said to make him look like that.

After a moment he smiled at her.

"Of course not. Although Muriel has a gift for twisting things — into, shall we say, circumstantial evidence? Lani, don't look like that. I can't bear it. I can't endure to have you so unhappy. I wish I could make you understand Muriel. God knows I don't understand her, wholly. I doubt if she understands herself. As you say, she doesn't love me, she doesn't want me. But she will not give me up. Or so she says. Yet I am not altogether without hope. The last word hasn't been spoken. She's — mercurial. Perhaps someday she'll tire of this crazy life of hers, find someone she believes she wants enough to — " He shook his head. "I don't know," he said flatly.

After a moment Lani asked:

"What are we to do? We can't go on like this."

"I know." He looked at her for a moment without speaking. Then he said gently:

"The last time you were in New York — do you remember?"

"I remember," she said steadily.

"Things have changed," he told her. "You no longer have anyone you need consider. If you remain here, set up your own establishment, make a new life for yourself, new friends, new surroundings, can there not be room for me? As you just said, we can't go on like this . . . marking time. I love you too much. And you — answer me honestly — do you not love me too much? What we have is lovely and exciting, but it isn't enough . . . or at least, not for me. You understand, don't you, Lani?"

She understood. She bent her head a little, said something too faintly for him to hear. He went on, urgent, demanding, compelling her eyes to his own. He said:

"Don't say anything — now. Don't make up your mind. Think about it. And when you have thought, let me know. But before you make up your mind I must be honest with you. About myself. About Muriel. As long as I do not try to force her to a divorce, she will make no trouble." He added quickly, "I have her word for that. She to go her way; I to go mine. And I would protect you in every possible way. Lani, it's hideous to have to talk of things like discretion now. But fair to you. I wouldn't jeopardize you in any way, darling. You'd have your own life — and make a place for me in it. Caution is a narrow, cold word, but for your sake — "

She said suddenly:

"It's horrible to sit here and plan and — "

"I know. But if you love me enough," he urged her, "the things which seem furtive and sordid wouldn't matter. We would have each other, we could take what we could and be grateful for it. And surely in this case the end justifies the means."

She said slowly:

"I'm accountable to no one but myself, I know, Dexter. But — "

84

"Don't answer," he said. "And don't blame yourself — for anything. Any blame has been mine. Any future blame will be mine. Remember that. When you have thought about this, when you have reached a decision, send for me. And remember that I love you . . . enough to hurt you like this. For I am hurting you," he said, "and I'll go on hurting you, I suppose."

She said, "I don't mind." She tried to smile at him. After a moment she added, "All right, Dexter. I'll — send for you after I've thought . . . I — I wish I could make up my mind now. But you can't do things like that, can you? At least," she added, "I can't."

A little later they went out of the restaurant together into the sunlight. Dexter called a taxi and put her in it. She looked back and saw him standing there, hatless, looking after her.

For three days she saw no one except the people in the hotel. She went for walks, long hard walks in the Park, around the reservoir. She went to a movie, alone, sitting in the back of the house watching the screen, the vicarious love and sacrifice, and seeing nothing. She tried to read, nights. She made no sense from printed words.

She marshaled all the arguments. She would hurt no one save herself. Her mother was gone, there was no one else. She thought,

85

No matter how discreet we are there will be gossip. Yet how could gossip hurt her, when there was no one who cared? She thought, Perhaps in time Muriel Warren will see how futile it is, to stand in his way like this, perhaps in time she will free him.

She found that she wanted desperately to call him, to say, All right, it will be as you wish it. Yet she could not.

She remembered a trivial thing . . . how once, as a small child in London, she had committed a tiny crime and had run, with the tears streaming down her face, to confess it. Her mother had caught her and held her and kissed her swollen eyes. And Lani had said, weeping, "You needn't have known, but I had to tell you. And I didn't want to, I didn't want to!"

She remembered Mary Aldrich saying, "You can't help it, darling. It's your missionary ancestors. Stern and rockbound coast." Her mother had laughed, and yet the tears had stood in her eyes. "New England conscience," she had said; "you'll always be honest, no matter how much you hate it. Poor Lani."

She wanted to go to Dexter. To say, I am here, I am yours, completely. But something held her back. It was not fear. It was an innate integral shrinking, a hard, inviolable core within her which would not surrender; it was as if her spirit drew a sword against the demands of her body.

On the fourth evening, in a room full of Dexter's flowers, she sat across from him, watching the flames flicker in the little hearth. They had been talking for two hours and she was sick with fatigue. He said, at last:

"It all boils down to this, Lani. You don't love me enough."

She looked at him wearily.

"I love you," she said, "more than enough. But I'm at odds with myself. If it were just loving . . . but it goes deeper than that. So I'm going away."

He sat very quiet. Then he asked:

"That's your answer?"

"No. I think that if I get away, for a while . . . by myself, out of New York, away from you . . . you see," she added, trying to smile, "here I have only to put out my hand to a telephone and there you are . . . I mustn't, on an impulse, Dexter, or because at that moment I'm wanting you so much. So I've made my plans. I'm going back to the Islands. I cabled my cousin, Helen Gaines, yesterday. I have had her answer. My passage has been arranged, and train reservations. The Washington lawyers will take care of everything here. I'll go out for a visit, two months, three. I don't know. I won't write you. Perhaps when I'm away from you, when I have a better perspective, I'll know. And as soon as I know, I'll cable. Please understand. I must be sure."

He said slowly:

"All right, if that's the way you want it, Lani. I can wait. It's been my fault. I spoke too soon, you have had difficult adjustments to make." He rose and took her in his arms and kissed her and she clung to him, tearless, her face very white and drawn with fatigue. She said, low:

"You're all I have now . . . but for a little while I have to be alone."

A week later she stood on the boat deck of the big white ship and watched it pull away from the docks at San Pedro. People were laughing, throwing long confetti streamers, there was music. The decks below were crowded, up here there were fewer people, a handful of passengers, some members of the crew. The March wind was soft in Southern California, it smelled like spring.

She thought, I'm going back to the place where I was born; I'm going back, alone.

The ship moved slowly, toward her anchorage over two thousand miles away, over the fathomless water lying between the United States of the mainland and the United States of the Hawaiian Islands.

Leaning on the rail Lani watched their progress, the slow tears falling unheeded down her cheeks, salt and bitter in her mouth. Her mother had said, "There's no return to Eden." But she was returning — was it return, she wondered, banishment, or escape?

Chapter 6

On the morning they docked Lani woke early and lay still in her bed listening to the water sliding by, to the familiar sounds of the ship which speaks with little voices and is never still.

It was warm, as it had been for two days. She rose and went in her bare feet and thin nightgown to the *lanai* which opened from the stateroom, a small private domain furnished like a veranda, and in reality part of A Deck, forward. Here she could lean over her railing and look her fill at water and at the shapes of islands rising suddenly from the sea. She thought, straining her eyes to see Molokai, strange and unsubstantial in this light, that for the last day or so the air had been softer than any she remembered, the water a more miraculous blue, bluer even than her dim recollection.

She had packed, and presently the stewardess would come on duty and bring her coffee. She left the *lanai* reluctantly and returned to her stateroom to dress. Looking at herself a little later she saw grave eyes and a rested face touched with the color of excitement.

She had done nothing on the trip but eat and sleep. Her meals were brought to her on her *lanai* and much of the first two days she spent in bed, dreaming a little, sleeping a little, but for the most part lying quiet, listening to the sea sounds and trying to bring some order to the chaos of her thoughts.

The thought of her mother was a dull continuous aching, as if she had lost a limb and it still pained her. But her longing for Dexter Warren was a harsh, stabbing pain, which came and went, breath-taking in its intensity.

During the trip she had not made friends among the passengers, had spoken to no one until yesterday when she went out on deck and watched them swimming in the pool. She had talked to the captain, at whose table she had been placed, and to whom she had sent a note thanking him for his courtesy but asking to be excused. In return he had asked her to have tea with him, the day before they landed, in his quarters. He said, when she appeared, that he felt she would prefer this rather than attend one of his before-dinner parties. And she had been grateful to him.

He knew, it appeared, about her mother; and he had known her father, and his people.

He talked to her of them, over the teacups, friendly and concerned. And when she said, "I feel I've been very rude, shutting myself away as I have, during the trip," he shook his head.

"You've been wise," he told her.

The stewardess knocked, and came in with the coffee. She said, smiling, "You must go on deck, Miss Aldrich, it would be a pity to miss anything."

So presently Lani went out on deck where most of the passengers were gathered and took her place among them — men and women, pretty girls, old people, children, all laughing and excited. But Lani's excitement had passed and something deeper had replaced it. She looked across the rail and saw Oahu — anchored in the sea. They had passed the southernmost tip of the Koolau range, and Makapuu, and now the tawny round shape of Koko Head was in view, and presently Diamond Head, crouching, her ancient feet in the sea, the guardian, unforgettable shape, dull rose, saffron and green. And between the heads the fabulous valleys, the color of emeralds.

Here the sea was emerald too, and jade and cobalt blue. And someone cried that you could see the white surf breaking at Waikiki, and, on the beach, the Royal Hawaiian hotel, coral tinted against the sapphire sky.

Honolulu lay just ahead, the Aloha Tower pointing the way to heaven. And presently the engines were stilled, the tugs came out and people came aboard, their arms full of flower garlands.

Everyone was meeting someone. Lani felt a small, forlorn pang. She was coming home to a home she did not well remember, and she was alone.

Someone spoke to her and she turned . . .

"Uncle Fred!"

He seemed taller than ever in his white clothes. He put a dozen fragrant leis about her shoulders and they were heavy and cool and smelled of paradise, pikake, gardenia, ilima, the royal flower, carnation, plumeria, crown flowers.

He said, "I knew you'd come."

"It was dear of you to meet me," she told him, her throat tight with sudden tears.

"Helen telephoned me as soon as she had your cable. She expected to fly from Hawaii and be on hand," he told her, "but she couldn't get away. I'm hoping that you'll come directly to me. Jim's mother presides over my establishment, you know. I wouldn't let her come with me this morning, I wanted to meet you — alone. Which was selfish of me. Helen demands your immediate presence at Waipuhia, of course, but I've told her firmly that you're staying on in Honolulu first."

She said, "But I can't impose — "

He looked at her a moment. He asked:

"Alan's daughter — and Mary's — imposing?"

She had hurt him. Lani put her hand on his arm and tried to smile. She said, "Forgive me. Of course, I'll come . . . if you and Mrs. Gaines — "

"She won't like that," he interrupted; "After all, she's a bona fide relative, not a courtesy one, like myself."

"Cousin Helen then," she corrected herself; "if you'll plan for me, I'll be delighted. I hadn't any plans, really, I thought I could stay at the Royal Hawaiian for a while, and then visit the Gaineses . . . but — "

He said, "You'll stay with us, first. Oh . . . I'm sorry, but reporters are headed our way. Do you mind? You see, you're news. Island born, returning after all these years."

"I don't mind." She drew a deep breath. She said, "Things smell different . . . ever since early this morning I have been smelling flowers. It can't be my imagination."

The reporters came up, a pretty girl, a young man, a Japanese cameraman. Lani posed alone by the rail, and with Frederick

Bruce, answered their questions in her gentle friendly way and they went away, smiling. They, too, had brought her leis; she was laden with them. Others came up, with their garland offerings, people whose names she did not know or could not catch and whom she had never seen before. She said slowly:

"I've never landed here before, of course . . . but I went away. I have very little memory of that sailing."

"Your mother was very ill," Frederick Bruce told her, "a nurse was with her, and you had your own nurse. You cried a good deal, I remember."

"I remember only the flowers," she said.

They were under way again, approaching anchorage. The sun was golden and from the dock the sound of music reached them and Bruce took Lani's arm and guided her to a place at the rail. The Royal Hawaiian band was playing, and a big dark woman was singing. She wore white as if it were royal purple and her lovely voice floated out, singing to welcome the ship and her passengers to the Islands.

"I want to laugh," said Lani suddenly, "but most of all, to cry."

"There are people," commented Frederick Bruce, "who decry all this display of flowers and song, as part of a commercial sort of hospitality, a general publicizing of the Islands for the tourist. Maybe we do like our tourists to have a good first impression. Yet it goes deeper than that, Lani. It is authentic, a symbol, an expression of the Island spirit. You will learn that after a while."

People came up to speak to him, passengers returning for the second or tenth time to holiday in Hawaii, or passengers returning home after a pleasure or business trip to the mainland. Lani watching him, thought, He's very well liked, everybody seems to know him.

There were several men and an elderly woman who knew her as well, had known her as a child, and her parents. They all said much the same thing to her, "We knew you were on board, but we did not wish to intrude. Now that you are here you must give us the pleasure of seeing you, often." And one, the woman, said, "We're so glad you've come home."

They went down the gangplank to the big echoing sheds where Bruce's car was waiting. The driver spoke to Lani, smiling. "Aloha," he said, and gave her the lei which was over his arm. He was Chinese-Hawaiian, a short stocky young man with a brown round face.

"That's Pete," said Frederick, when they were in the car, "he's been with me from a pup. You'll get to know him."

Afterward she could remember no details of that first drive. She had a dim memory of narrow streets, of many people, of broad avenues of palm trees and blue water, of gracious buildings and parks, of African tulip trees just past their glowing prime. She sat back in the car and smiled dizzily at Frederick. She said:

"My trunks and — '♥

"All arranged," he said promptly; "your hand luggage is in the car and the rest will be along presently."

She said, "It's very dreamlike . . . I seem to have no volition . . . yet I like it."

He said gently, "There is healing in these Islands. You will find it so, Iolani."

Frederick Bruce's house, out Diamond Head way, stood in gracious gardens. Long and low, it faced the sea, wide windows looking over that ineffable changing blue, and the broad *lanai* running straight around the house. Entering, Lani drew a long breath of sheer delight. It was like coming home, she thought, yet she had so little recollection of home.

Jim Bruce's mother was waiting for them. She was a little brown woman with short curly hair growing gray, and a small face of the most pleasant plainness. She smiled at Lani and said, "You wouldn't remember me, of course," yet when Lani felt her thin strong arms around her, it seemed to her as if she had never forgotten.

The room to which they took her was big, many windowed, and looked upon the sea. It opened on a *lanai* — "You can lie here in the sun," Betsy Bruce told her.

Pete had brought up her hand luggage, Frederick Bruce had gone, the two women were alone. Lani raised her hands to her throat and began removing the fragrant, heavy garlands. The room was full of flowers, and great baskets stood on the *lanai* . . . water lilies, mauve, purple and blue, torch ginger, tuberoses, gardenias — she had never seen as many flowers and said so, with delight.

"You can look at the cards later," said Betsy, "everyone is so glad you've come. The gardenias are from Jim," she added.

Lani had thought that she never again wished to see gardenias. She said now, uncertainly, her throat aching, "It was kind of him, Mrs. Bruce."

"Not Aunt Betsy? Well, perhaps you'll come to that, in your own good time," said the older woman. She beckoned the girl out to the *lanai* and they looked together, over the gardens, to the sea. She said quietly:

"I loved your mother and father, and as a little girl I loved you. You're still that little girl, Iolani. Everyone who knew your parents is ready to welcome you, and many who did not have that privilege. They will kill you with kindness if you let them. It's entirely up to you, my dear. You can do as little or as much as you wish, you can see as many people or as few. Helen wants you to come stay on the Big Island with her and there are numerous other invitations for you already. I want to know just how you feel about things . . . you have the excuse of your mourning . . . but then you do not need any excuse. I have not accepted any invitations for you, nor issued any."

Lani looked at her gravely. She said:

"I'd like to know people." She added, after a moment, "My people, after all, aren't they? It doesn't make any difference — I'm not in outward mourning, I mean. My mother hated it, she wouldn't wear black for my father and heaven knows — " her voice faltered and then steadied — "she'd want me to be part of things," she concluded.

"That's what we all hoped you'd feel," said Betsy. "The parties here are frequent," she went on, smiling, "but simple . . . you'll soon understand. People swim, play tennis, go to beach houses and fly to other islands . . . they dance under the stars . . . they have friends in their own homes for a *luau* — or have you forgotten the Hawaiian feasts? They ride horse-back and go camping. Night life, as you know it on the mainland, doesn't exist. Oh, perhaps with a percentage of people, tourists, and those who have homes here for a few months each year. But you won't see much of that, except as a spectator. You'll see the Islands in which people live and have their being. Our men work very hard. Take Jim, for instance. During the week he calmly leaves any party at nine . . . he has to be up at four, you see. Weekends he can permit himself more lati-tude," his mother explained, smiling. "And the men in Honolulu get up early, accomplish a great deal, and get through in time for tennis or golf and a swim."

Someone knocked. Betsy said, "Come in," and turned back into the room, Lani follow-ing. A small Japanese girl in a kimono, her bare feet in clogs, stood waiting. Betsy said briskly:

"This is Kazue. If you will give her your keys she will unpack for you. I'll leave you in her hands for a little while. Your trunks will be here any minute, and Kazue will see to them. Are you sure you have everything you want?" •

"Everything," said Lani, "and thank you, Aunt Betsy."

Kazue had the keys, she was unpacking the

traveling case, the small suitcase ... deft, silent. Lani, sitting down on a chaise longue, watched her. She said ruefully, "I'm afraid that frock is badly wrinkled, I threw it in anyhow."

Kazue's English was fluent, and almost without accent. She said:

"I will press it for you, Miss Iolani, and anything else that needs attention."

She was tiny, her hands incredibly efficient. Lani commented:

"You speak such excellent English."

"I was born here, I am an American," said Kazue. "I went to school in Honolulu — American school, and Japanese school too." She smiled, a little. She added, astonishingly, "We don't remember each other."

"Remember?"

"My aunt," said Kazue, "was Mrs. Aldrich's cook. You and I were born on the same day, Miss Iolani. When I was very small my mother took me to see my aunt. They let us play together, in your garden. There were fish, in a pool. I remember that."

Lani rose and went over to take the small brown hands in her own. She cried, "But, Kazue, how wonderful to find you again!"

Kazue said:

"We all knew you would come back, Miss Iolani. When Mrs. Bruce learned you were coming she sent for me . . . I was working in Kahala. I am to look after you, and go where you go, if you want me."

Lani said, touched, "Of course I want you, Kazue."

"That is good," said Kazue gravely. She took a negligee and slippers from the traveling case and laid them at the foot of the bed. She took the white shirtwaist frock over her arm. She said, "If you would like to change, Miss Iolani, I will bring this right back to you."

She smiled, and slipped quietly from the room. Lani looked around, standing there. The big bed, the deep chairs, the *lanai* beyond. She drew a deep breath, conscious of the fragrance surrounding her, and looked through the arched opening across the *lanai* to the sea, experiencing a new happiness, of a kind she had never known, a sense of well-being, of contentment. She thought of her mother; she thought, How could you bear your exile?

She took off her clothes and put on the negligee. Kazue had hung the leis from the posts of the bed, draped them around the dressing table mirror, hung them on the doorknobs. Lani went over to them, took them in her hands, feeling the texture of the flowers. Her mother had talked to her about this custom, and very dimly she recalled it. But she had not understood it. Now she began to understand that Hawaii speaks to the stranger as to her own people, native or adopted, through her flowers, symbol of welcome, of affection.

The bathroom adjoining was enormous, the shower was bracing. When Lani returned to her room Kazue was there, the white frock pressed to perfection, the short pleated skirt as if it had just come from the shop.

Betsy came presently to see if she was ready and Lani took a carnation lei from the multitude and put it about her neck. The candy stripes, pink and white, were lovely against her skin, and the dark cloud of her hair.

"Want to see the house?" Betsy asked. "Fred's back at the office but he'll be home for lunch."

Later they sat on the garden *lanai* where luncheon would be served. The shell ginger was in bloom, falling pink and white and waxen on its long tendrils, and the plumeria trees, and Betsy said, "Wait until you see the shower trees and go with us to Punahou to watch the night-blooming cereus open. You'll never forget it. And you'll never tire."

Toward lunchtime Betsy stopped talking long enough to ask, "Cocktail? I talk so much I forget time." But Lani shook her head. "No," she said, "if you don't mind."

"I don't mind at all, I don't like 'em myself.

We'll have pineapple and passion fruit juice, instead. Fred likes it too."

One of the houseboys came out, a young Japanese, and Betsy gave her orders. Presently the tall frosted glasses of juice appeared and while they were drinking Frederick Bruce came. He said instantly:

"You look rested and at home."

"I am," said Lani, smiling.

"I've talked her to death," said Betsy contritely, "told her all the gossip, asked her a million questions. She shouldn't look rested, she must be worn out. Lunch is ready, Fred. Iolani, I hope you aren't allergic to crab," she said anxiously.

"I'm not allergic to anything," Lani told her.

"Good. And you mustn't mind the way I run on. Jim calls me Betsy Brook — Betsy because he has no respect for my gray hairs and Brook because I go on forever. And now, let's have luncheon."

Chapter 7

March slipped into April, April went serenely toward May, with the first of the shower trees flooding the city with pure gold and rose, and Lani was still in Honolulu.

She had kept her word, she had not written Dexter — unless you can count the letters she had torn up and put in the wastebasket. No word had come from him . . . he had promised her that none would come. Yet every boat and clipper day she had looked through her mail with wild-hope, a quickened heart.

Distance, absence, she had thought that these would show her everything in its right perspective. But in this effortless life she had reached no conclusion. Always under the surface she seemed to be in ceaseless conflict with herself. And when she had reached Hawaii she had been tense to the breaking point, mind and body almost numb with fatigue, with spent emotion, with sorrow. Now the fatigue had gone, gradually the tension lessened, and she was trying to think again. Once she was wholly herself, she believed, she would be sure, she would know, she would be able to justify the rightness of her love for Dexter and would know once and for all that she could return to him, without misgiving. Helen Gaines telephoned regularly and plaintively from the Big Island and demanded to know when in the world she was coming over. But Betsy was always on an extension to say firmly, "We can't spare her, Helen, not yet."

Jim himself had a word to add. He flew over one Saturday, shortly after her arrival, and greeted her as if he had left her only the day before. He said, taking both her hands in his firm hard grasp, "It's good to see you. And you're looking wonderful."

She was. She had tanned for the first time in her life, an even pale gold against which her eyes were startling. She had put on a little weight. She was sleeping well for the first time in so long. She swam every day, at Waikiki or at the beach homes of the Bruces' friends, and the warm clear water flowed over her like a benediction. She was learning to surf, and she had been out innumerable times in the outrigger canoes. She had experienced her first *luau*, in a Hawaiian garden, to Hawaiian music, Hawaiian voices raised in the old chants and the newer songs, and pretty garlanded girls had danced for her. She had explored the Island, and driven up Nuuanu — "The Long Hall of the Rains" — and over the sheer Pali, with its wind and mist, its breath-taking view of plains and sea, she had ridden up Tantalus, and stood at sunrise in the old crater of the Punch Bowl where the Great Cross looked out over the city, and listened to the Easter service. She had made friends, old and new, she knew her way about King and Ford streets, she had become accustomed to the medley of races which flowed through Honolulu and became, somehow, harmony.

He said, "I see you like us." He smiled at his mother. "But when are you coming to the Big Island? It's time you saw some of us at work . . . especially me."

His uncle said tolerantly:

"Jim thinks that no one works in Honolulu."

They were dining on the *lanai*, with tall candles burning steadily, and a full moon over the sea. Flower scents drifted to them, and the sound of music. Far along on the rocks men were spear fishing, you could see the glow of their torches, reduced by distance to the size of fireflies.

Lani said, "I know better than that. Uncle Fred's taken me to his office . . . yet how anyone could work in such offices! Patios and fountains and palms!"

Jim said grimly:

"I don't work in patios. Come on over," he urged. "Mother'll take you on the rounds first, Volcano House and all the rest, and then we'll claim you for months and months."

Later, she looked over at him, sitting in a canvas swing, his cigarette glowing, talking shop with his uncle. She thought, What a nice person he is, open, friendly, entirely unsubtle. And said so, to his mother.

Betsy said:

"He's a good boy — Fred has great hopes for him. He works his head off — and never grumbles. He has an exacting job, Lani. And he loves it. Waipuhia's a big plantation and Bill Gaines hasn't been really well, for a number of years. The assistant manager is something of a slave driver — and he and Bill don't always see eye to eye. Jim's next in line, so to speak, in a job which calls for considerable tact. But he's never known anything but sugar. That's his life."

Lani commented lazily:

"I don't know how he's escaped matrimony all these years. He's very attractive."

His mother laughed. She said, "He hasn't had much time for girls. There was one, years ago — they grew up and went to Punahou together and on to the university. You've met her, Lani; she's Dorothy Ballinger now — married a classmate of Jim's. That was the only time he seemed — well, serious. He claims that he'll follow in Fred's footsteps and remain an eligible bachelor. His standards have become very exacting."

"What's that about bachelors?" Jim called.

"Your hearing's too good," said his mother. "Lani was merely remarking on the fact that you've kept your freedom."

"And how," said Jim heartily, "although now that she's here I might weaken . . . but then," he added, "I don't get to see her; it's pure propaganda, keeping her in Honolulu."

Lani laughed. She said:

"If you've withstood romance and the prettiest batch of girls I've ever seen, I'm afraid that — "

He interrupted briskly, coming over to sit beside her.

"Visiting firemen have their allure," he said; "look at all the tourist glamour girls who walk off with our best young men . . . to say nothing of our best girls who go to the mainland and fall in love with some lucky guy from Chicago, San Francisco, New York. We're all acclimated here, trade winds, tropic moon, palm trees rustling . . . it isn't any more romantic to us than New England blizzards to New Englanders. It's home, it's where we live, it isn't just a place on a map or a stop on a cruise."

"I never thought of it that way," said Lani. "Are you arguing that you'll have to look for romance in a snowbank?"

Fred Bruce chuckled. He said:

"We don't give him time."

"I'll take time," said Jim, grinning, "I've a vacation coming to me. And if you'll come to the Big Island, Lani, I'll spend it with you. We might even find a snowbank . . . Mauna Kea is snow-capped still."

He put his arm around Lani and hugged her. When she did not struggle he let her go. He said, disgusted, "I like a girl who puts up a fight!"

"Why should I?" asked Lani. "Why should anyone fight anything — here?"

He said with mock horror:

"Don't let the tropics get you, woman." He thought, rather startled, that it was a long time since he had . . . well, not too long. Every now and then a girl came along who submitted to the atmospheric conditions and so you danced with her, and kissed her, once or twice, and said a lot of things you didn't mean. And that was that. She didn't mean them either. If you thought she might you shied off, having common sense. Lani, however, was not just any girl. She was — part of the family, she was beloved. He liked her enormously. He hoped she liked him. He hoped, too, that the strange little look he surprised now and then in her eyes, that shadow, would pass. He said, as Lani laughed at him:

"If you don't come to the Gaineses' soon, Lani, I'll kidnap you by force."

He flew back the next day and Lani was conscious that she missed him. He had brought a fresh salty briskness into the dreamlike drifting of this new life. She was aware that she drifted, asking nothing of today, and less of tomorrow. But it was healing, and she needed healing. Yet there were times when the charm, the almost intolerable beauty of her surroundings, the gentle gaiety, hurt her beyond endurance, when the knowledge that beauty unshared by the beloved one can be a burden wounded her past tears.

Her only word of Dexter was indirect. Ellie wrote that he had not been seen in Washington "for lo, these many weeks." She added that she understood he'd returned to Florida, although Muriel Warren had left there for a trip. She added that she'd like to know when Lani was coming back. What were her plans?

Lani had not answered. There was nothing she could say. If Dexter were here . . . if she could see him suddenly in the hot, vital sunshine, if she could turn and find him beside

her in the soft velvet of the enveloping nights
. . . But she could not. She had exiled herself
and she could not return to him or recall him
to her until she could tell him with the full
consent of her entire being, body and spirit,
that she was ready to do, to be, as he asked.
Or if that consent was lacking, she could tell
him that he must let her go.

She could not answer Ellie's letter, for she
had no plans. If she came to the conclusion
that she must give up Dexter, exorcise the
enchantment from her heart, destroy the
image, then perhaps she would find it less difficult to live here than anywhere else in the
world . . . to remain, never to return. Once
she spoke wistfully to Betsy. She said, "I
haven't any home really. Perhaps I could find
one here, of my own . . . a little place by the
sea, with Kazue to look after me."

Betsy had said soberly, "You have a home,
with us. That's how I feel and I know it's how
Fred feels too."

"I couldn't," said Lani; "you can't just
open your doors and take me in forever — it
isn't fair to either of you. I've given you
enough trouble as it is, breaking into your
lives this way."

"We opened our hearts as well as our
doors," said Betsy, "but I understand. You're
finding yourself. This interlude will help you.

If you decide to make your home here I'll go househunting with you when you are ready, and I'd love it. But don't rush into anything, Lani; give it time and thought. It's still strange and new to you. You'd have to be very sure that it is what you want."

Lani thought, I am not sure of anything.

She had acquired, with her golden tan, a few words of Hawaiian, and a *holoku,* the graceful frock, which many of Betsy's friends wore at *luaus* and sometimes at dances, the genesis of which lay back in missionary days when startled missionaries evolved a garment with which to cover the young brown bodies of their female converts. Lani's *holoku* was glorified, pale-yellow satin, and she wore it charmingly, and learned to manage the little train. But once in a shop on Fort Street she saw an old Hawaiian woman, carrying her years and weight as though they were flowers, wearing a *holoku* of gray cotton, the straight front, the fitted back, the train, and on her thick hair a funny little black straw hat. Lani watched her walk, with beauty, in dignity, and wondered if she would ever wear her yellow satin again without being conscious of her inadequacy. But she liked it and the short, voluminous, shapeless Mother Hubbard, which they called a Mo-mo and which, in a gay print, Betsy had given her. "If you have to

113

cover your bones," said Betsy, "when you're lying out on your *lanai,* this will do the trick — without restrictions!"

The first of May came, Lei Day, with every man, woman, and child garlanded in its honor, and Lani went with Betsy and a crowd of young people, a Washington girl whom she knew slightly and who was at the Moana, and some of Betsy's friends, to see the exhibit of leis, in the Park, listen to the band and look with admiration and envy on the beautiful Island girls who had been chosen, each from her own island, as Lei Day Queen. In the evening they went to a party at the home of Betsy's cousins, high up on Tantalus. There were a number of Navy and Army officers there, among them a man whom Lani had last seen in Washington, at Ellie Underwood's.

He was Navy, a lieutenant commander, exceedingly able and personable. There had been dancing on the terrace and the first Lani knew of Mannering's presence at the party was when he cut in.

"May I?"

"Sam Mannering! Is it really you?"

"Indubitably . . . My ship just made port two days ago. It's pretty swell to be back in Pearl Harbor again. How long have you been down here?"

114

"Since March. I'm visiting friends . . . the Bruces . . ."

"Like it?"

"Love it. I was born here, you know."

"I didn't know. I never knew enough about you. Remember? I mean either you had a date or I was sent somewhere — same old story, New York, San Francisco. But now that you're here — "

"We're leaving for the Big Island tomorrow," she said, laughing.

"You would! But you'll be back?"

"Of course. Isn't this one of the loveliest places you've ever seen?"

"They're all lovely. And sooner or later you see everyone you know against this background. There's a saying to the effect that if you stand on the corner of Fort and King long enough your entire acquaintance will pass you. Lord, the Army's cutting in!"

"The Army" was Captain Collins, whom Lani had met earlier in the evening. He said lightly, "Looks as if the services would begin to clash, here and now. How about it, Sam?"

They were old friends. Lani said, looking from one to the other, "If I could have a glass of something or other — ?"

"Champagne punch? A highball? Name your poison."

"Papaia juice," she decided, and presently

found herself in a deep wicker chair in a corner of the terrace with the Army on one side and the Navy on the other.

She raised her glass to them. "To the services," she said; "and I feel very well fortified."

There was no prettier girl present, not even Jim Bruce's ex-love Dorothy, who danced by a moment later in the arms of her good-looking husband. Mannering and Collins regarded Lani appreciatively ... in her white cotton frock with a brief bodice and a long full skirt, splashed with dusty-pink and mauve flowers, a lei of tiny pinky-purple orchids, a bracelet of them around her wrist. And Mannering said, smiling:

"Collins here, he's an old married man. He dares not speak with my authority." He raised his glass. "*Aloha nui,* Lani," he said, "and lots of it. You're prettier than ever."

Collins said, "Even a married man is permitted to stop, look, and listen. Sam, you old hound, what have you been doing with yourself?"

"Trying to get back here," said Sam promptly. "Don't we all?"

Collins laughed. He said, "Sally, my wife, and I went on leave recently back home. It was wonderful, at first. Then we got homesick. We returned last week on the *Lurline* . . . very gay, thousands of tourists, all sizes and ages — you know, all oh-ing and ah-ing and wondering if there would be a girl doing the hula under every palm. Sally and I were out of our minds waiting for the tugs to come along . . . we could see the first ones with a dozen of our friends on it but a cruiser snaked out of the harbor and people got aboard and held things up . . . you know, Sam, the *Trade Wind II*, the elegant little job that belongs to the Renfews."

Lani asked, "Renfews?"

"You haven't met them? New Yorkers, very gay," said Collins, "always making the wassails ring, or is it the wattles? I never knew. They have a house across the Pali, on the windward side, and spend a few weeks here every year. They were meeting the Glamour Girl of the week, one Mrs. Dexter Warren. Seems that she was coming by clipper for a few weeks' stay but when she found the clipper wouldn't accommodate half a dozen trunks she decided to take a boat."

Lani felt definitely, physically ill. She asked carefully:

"Mrs. . . . did you say Mrs. *Dexter* Warren?"

"I did," said Collins. "Tall, beautiful — " he blew a kiss — "and always knee-deep in admiring males. I never had a look-in;

117

besides, Sally distrusts blondes — almost as much as brunettes."

"That's tough on Lani," remarked Sam.

"Oh, not her sort of brunette," said Collins, and Lani laughed, very creditably.

"That's no compliment," she told him. "Was Mrs. Warren alone?"

"I never saw her when she was, worse luck," said Collins cheerfully, "but if you mean was her husband along, if she has a husband, no."

Lani said after a moment:

"I know her husband, I met him in Washington." She was astonished that she could speak so evenly.

"What's the matter with him?" demanded Collins. "Big Businessman, no time for the Little Woman? He shouldn't let a beautiful menace like the man-eating Muriel loose."

"Gossip," Sam warned.

"Not at all. Amazed that you haven't met her. Oh, I remember, the Renfews were whisking her off somewhere, Maui, Kauai, I don't know. A hundred and twenty pounds of dynamite," he added; "these carefree old islands will never be the same again."

It must have been in the papers, thought Lani, but then she reflected, I haven't looked at a paper for days. Uncle Fred tells me anything of importance in the headlines or I listen to the news on the radio.

They reached home late and Betsy watched Lani prowling about the downstairs living room and *lanai* with some curiosity. Fred Bruce had yawned his way up to bed, he was always reluctant to keep late hours, and he had spent most of the evening talking orchids to his host. They each grew them, passionately, as a hobby.

"Looking for anything, Lani?"

"A book," she said, "I thought I left it here."

Of course the paper, several days old, wouldn't be available. She went upstairs to bed, to lie awake listening to the wind in the palms, her arms crossed behind her head, watching the stars out beyond the *lanai*, smelling the flowers and the sea.

She thought, I won't be likely to meet her.

For the first time shame burned up, from her toes to her eyes, flooding her body. She moved restlessly under the cool touch of the sheets. She thought, I couldn't bear to meet her.

Yet, meeting Muriel Warren would be a challenge. She would be cowardly not to accept it. She had been cowardly to drift all this time, shirking her decision. Why should she shirk it? It wasn't fair to Dexter nor to herself. She thought, I've tried to face it fully, all the implications, and I know that I'm in love, wholly and forever. Nothing matters but that. And when I return from this visit I'll cable Dexter and tell him so and then I'll go home — to him.

She experienced a moment of loss, of sorrow, as if she had already gone, as if she had left these islands behind her. Perhaps someday, she comforted herself, when Muriel Warren had come to her senses and to an end of her selfishness, she and Dexter would come here, together.

Chapter 8

They had a very early breakfast the next morning before driving to the airport. Betsy was going to take Lani over and stay for a few days. Kazue went too, to look after Lani and to see some of her innumerable relations who were at Waipuhia.

Early as it was, the shopkeepers were opening their doors, the traffic was heavy. Pete drove the big car out past the pineapple cannery, past the mullet ponds. The airport sprawled in the sun, the big planes were tuning up. The hand luggage was weighed . . . for Lani's trunk would follow by interisland steamer.

The engines raced, the plane moved off down the field, rose and flew out over land grown tiny, out over the water, purple and jade in the shallows, indigo in the depths. The breakers looked like static whipped cream.

Betsy was reading the morning paper and chewing gum furiously. Kazue was reading too. There were half a dozen other passengers, a quiet, massive Chinese, a small Hawaiian child with her parents, businessmen, a couple of voluble tourist women in their late fifties. Lani leaned back and looked out the window next to her. A ship on the face of the ocean was a toy, leaving a white wake like a narrow ribbon. The blue fishing sampans were dots on the water, and now they were passing over Diamond Head, and looking down into the circular cavity.

"Molokai," Betsy said, and Lani looked down at the rocky coast, the white sweep of beaches, and at the smaller tawny island of Lanai, the pineapple island, the great plantations of pineapples checkered gray-green below them, crisscrossed with rosy paths, the rose-red of volcanic earth.

Maui loomed up, with the magnificent towering mass of Haleakala, towering into the crystal blue, and presently the scalloped coast of Hawaii, with its waterfalls tumbling to the sea, its sugar plantations like toy villages, its young mountains still in the making.

A car waited for them at Hilo, and as they drove south Betsy said:

"Sometimes I think I love the Big Island best. Jim was born here, you know, it was here I came as a bride."

"I've heard," said Lani, "that it always rains in Hilo."

"Not today, at any rate," said Betsy, smiling.

"Tell me about the mountain, the volcano."

"There are five mountains: Kohala, Hualalai, then Mauna Kea in the northeast and, in the south, Mauna Loa . . . These two rise over thirteen thousand feet and Mauna Loa's crater still burns, Lani. Kilauea, where we are going, is on its east flank . . . but there hasn't been much activity for some time. I'm sorry, I'd like you to see Kilauea when Pele, the fire goddess, stirs in her sleep. Perhaps you will someday."

They drove through green fields of cane, and past tree ferns twenty feet high, past the lehua trees whose red blossoms Lani coveted. But their Hawaiian driver shook his head regretfully. "If you pick them it rains," he said with finality.

Presently they were in the Hawaiian National Park and driving through the forest of tree ferns to the plateau, with the mountain beyond and the heaped black lava, desolate and forbidding. Across the enormous crater Mauna Kea dreamed in the sun, under her tiara of snow.

Lani stood and looked down into the crater. Steam rose in little wisps, there was the smell of sulphur. From the ground all around them the steam rose idly.

"It is superb," said Betsy at her elbow, "when the goddess wakes and the molten lava boils in the fire pit. . . . Last time I stayed here as close as I could, all night, and nearly scorched the shoes off my feet. Jim was furious at me!"

The driver brought them bright red berries, the ohelo, sacred to Pele and under his smiling instructions Lani knelt to drop them into a fissure of the ground through which the steam rose lazily. The sound of an automobile horn startled her for a moment and a great gush of steam still more. Betsy was laughing when the girl rose to her feet. She said, "Pele accepts your sacrifice," and the driver laughed too. But, he explained earnestly a little later, it was not quite like that. It was the vibration of the horn that caused the sudden activity.

They went with a ranger into the depths of the Fern Crater, the tree ferns towering above them, the sunlight so thick that it was almost tangible, and birds singing in the stillness. They walked through the lava tube, a black cave from which the sun was excluded, and a little later lunched at Volcano House, where a fire burns on the great hearth always because it is cold at Kilauea, four thousand feet above the sea. And presently they got back into the car and drove on by the Hamakua coast road to Waipuhia.

The manager's house stood high, facing the sea, but from the gardens at the back one looked straight up the face of Mauna Kea, with her snow indifferent to the blazing sun, under the cobalt sky. Lani looked through a mauve-blue haze of jacaranda trees and knew she would remember it all her life.

Helen Gaines was at the door to meet them, a tall, spare woman with prematurely white hair and young blue eyes. She said, kissing Lani's cheek, "You're very like your father, you know," and her eyes were misted and soft. But presently her husband came limping on his crutches to hold Lani's hand and exclaim over her. He said:

"It took you long enough to get here. How are you, Betsy? Putting on weight, or I'm a monkey."

"You are," she said firmly. "How's the leg?"

"Not what she used to be," said Bill. He was fifty-odd, his lean face lined, his eyes as eager and young as his wife's. He said to Lani, "Jim'll be along presently. Meantime, and always, this is your house."

She was given a room overlooking the sea, and she could see the fishing boats. And when she had bathed and changed Helen took her out into the gardens and to look at Mauna Kea, rosy with sunset.

"Betsy and Bill are gossiping their heads

off," she said. "I wanted you to see this in peace and quiet . . . it's lovely, isn't it? And I'm proud of my gardens."

Jacarandas, tall and delicate, lilac, mist blue, and the burning red beyond of the royal poinciana. Cup of gold lifting its goblets, and everywhere you looked an ordered wilderness of bougainvillaea, of bignonia, of shower trees, rainbow and gold and rose.

"When things get a little difficult," said Helen Gaines, "as they sometimes do, I walk among the flowers and look at the mountain. Or I go through the house and stand on the *lanai* and look at the sea. And after that it seems to me that I can endure anything."

Jim came up to the manager's house for dinner from the bachelors' quarters, and Frank Davidson, the assistant manager was there, a dark, aggressively good-looking man. It was he who sat with Lani later and somehow managed to keep Jim Bruce at his distance, without ostentation. He was not, he told her, Island born and he had not been home to the mainland for ten years. He was from Massachusetts, he said. He added, "I get homesick now and then, but I'll never go back."

Later when she was getting ready for bed Betsy knocked and came in. She said:

"Jim's ready to slay Davidson. He didn't have a chance to talk to you all evening.

How'd you like Frank, by the way?"

"He's attractive," Lani said readily.

"And bitter. His wife ran away with another man shortly before he came here. They were living in Puerto Rico at the time, where Frank was learning the sugar business. After the divorce he came to the Islands. He's played the field ever since."

It was a definite warning and Lani could have laughed aloud. She was, she believed, as completely armored against Frank Davidson's charm — or that of any other man save one — as any girl alive. Betsy lingered, looking at her.

"Jim can't decide what color your eyes are," she remarked.

"Neither can I," Lani admitted.

"It's interesting," said Jim's mother thoughtfully, "at least to me. You see he hasn't worried about the color of any girl's eyes for a long time."

She kissed Lani and turned to go, a small, engaging figure in a pretty kimono.

"I see Kazue's unpacked for you."

"She did. I told her to run off and not bother with me, I could put myself to bed. She spoils me," said Lani.

"She loves to," said Betsy; "we all do. Helen said, a few minutes ago, 'If only she'll stay here with us, and be happy.' "

I'll stay, thought Lani, lying in the big bed. But — happy? She thought, At least I can be content.

The door was open between her room and Betsy's. She called and Betsy appeared in the doorway, her hairbrush in her hand.

"It's nothing. Just do you know some people named Renfew?"

"Oahu, on the windward side?" asked Betsy. "I've met them, everyone has, here and there. Mainland people, they have rather their own crowd. Why?"

"No reason. Someone spoke of them last night. Good night, Aunt Betsy."

"Good night, my dear."

The door closed, the light vanished. Lani slept presently, dreamed herself back in Dexter's arms, woke with her heart pounding and the tears wet on her cheeks and stayed wakeful, and longing, long enough to hear the mill whistle at four-thirty. And afterward, slept again, uneasily and apprehensive.

In the morning things seemed very different. The hot golden sunlight on flowers, the marvelous air, Mauna Kea beneficent above and the sea smiling below. Lani thought, dressing, I'm stupid to be so frightened; it isn't likely that we'll ever meet . . . and if we do, what of it? She knows there's someone. But not my name. She's never heard of me.

Now that she had made up her mind, nothing could disturb her, ever again.

The days went by serenely. She had her first glimpse of the superb efficiency of the sugar mill, with its heavy, sharply sweet odors, she saw the hospital, the bachelors' mess, the clubrooms, the swimming pool, and the rows of red-roofed cottages in which the workers lived. She picnicked on the beach and swam, by moonlight, and she rode, with Helen and some friends from Honolulu, far up into the forested flanks of the mountain. She did not see much of Jim Bruce except during the evening when he came up to the house or took her to a plantation motion picture — once it was a Japanese picture, very strange and exciting — but she saw a good deal of Frank Davidson, who always seemed to be able to escort her on inspection tours, whether of plantation store, recreation field or gymnasium.

She grew fond of Helen and Bill who, despite the pain he still suffered, despite his obvious restlessness, was extraordinarily uncomplaining. He managed to get to the office every day, by car, and the men came there to make their reports to him. She was astonished at the community life, the social activity, the friendliness. She had met most of the skilled workers and their wives at an evening party

Helen gave for her, and liked especially the spare Scottish chemist and his tiny wife, with their sun-browned faces and their burr.

She saw the school in session, children playing and working, children of Chinese and Japanese blood, a few with an admixture of Hawaiian, Filipino children, Portuguese, American. . . .

Early in June Jim Bruce had his vacation and flew to Honolulu to be with his mother over Kamehameha Day and to see his uncle. On his return a trip had been planned, to visit his closest friends, John Roberts and his wife, who lived on a cattle ranch on Hawaii. Helen was going too, her husband had urged it and she badly needed a holiday.

"But they don't know me," Lani protested.

"As if that made any difference. Their hard luck, that's all. They want you," said Jim, "they're the most hospitable people this side of heaven."

"Who isn't, in the Islands?" said Lani.

"They always have a houseful," he said carelessly, "you'll enjoy Johnny, he's tops, and so is Alison. Wait and see."

"Mrs. Roberts wrote me a charming note," Lani began doubtfully, "but — "

Helen Gaines broke in. "Of course you must go; they'd be hurt if you didn't. We would have seen them before this, we think nothing of driving over there and back for an evening, but Johnny's been terribly busy, Alison has been in Honolulu visiting, and poor old Bill hasn't been able to get around . . . a series of circumstances."

Frank Davidson, during Jim's absence, was pleasantly attentive. He and Lani rode one evening up the mountain, made a fire and cooked their steaks. The snow line had lessened considerably but there was still a breath of delicate cool air from the peak and, as the sky was drained of color, the dreaming distant sea a dusky wine, the stars stole out, silver, enormous, and the little light from their campfire was a lonely flare.

The horses stood by contentedly while Davidson broiled the steaks and poured the good strong coffee. He said, "I was almost glad that Helen couldn't come, much as I love her. I don't have you to myself very often."

"Thanks," said Lani, laughing, "and make mine rare."

He said:

"Jim neglects his opportunities, as usual. If I were his age — and free — "

"Free?" asked Lani. She was sitting with her back against a tree stump. She added quickly, "It's curious up here, isn't it . . . the temperate zone, or isn't that the right term? I can't get used to the difference in the trees . . .

the first time we drove up the mountáin, in the car, and I saw apple trees I couldn't believe it."

He said, "You regretted, didn't you, that you were about to ask me why I was not free? You know about me, everyone does. This is a small place . . . friendly, serene on the surface . . . but there is plenty of gossip. There is bound to be in any community so closely knit . . . not just this community — the Islands are small, every circle overlaps. No man is free who is a failure."

She said gently:

"You aren't a failure, Frank." 🖋

"A man whose wife runs away from him," he said bitterly, "is a failure — as a man. And that's all that matters, isn't it? Oh, someday Bill will be transferred to another plantation or perhaps sent to work in Honolulu and I'll be manager. It's been promised me. But that isn't what I meant."

She said, "Tell me more about the work."

"You're stalling," he said. "I had my first taste of sugar in Puerto Rico and learned from the ground up, riding twelve hours a day, time-keeping, overseeing, inoculating the bulls they used there then. It wasn't a picnic. Then I drifted out here and worked my way up too. It wasn't at all like Jim, for instance, born into a sugar family, generations of it, knowing

132

what he wanted from the time he was in knickers . . . and everything made easy for him."

"That's not fair," she said hotly. "He's worked too, at the university, at the experimental stations, and now here, after experience on Kauai . . . just because he's Fred Bruce's nephew doesn't mean — "

He said, "You're loyal, aren't you? I forgot that you're Island born too."

He moved closer to her. He said, "I'd like to fall in love again. Sometimes I think I've lost the capacity. Here, with you, halfway up a mountain, with the stars shining and the night closing in, I thought . . . But it's no go. Not that there haven't been women . . . not your kind of women, of course, but perhaps kinder. That's a pretty bad pun. And you have to be careful. No scandal on the plantation. Keep your eyes and your hands off the other men's wives . . . not that I've had any urge . . . therefore the sort of women whom you wouldn't understand at all."

She could not see his face, lean and bitter, with narrow black eyes, a close, hard mouth. She moved away, uneasily. She said:

"You'll be sorry tomorrow that you've talked to me like this, Frank. Suppose we forget it. And hadn't we better go back now? It's awfully dark."

"There's no real twilight here," he muttered. He said, after a moment, "Don't be frightened. Not of anything. And the horses know the way."

Riding back through the still night they did not talk.

Jim came back and they drove over to Wahi-O-Hoku for their visit to the Robertses', not far from the great Parker Ranch, and in the mountains. The name, Helen explained, meant Place of Stars.

The ranch house was long and ramblmg, fitting into the curve of the hills. Alison Roberts met them, a little dark thing, vivid and alive, flinging her arms around Helen and Jim, kissing them impartially and smiling with frank friendliness at Lani.

"Johnny's miles away," she said, "but he promised he'd be in early. The gang's gone down to the beach house, I stayed here to meet you . . . they took a picnic lunch, they'll be back for supper . . ."

The main living room was beamed, enormous, and half a dozen dogs lay sleeping on the great hearth where a fire burned. "It's cold here," said Alison, "and we've had rain for several days, thank heaven. I'll take you to your rooms . . . Jim, you're in the bachelors' dorm as usual and I've put Miss Aldrich in with you, Helen; you'll share a bath."

134

"Lani to you," said Lani, smiling.

"Much better," said Alison, squeezing her hand. "I keep forgetting you were born here. I wish I'd been. But Johnny found me teaching school in San Francisco . . . sometimes my own kids gang up with their father against me; after all, I've only lived here for twelve years!"

"Kids?" said Lani. "How marvelous."

"Twins; they're ten, a boy and a girl . . . Helen, you didn't tell her," said Alison reproachfully. "They went off on the picnic. Helen, it's wonderful that you've acquired the land next to ours. When are you and Bill going to build?"

"In the autumn, I think," Helen said. "Bill's been so handicapped, and he hasn't a thing on his mind at the moment but the crop."

Lani was in the tub, a little later, when she heard her hostess and Helen talking next door in the bedroom; the walls were very thin.

"Who've you got here," inquired Helen, "anyone I know?"

"The Renfews, from Honolulu," said Alison. "Know 'em?"

"Slightly," said Helen. "For heaven's sake, how long has this been going on?"

"I never laid eyes on them before," Alison said defensively, "but Johnny met them . . .

and then Mrs. Renfew's brother turned up, he and Johnny were classmates at Yale ... not very close, I judge, but he wrote him, and this is the result. They'll only be here a couple of days longer and then we can settle to a real visit. They've a mainland woman visiting them too — a Mrs. Warren. Boy," said Alison, sighing, "is she sumpin'! When I see my face in the mirror it looks like a coconut to me. Poor Johnny."

Lani lay still in the tub, the water, cooled slowly. She thought, It isn't possible. Under the same roof, she and I. But, as Frank warned her, the Islands were small.

She let the water out, stood up and turned on the shower, warm, then tepid, then ice cold. She shivered under it, shrank from the biting shock. After a moment her blood began to run fast and she shook her head under the tight cap, bracing herself for the encounter.

Presently she dressed, in a long slim skirt and an evening sweater, turquoise and gold, with long tight sleeves. Helen had warned her that she might find the mountain air chilly at Wahi-O-Hoku. Looking in the mirror she wondered if her feeling of tension was revealed in her reflected face. But Helen, looking over her shoulder, said affectionately, "You look lovely, but then you always do."

Helen wore velvet slacks and a stiff brocade

coat. "All very informal," she said. "I hear Johnny and Jim roaring outside. Let's go."

Johnny Roberts had returned to the ranch house half an hour ago, had showered and changed. He was an enormous man, wide-shouldered, almost as tall as Dexter Warren. He said, holding Lani's hand:

"Welcome to Wahi-O-Hoku. Did you know that your father used to stay here often in my dad's time, with Fred Bruce? They often went hunting. I was just a kid, on the mainland in school, but I remembered him summers."

Helen coughed and Alison said quickly, "Johnny, you galoot, the fire's smoking."

It wasn't, but Johnny, scarlet, went and kicked at the big aromatic logs. It was then that Lani realized that it was from this house that Alan Aldrich had gone to meet death at the hands of his best friend. It must have been. She closed her eyes a moment, stunned and sickened, and presently Johnny came back to put his big arm around her. He said, "I'm so damned sorry."

"That's all right," she said, "I didn't know about it until recently." And Helen said softly, "We wondered . . . I mean when we suggested this visit Jim was dubious."

"Please," said Lani, "don't think about it. I promise I won't."

A car drew up and someone shouted.

137

"They're back," said Alison, and went, in her Chinese coat and trousers, to the door.

The twins tumbled in, brother and sister, Liliha and Gideon . . . tall, thin, brown all over, with their father's bright blue eyes. The dogs rose to meet them and there was a general scuffle and Alison pleading, "For heaven's sake, will you kids go get washed?" and behind the twins, the Renfews and their guests.

Charlie Renfew was fat and fifty. He wore Johnny's dungarees, which were much too long and fitted him in the wrong places. A battered hat was on the back of his head, and his red, amiable and inane face was beaming. Johnny's leather jacket was too wide across his shoulders for him, too tight across the stomach. He was saying, "I don't know why we didn't buy a place here . . . Johnny, that beach house of yours is swell."

Gertrude, his wife, was short and thin. Her fingernails were very long and red and her small face petulant and lined. The clothes which Alison had lent her, heavy slacks, a sweater, did not in the least become her. She said, crossly, that she had sunburned, her skin would be ruined.

Her brother, a negligible man of Johnny's age, stood beside her. His name, Lani gathered in the ensuing babble, was Howard Wilkins. She acknowledged the introductions

138

automatically, unconcerned by Wilkins's open stare of interest. She was looking at Dexter Warren's wife, feeling, as she did so, an intense, ice-cold excitement.

Muriel Warren gave her a smooth long hand. She was wearing her own beautiful clothes . . . a pair of dark-blue flannel slacks, superbly tailored, a turtle-necked cashmere sweater, very revealing, and a little leather jerkin. She carried a big lauhala hat in her hand. Her fair skin was untouched by sun or spray and her long eyes were a brilliant, unusual brown. Her short hair cut close to her head was consciously blond. She told Alison in a deep, lazy voice, "My dear, the most divine place . . . I won't be happy until I have one just like it."

They were gone now, to change. The room was quiet. Johnny sat near the fire, on a bench, his arm around his wife, and a dog at his feet. Jim sat on the floor beside Lani, smoking, and Helen was turning over the pages of a magazine. She said:

"Women like that infuriate me."

"Like what?" asked Alison.

"Like Mrs. Warren. Out of a bandbox. It's incredible. And what a figure!"

Jim spoke. He said lightly:

"I think she's the most beautiful creature I ever saw." He turned his head to look at Lani.

"What's your opinion?" he asked her.

"Essence of tact," grunted Johnny. "You'll never learn, old boy. To ask one *wahine* what she thinks of another *wahine's* looks. You've more nerve than I have!"

"Lani's honest," said Jim, "and above pettiness. She can afford to be."

"Thanks; she's lovely," said Lani evenly.

"Boy," said Jim, rose and stretched, laughing, "boy, what a dish!"

"Not your dish," Alison warned him; "she's been ordered."

"Wilkins?" inquired Jim. He shrugged, "I should worry!"

"Wilkins and twenty-three others," said Alison, "from what one hears. Besides, there's a husband in the background. She doesn't talk of him much but he's probably on the Renfew side, fat, bald, and given to one highball too many."

Johnny said gently:

"You're talking of your guests, Alison."

"I'm sorry, Johnny," she smiled at him, "but in a manner of speaking, they aren't the guests I'd select. This tide of old college days stuff, to say nothing of letters of introduction, washes up some queer fry at our doorstep."

Her husband said inexorably:

"Moreover, the walls are thin."

"Not with the showers running," said Alison, "and you'd better get busy about drinks."

Johnny departed with his extraordinarily light tread. Alison said, sighing:

"He's so much more charitable than I. Forget what I said, all of you. Tomorrow night we're having a big party. Don't let it frighten you. People from miles around. Frank Davidson's coming, he telephoned me at noon, and tons of others. A *luau* for the Renfews. Next day they go and we'll have our own kind of fun. I can't wait to show Lani the beach place. And I was wondering, Helen, when you're going to take her over to Kona."

"All in good time," said Helen; "you forget she isn't a tourist. She's here — for keeps, I hope."

Jim said raptly:

"Helen, you couldn't find it in your heart to invite Mrs. Warren — without the appendages — to Hale-O-Ka-Moana, could you?"

"I could not," she said severely.

"Well," he said thoughtfully, "I'm on vacation." He was sitting down again, crosslegged, playing with one of the pups. He reached up a free hand and caught at Lani's. He said, "Lani's with me, aren't you?"

Mrs. Renfew and Mrs. Warren appeared for dinner in formal frocks. If they were chilly they did not show it . . . one had a little chin-

141

chilla wrap and the other a soft sable, to ward off arthritis. There were drinks and then dinner, after which they sat around the fire and talked. But at nine Johnny rose.

"Sorry," he said, "my bedtime . . . you mustn't mind me."

"He gets up at all hours," explained Alison to Lani. "We won't see him again till noon — if then."

"How about you, Jim," Johnny asked him, "coming to bed? You'd better if you're riding with me tomorrow."

"I've changed my mind," said Jim, grinning. He was sitting by Muriel Warren. "I've lost my interest in cattle, suddenly. I'm riding with Mrs. Warren and Lani — "

Mrs. Warren looked at Lani, apparently for the first time. She said:

"I thought you were from the States."

Helen said, smiling:

"We are part of the States — we say the mainland here, Mrs. Warren."

"Oh, sorry," said Muriel. "I forgot. But your name?" she persisted.

Lani repeated it.

"I see." Muriel looked thoughtful, the bright brown eyes widened. "Aldrich," she said. Then she smiled. "Oh, now I remember; I didn't connect . . . I think you've met my husband, haven't you?"

142

"Yes," said Lani steadily, "in Washington, several times."

"That's it," said Muriel, "you're the girl Ellie Underwood told me about." She leaned forward, her face alight with interest or perhaps malice. And Lani thought, Oh, *no*, not *Ellie*, she wouldn't, she's too loyal —

She said, hoping it were true:

"Ellie's a very good friend of mine."

"Of course," said Muriel warmly, "I'm delighted to meet you." She turned her brilliant eyes on the others, and said gaily, "This is my latest rival, the girl poor old Dexter lost his head about not so long ago. And I don't in the least blame him. You know, of course," she asked Lani, "that he's joining me in Honolulu? Any day now — I expect him by the next clipper."

Chapter 9

Muriel waited, her bright searching eyes on Lani's face. This was no rhetorical pause, she expected an answer. Lani spoke slowly. She said:

"No, I didn't know, Mrs. Warren."

Muriel's eyebrows lifted. She cried, "Darling, don't tell me you don't keep in touch! Although Dex loathes letter writing." She turned her regard on the others, explaining, including them in the conversation, "Half the time when I'm away I never hear from him," she said; "then there's a telephone or a series of contradictory wires, or he just turns up. You mustn't mind," she added, in an audible aside to Lani, "he's *like* that. He knows you're here, of course?" This time she did not wait for the reply but went on, "He'll adore seeing you."

Lani felt curiously cold. As if she were dying. She was not aware of the comfortable warmth of her sweater or of the heat from the blazing logs. She shivered, very slightly.

Her palms were like ice. Muriel Warren knew. She had known all along. And Dexter was coming to the Islands. Lani was aware of a sudden crazy triumph. He hadn't been able to stay away, he had had to see her, he had come to her, to wake her out of this dream life which held her, which prevented her from hard straight thinking. He was coming to compel her to make up her mind. She drew a deep shaken breath and was suddenly conscious of the people around her, of Muriel's audience. Johnny and Alison were listening with the bland, blank courtesy of people not particulariy interested, not troubling to look below the surface of an idle conversation. Howard Wilkins and the Renfews seemed amused, however. Charlie Renfew's face was redder than ever, he slapped his knee and remarked genially that Dex was the limit; he added, "But if I may say so, he has damned good taste." His wife did not speak but her petulant face was alive with curiosity. Her brother, pulling at his absurd mustache, smiled. Helen, leaving her magazine to join them, looked at Lani gravely, and Jim's blue regard was definitely disturbed, looking from Lani to Muriel Warren.

Muriel opened her evening bag and exhibited a square, heavy gold box, the clasp in rubies. She opened it and offered Lani a cigarette. Lani took one mechanically and Jim rose to present his lighter. Her hand shook and she steadied it against his. She was astonished at this betrayal, she felt so completely unmoved, so numb . . . as if she were dying, she thought again, no, as if she had died.

Jim looked over at Alison. You could count on Alison. His glance commanded. Do something — anything. And Alison asked quickly:

"How about some contract? Johnny won't play, he's headed for bed, as usual."

Gertrude Renfew said:

"That's a divine idea." She was a restless woman, she had been appalled by the thought of another evening during which people did nothing or went to bed at practically indecent hours. There'd be plenty of opportunity later to talk to Muriel and find out what this was all about. She knew Muriel rather well. There had been something behind her remark, it wasn't the easy, exaggerated compliment one woman pays to another. Alison, for instance, could put her arm around a girl and say, "My Johnny's crazy about you," and it wouldn't mean a thing. But Muriel wasn't Alison by a long shot, nor did Dexter Warren bear the slightest resemblance to Johnny. Dexter, thought Mrs. Renfew, certainly picked them young. She didn't like Muriel's husband especially. "Terribly attractive, of course," she

said, if asked for her opinion, "but so unstable
... I'll take my old man any time, waist-
line, blood pressure and all." Naturally she
wouldn't admit, even to herself, that Warren
had never found that she merited an interlude
of unstability.

Johnny was putting up the bridge table,
Alison was busy getting out the cards. She
cried, "Shall we cut?" and Helen and Jim
moved toward the table. Jim jerked a thumb
at Lani. "Come on, Lani," he said, "if you
draw me for a partner you couldn't be unluck-
ier."

But Muriel had other plans. She said,
"Count me out — and Lani too. You don't
mind, do you?" she asked the younger woman.
"I want to talk to you. We've so much in common!"

There was nothing Lani could do. She
found herself on the big divan in front of the
fire, with Muriel beside her. The others cut,
and the game began. Alison and Renfew,
Helen and Mrs. Renfew. Johnny drew Jim
away from the fire. "Come out," he said, "and
get a breath of air ... besides, I haven't seen
you for a coon's age — and if you aren't riding
with me tomorrow — "

The four at the bridge table settled down.
Gertrude Renfew took her contract seriously
if no one else did. The slur of shuffled cards,

the voices raised, bidding . . . the comments when the hand was played. . . . "But, *partner*," said Mrs. Renfew querulously. . . . There was some discussion of systems and Renfew saying, "All too deep for me, I leave that sort of stuff to Gertrude . . . mind if I mix myself a long one? Anyone care to join me?"

The fire sang to itself, it possessed an intense, vital life of its own. A dog dreaming on the hearth barked sharply, twitched and thumped his plumy tall. Muriel was running on about Ellie Underwood, about the Washington people she knew.

"You don't know him? My dear, everyone does!"

Lani said, out of her nightmare:

"But we weren't in Washington very long, Mrs. Warren."

"Oh, do call me Muriel. I loathe formalities. Anyway, we're practically related, aren't we?"

"Are we?" asked Lani.

"Of course. I adore all Dexter's girls," said Muriel gaily. She did not keep her voice down. "Agnes Palmer and I were the greatest friends. You've met her . . . no? Oh, how stupid of me, she was before your time. Tell me — " and she leaned closer, so close that Lani could see the incredibly fine texture of her skin, the silky texture of the fair hair, and catch the faint fragrance of some heady, unusual scent.

"Tell me," repeated Muriel, "do you know anything about his latest mad enthusiasm, Susan Tait?"

"I'm afraid not," replied Lani. She spoke evenly, out of the dark dream. "Is she — someone in Washington?"

If she could hold the conversation, guide it, refuse the implications . . .

Muriel shook her head. Her hair was rolled in a multitude of curls, long smooth curls captured at one point with a jeweled clip, and little carefully careless curls. She said, "You *are* behind the times! She's a career girl. New York. Very successful, a dress designer. Dex met her on his last trip to South America. And he went right overboard. He's so terribly susceptible."

Lani gathered all her forces. She looked straight into the brilliant narrow eyes. She asked pleasantly:

"And you don't mind?"

Muriel shrugged her handsome shoulders.

"Mind? Why should I? We understand each other perfectly," she answered, and Lani could read the warning, it was plain enough. "He's never serious . . . except, of course, at the moment. I knew when I married him that he'd always be attractive to women. Lord, I

149

wouldn't want a man who wasn't. Too dull. Look at poor Gertrude, married to Charlie Renfew." She had the decency to lower her voice, a little. She laughed. "I have fun too," she concluded lightly.

Lani said, "It's a charming arrangement."

"You mean, you don't approve? How naïve," commented Muriel. "Do you mind if I give you a little advice?"

"Not at all," said Lani, "go ahead."

"Don't waste your time," continued Muriel, "on men like Dex. I mean, seriously. Only a very plain girl can afford a tragic love affair, too much emotion is disastrous to a beautiful woman and, besides, it isn't necessary. And you are quite beautiful, you know," she said musingly and studied Lani deliberately. "Much prettier than Agnes Palmer, that crazy little kid — do you know she actually came to me and demanded that I give Dex a divorce? 'But, good heavens, child, what for?' I asked her, 'He doesn't want a divorce, no matter what he's told you. He's safe where he is — and quite, quite comfortable.' I was sorry for her, really, she was so completely shattered. I haven't laid eyes on the Tait woman," she went on, "but they tell me she's chic rather than pretty. So there you are. And there *you* are," she added, as Wilkins appeared at her elbow, bored with sitting with the contract players and kibitzing.

He suggested coaxingly:

"Let me get your coat, Muriel, we'll go out for a walk. It's marvelous out, really."

"But I'm happy where I am," she said, unmoving.

Lani rose. She said, "If you'll excuse me — "

She moved away, blindly, toward the bridge table. Wilkins looked after her. He asked:

"What did you do to her?"

"Nothing. Gave her some good advice."

"She looked as if she'd seen a ghost."

"Perhaps she has," agreed Muriel. "Sit down, do. I hate men who prowl."

He said gravely, "You're a very cruel woman, Muriel. I wish to God I weren't in love with you."

"It's fun while it lasts," she asked, "isn't it?"

"But you aren't the least in love with me, are you?" he asked, low.

"No, darling. I've never been in love with anyone except, a long time ago, one man — a little."

"Warren," he said, with his weak mouth firming into a straight line.

"Yes, of course. I even forgot to feel superior. Boss's Daughter Marries Hard-Working Young Man. I forgot everything," said Muriel. "We went to Italy for our honeymoon. It was rather like one of those pretty pictures people laugh at nowadays. Venice and balconies and gondoliers. Very Royal Academy. Very, I might say, eighteen-ninety, although it was only about fourteen years ago."

"What happened?" asked Wilkins. "Not that I want to know."

She said lightly:

"A pretty chambermaid, believe it or not."

"Why don't you divorce him?" urged Wilkins. "You can't love him — now."

"He makes money for me," she said, "and he's rather nice to have around, when he is around. Don't be absurd, darling. . . . Let's take a look at the contract players; your little sister looks as if she'd swallowed two canaries."

Lani had left the bridge table, she was standing at the door, looking out. She saw the glow of Jim's cigarette, on the steps there in the dark.

"Come on out," he called.

Alison spoke from the table. "Old coats over on that chair," she said, "better put something around you, Lani. And close the door, there's a dear."

Lani picked up a coat. It was Johnny's. She shrugged herself into it. She was tall but it hung around her feet, there was room for two of her in it. It smelled of earth and tobacco.

It was very dark outside. There was no *lanai* on the front of the house, just the wide steps leading into the living room. Jim made a place for her beside him. He said, "Look at those stars, girl, look at them."

"I'm looking," said Lani.

Johnny said in his deep, slow voice:

"Mainland people come here and demand to know why I've buried Alison among the hills. They say they'd think she'd go crazy. We think people are crazy to live in cities," he added. "The kids feel that way too. When we take them to Honolulu they're unhappy as soon as the first novelty wears off. They like it here, up practically at dawn and bed after supper. Later they'll have to go to Honolulu to school. For the moment they're all right. We have a good teacher in the little school here, and Alison helps. This is a good life, Lani."

She said, "I can believe it, watching you together."

"Alison," said Johnny, "loves it. She rides, she spends lazy days at the beach house, she knows everyone for miles around. . . . Hello, Moki, what's up?"

One of his men had come around the corner of the house from the bunkhouses, a tall, heavy Hawaiian. Johnny said, "Apologies," and went down the steps to meet him. They stood talking a moment and then Johnny walked off with Moki following.

Jim Bruce threw away his cigarette. He said, "It's like being on the top of the world. Like it here, Lani?"

"Very much."

He thought, That woman upset her, she's different. Poor kid — He was astonished at the revulsion of his feeling against Muriel Warren. He'd been definitely disturbed by her, her looks, her smooth sleekness of manner, her half-promise . . . she had only to look at a man, any man, and she was pledging something . . . anything. Not that she'd keep it. But he had seen Lani's unguarded eyes, as Muriel spoke . . . a little while ago.

He asked, "Know your Rupert Brooke?"

"Not very well. Why?"

She was grateful to him, and to the starry night, the quiet hills breathing of peace.

He said:

"He wrote a little sonnet once, called 'Waikiki.' I don't recall it all. But a little of it sticks . . . it goes like this:

"And new stars burn into the ancient
    skies,
Over the murmurous soft Hawaiian sea."

154

"It's lovely," said Lani, after a moment.

"Yet, it doesn't tell it all. . . . Those people in there," he jerked a shoulder, "Renfew and his wife, Wilkins, Mrs. Warren, they'd live here a thousand years and not know what it's all about. They'd pick up a few Hawaiian words. They'd say *pau* for finished, they'd talk about *pilikia,* when they meant trouble, and *welakahao,* when they meant raising hell. They'd babble on about climate and how picturesque it is and how you could do what you wanted here and no one be the wiser. They'd wear shorts and bathing suits and dungarees on King Street most likely, because this is the Islands and anything goes. They'd hire Hawaiians to sing for them and teach them to surf and canoe and give them a spot of *lomilomi.*"

"What?"

"Well, massage," translated Jim, laughing. "Haven't you seen 'em perform on the beach at Waikiki? Of course you have. Beach boys oiling the fat, elderly carcasses of silly women, or the prettier outer envelopes of youngsters? Sure you have. That's what I mean. If all the Renfews and all the Wilkinses and all the Muriel Warrens lived here all their lives they'd never belong — because they wouldn't have the slightest understanding."

"I know," said Lani.

He said abruptly:

"You don't have to answer this. You don't really know me ... even if we did play together once, very long ago, even if I feel as if you belonged not just to the Islands, but to us. So you don't have to answer, Lani. But did the Warren woman say something that troubled you, a while ago? Something did. Would it help at all to tell me about it?"

"I don't think so," she said, "but thanks just the same." She shivered again, slightly.

Jim rose and pulled her to her feet.

"It's cold under the stars," he said. And somehow it was more than just a phrase. She thought, *And lonely, too.*

"You'd better go in," he went on, "you're tired. Tomorrow's another day."

She turned, at the top step.

"Can I count on that?" she asked him gravely.

He needed no explanation. He said, as gravely:

"Of course, you can."

The contract game was still in progress when they entered, and Muriel and Wilkins were still deep in conversation before the fire. Alison asked, "Where's Johnny?" and Jim answered, "Moki came for him and they went off."

Alison laid down her hand. She was dummy. She rose and came over to them. She said:

"That will be the new Hereford. Johnny was worried about him." She turned to include Lani. "Johnny went off the deep end," she said, "and bought himself a prize bull. Cost a fortune, but worth it. Something was wrong with him this morning. Johnny said it wasn't serious — " She smiled at Lani. "What about tomorrow?" she asked. "Did I hear Jimmy dating you and Mrs. Warren for a ride? We've some pretty good horses, and I can fit you out — "

Lani thanked her, she had her riding clothes, she said. But, looking at Jim, "If you don't mind," she told him, "I think I won't ride, tomorrow."

"I'm sorry," he said instantly, "but I'll take Mrs. Warren and — "

"And Mr. Wilkins," suggested Alison, with the shadow of a smile.

Jim grinned.

"We could lose him — or push him over a *pali*."

Alison slipped her arm through Lani's.

"You look tired," she said; "if you want to turn in — "

"I am, a little," Lani said gratefully, "but — "

"You go to bed," said her hostess soundly,

157

"there isn't an ounce of formality here. Suppose we go to the beach house tomorrow, you, Helen, the kids and I? Johnny can't get away. Jim has his big date and the Renfews are driving to Kona. At least that was the last arrangement I heard."

"I'd love to," said Lani. She smiled at them both and slipped away. Muriel didn't see her go, nor Wilkins. They were quarreling now, low-voiced. But Helen Gaines looked after her and then at Alison.

"Lani was tired," explained Alison, returning to the contract table. She spoke over her shoulder to Jim. "Want to cut in?" she asked. "The rubber's over."

He shook his head.

"Think I'll go out again and wait for Johnny," he said.

Alone under the stars, enfolded by the hills, his eyes turned toward the distant sea he sensed but could not see, he thought of Lani. Surely there couldn't have been anything in that stupid remark? "This is my latest rival, the girl poor old Dexter lost his head about not so long ago." Yet he had seen Lani's eyes. If there was anything in it, would the man's wife be so openly malicious, so — ?

He shook his head. Women! he thought. Heaven defend us. He didn't understand them, he didn't want to. He thought, I don't know a damned thing about anything but sugar.

It was just as well. As he lighted a cigarette he heard Johnny coming back, alone. Walking out to meet him, he found himself preoccupied. What kind of man was this Dexter Warren who permitted his wife to go where she pleased and with whom — take Wilkins, for example? No, you take him, I don't want him — and whose name, carelessly mentioned, could bring that look into Lani Aldrich's eyes? He swore to himself. Lani wasn't the type to run after married men. She couldn't be. She was too fine, too honest.

Muriel Warren, he admitted, was a woman to stir any man's pulse. He himself hadn't been immune. That was odd too, if, as she had plainly intimated, her husband chased around with other women.

He didn't like Warren. He didn't know him, but he didn't like him. He thought, Lani belongs to us. Anyone who hurts her . . . well, he's in for *pilikia* and plenty of it!

Chapter 10

Lani went to the room she shared with Helen, grateful for solitude, for silence. She sat on the narrow white bed for a long time, one hand folded in the other. She told herself, Muriel lied, as Ellie lied to me once. Ellie was trying to warn me, a purely conventional gesture. Muriel was trying to hurt me. She's jealous . . . even though she doesn't want him she can't bear to have anyone else —

It couldn't be true.

She thought, But it is true. Malice had emanated from Dexter's wife, heavy and potent as her perfume. Malice — but also truth. Truth had been in the amused brown eyes, the husky voice.

Lani thought, So I've been one of a bright parade. Luckier than most, luckier than — what was her name? — Agnes Palmer. She thought, heavy with shame, *And I was going to cable . . .*

She had believed Muriel's presence a challenge, one which had shocked her into action, one which had forced her to make a decision. So she had made it. And it had been unmade for her. She knew she would not send that cable. Not that she'd need to, for Dexter was on his way to the Islands. If she saw him, if he explained, if he argued, if he implored, how could it make any difference? The damage had been done. She could never believe in him again. You can't love unless you believe.

Yes, you can love, even without belief, but you cannot build your life on such a love.

She felt bruised, beaten, informed by a blaze of jealousy she had never known could exist, for her . . . she could see his eyes, almost she could feel his touch, hear his voice . . . experienced eyes and hands, words he had used over and over. She thought, I must loathe him. But she could not. You don't fall out of love because a woman has told you the truth in a sleepy, malicious voice. You fall out of trust, you fall out of hope, you wake from a dream. That's your misfortune.

After midnight Helen came in, to find Lani sleeping. She moved quietly in order not to waken her. Before she turned out the light she stood between the beds and looked down at the younger woman. How defenseless she seemed in sleep, how vulnerable. Helen's heart quickened with tenderness. She and Bill had never had a child. She thought, If we'd had a daughter like Lani —

Curious, how much Lani looked like Alan, a softer, feminine edition, lying there with her eyes closed. Helen had been very fond of her cousin, had thought herself a little in love with him at one time. But they were cousins and her emotion had been partly hero worship. Then Bill came along and she knew that she hadn't really been in love with Alan.

She bent closer. Tearstains, sodden lashes. She snapped out the light and went to bed, sighing. If there were only something you could do for the child. But we must go slowly, she told herself, all of us — she doesn't know us yet, doesn't perhaps trust us. And she's desperately unhappy over Mary's death. But was this because of Mary, this look of drained exhaustion, of grief, in dreams remembered and renewed?

She thought, as Jim had thought, there couldn't be anything in what that silly woman said . . . no decent woman would say it if there were.

Lani woke early. A misty morning and a bird singing and the wind through open windows was clear and wonderful. It was a moment before she remembered that Dexter Warren was on his way to Honolulu, a moment during which she lay there, mindless and happy, because she was young and the day was new and beautiful. Then she remembered.

Helen was smiling at her from the other bed. She said, "It's only seven and Alison thought if we woke early we could get a good start. Put on old things, Lani; you'll probably get soaked in the sampan, if it's rough at all."

When they went out to breakfast Alison was waiting for them, in dungarees and a sweater. She looked about fourteen, not much older than the twins. Gideon said:

"We'll have more fun than yesterday." He made a face, screwing up his pug nose, and his mother said hastily, "We won't inquire about yesterday."

Today was Sunday. Tomorrow, mourned Gideon, there'd be school. But today was free. He grinned at his sister.

The Renfews weren't up, nor Muriel nor Wilkins. Jim wandered in, sniffing the coffee, dressed for riding. Johnny had been gone for hours, his wife explained.

When they went out to the station wagon Jim went with them. He said disconsolately, "Wish I hadn't been so brash . . . I'd much rather go with you."

"Nonsense," said Alison briskly, "a beautiful blonde! Be sure you lose the escort en route."

Helen, Lani, the twins and Alison drove to

the sea in the station wagon. It was still misty on the mountain when they left but the sun was clear and golden when they reached the little dock. Alison explained the wharf . . . some of the cattle was shipped from here, but most of it from farther down the Kona coast. The sampan was waiting, sturdy, broad beamed, a faded blue, with an ancient, smiling Hawaiian busy about the engine. They loaded the picnic basket aboard and were off, dancing over the blue water, watching the coast line unroll before them on their left. Lani sat up in the bow, hugging her knees, young Gideon, brown and thin, stretched out beside her. He was not a talkative child.

He explained, however, sleepily, that you could reach the beach house only by water. "No roads," he said drowsily, "all lava." He closed his eyes, and appeared to slumber.

Lani sat still, the spray cool and salt on her lips, her eyes on the unforgettable coast, the hills rising beyond. She thought, I won't have to see him . . . I won't return to Honolulu, until they've gone . . . I'll make some excuse to Aunt Betsy and Uncle Fred. Helen will keep me with her; she's urged me to stay all summer.

"There are two kinds of lava," said Gideon, so suddenly that she nearly fell overboard, "the *aa* and the *pahoehoe* . . . the clinkers, you know, the first kind, and the smooth flow, the second."

"Honestly?" asked Lani. She thought, She's always known about me just as she did about Agnes Palmer, just as she does about Susan Tait.

"Sure," said Gideon. He went on without stopping. "Pop's cattle, everyone's cattle eat *kiawe*. That's a sort of mesquite. We don't have much rain . . . they eat cacti too. *Haoles* don't believe that . . . I suppose you know what a *haole* is?" he demanded.

"Of course," said Lani, outraged, "a foreigner, really, anyone not Polynesian or Oriental."

"That's near enough," said Gideon, yawning. "Anyway, they do eat the cactus and then they don't need water. Anything else you'd like to know?"

She said, laughing:

"You needn't perform for me, Gideon. I'm not a tourist, really. I lived in the Islands until I was seven and perhaps I'm here to stay now. I don't know."

He looked relieved. He said:

"They ask the silliest questions, most of 'em. You should have heard that Mrs. Warren!" He looked disgusted. He added, "If you don't mind, I'll go back to sleep."

He opened one eye, winked it, closed it

again. He was a companionable little boy.

The beach house had a strip of white beach before it, and a half-moon of lava that made a natural breakwater. There was a tongue of lava running into the sea, which served as a rough wharf. They landed here, clambering over the jagged blocks of lava, and the sampan left them.

This was peace, thought Lani, the simple house, one vast room open to sun and air, the waves singing on the beach, the clump of coconut palms. . . .

Beyond, the lava was heaped in rusty, brown-black, fantastic shapes . . . between themselves and civilization, between themselves and the snow-capped shape of Mauna Kea, the lava spread, a static sea.

That was a good day. They swam in palm-bordered fresh-water pools, they lay in the sun. They ate when they were hungry, they slept when they were sleepy. Lani, lying on the big divan . . . "*hikiee* to you," said Alison; "the real ones were mats, one on top of the other" . . . felt numb. She could not think. She could only drowse, wake to smile at something one of the twins said or did, listen to Helen and Alison exchanging friendly gossip. No one spoke of the Renfews or of Muriel Warren. No one said anything that mattered. The sun seeped into your blood and bones, the wind was cool in the palms, the sky was cobalt, arched above you. Once it clouded suddenly and the warm swift rain came singing down and then was gone, as suddenly. The sun shone again, the sea was a restless magnificence, and there was a rainbow arching.

At three the sampan returned for them. "Damn," said Alison, repacking the basket and looking resigned when the twins unpacked it again to look for bananas, "I wish we needn't go back. But there's that party. You have to give parties for people like the Renfews, you know; they dote on 'em."

Returning, Helen sat beside Lani in the bow and talked of the beach house she and Bill intended to build, on the ground next to Johnny's. "It's just a dream, of course," she said, "because there's every indication that someday he'll give up managing plantations and go into Fred's office. It will be fun living in Honolulu again," she went on, "so many of our best friends are there. But it will be a wrench. After all these years I've become identified with the other sort of life, with the people who live it. There's more in being a manager's wife, Lani, than just keeping house and entertaining people — friends, strangers. . . . I know every man, woman and child in Waipuhia . . . their troubles, their joys, their illnesses. It's a very satisfactory life, if you take it — humbly."

"Humbly?" asked Lani, arrested.

"Now and then," said Helen, "you may meet a manager's wife who grows in instead of out . . . you wouldn't know what I mean . . . who feels a little on the regal side, queen of the community, dispensing patronage, insistent on caste, on rank. Rather like things you run into sometimes in Army and Navy posts. Well, there aren't many of them, on the plantations, for which thank heaven, but where you find one you also encounter considerable heartburning, gossip, and dissatisfaction. It isn't an easy job at best, you know. You can't like everyone, no one can. And there's always something going on, in so close-knit a community — always someone who stands out, apart, who won't fit in. Always some unhappy wife who'll confide in you. Or someone who drinks too much. Or someone who doesn't drink at all and has that holier-than-thou attitude. There's a certain amount of social exchange, there must be, it's all the life some of us have, and jealousy and — You'll understand when you live with us a little longer. But it's been a good life," she said, "and when it is over I shall miss it greatly, no matter how much fun Honolulu may be. Bill rates a change, he's worked very hard, but he'll hate

168

adjusting himself to an office."

After a moment Lani asked:

"If and when Bill leaves Waipuhia I suppose Frank Davidson will be manager?"

"It's on the cards," said Helen carefully, "and he's a very good man if not as popular as some — as Bill himself, as Jim."

"What about Jim?"

"He's still too young," said Helen. "Someday he'll be manager somewhere, and a good one. He isn't interested in sugar from a production and cost standpoint only, you know. It's part of him. He sees it not as a means of earning a livelihood, but as something vital and important. And he likes people, he gets on with his superiors and with the people under him. His men are crazy about him, they think he's gold. He's ironed out any number of difficulties. Frank's hard, you see. Perhaps it isn't his fault. He's a stickler for discipline, a terror if there's a malingerer around. He and Jim cross swords very often but respect each other. Jim's not so hotheaded as Bill," she added; "when Bill and Frank have a difference of opinion, sparks fly." She shook her head. "This must bore you. I wonder how Jim made out — today. I thought the beautiful Muriel had her eye on him once or twice."

"Anyone," said Lani, "would look at him twice."

"He's very popular," said Helen, "more than one girl has tried — but it's no go. He says he's waiting for a girl like Alison. But there's only one of her and Johnny found her first. Whatever girl he waits for will be lucky. I'd hate to see him sidetracked," she added thoughtfully, "but I'm not worried. He doesn't sidetrack easily. If I had a daughter, I'd break my neck to see that Jim — "

She stopped. Lani wasn't listening. She was looking out over the water with the expression of a woman who does not see the beauty which fills her eyes.

When they reached the house they found Jim sitting by the fire with the dogs around him. Alison dropped into a chair. "I'm so sleepy I can't stand up," she complained. She regarded her children tolerantly. "Run away, wash your faces," she said, "and get into something presentable." She explained to Lani that the doctor from the nearest sugar plantation was coming with his wife and two boys. "The kids will eat with my pair," she said; "one of them's a devil on wheels. What will happen I haven't the remotest idea. Lucky there's a cubbyhole for them to devastate. I suppose I must look after things. Lord, I'm an abominable hostess."

She laughed and Jim remarked that her hostessing suited him.

"Before we trail off to see if the hot water's *pau*," Alison demanded, "give us your report. Where's everyone?"

"The Renfews haven't returned from Kona," he replied obediently, "Johnny hasn't shown up — Mrs. Warren, Wilkins, and I were home by three. We didn't get going till almost noon. The lunch you had packed for us was elegant. I was the only one who ate much. Wilkins was a trifle dour when we started. I think the girl friend had twitted him about his riding. He fell off only twice. It didn't hurt him. But I think he's saddlesore."

"Does she ride badly?" asked Alison hopefully.

"She rides very well," said Jim, grinning.

The guests were arriving when Lani came into the living room. Frank Davidson was already there. He said, taking her hands, "Have you any idea how we've missed you?"

"Royal or editorial we?" demanded Helen, overhearing. "What about me, and how's Bill?"

"Fine. He sent word you were to stay away as long as you liked."

"I don't believe it," Helen said. "I'll telephone him tonight and check."

They had all assembled before Muriel made her appearance. Most of the women looked at her with an entirely natural rancor and the

171

men with equally understandable appreciation. She wore a long, tight frock of lamé the pale-gold color of her hair. It was artfully draped and left little to the imagination. The plantation doctor whistled under his breath. His was, perhaps, an academic interest in anatomy. She wore a barbaric hunk of emeralds at the high neckline and another around her wrist. Gertrude Renfew, in an elaborate flowered print, looked fussy and insignificant beside her.

The local women all wore *holokus*, including Lani. Muriel drifted over to her presently. Standing beside her with a cocktail glass in her hand, her cool, amused look was indifferently friendly. She said:

"You look quite charming . . . but some of them . . . my dear!"

Jim heard. He said instantly:

"As a rule it takes the dignity and, yes, the weight, of the older Hawaiian women to carry off the *holoku* — but Lani wears hers beautifully. Rested after your ride?" he asked Muriel.

"I wasn't tired," she answered. She added, "You missed a marvelous time, Lani. I've learned so much about sugar." Her intonation was faintly mocking and Jim colored slightly. It was difficult to remain impersonal with such a woman. Lord knows he had tried, in his growing dislike of her.

His change of color did not escape her. She went on, laughing, "Poor Howard. It's a miracle that he can sit down."

The *luau* was ready, the huge dining table stretched to its full length. Chicken and pork *laulaus*, cooked and wrapped in ti leaves, bowls of poi, salty salmon, squid cooked in coconut milk. Ti leaves were scattered on the table; they ate with their fingers and washed them later in bowls of warm water in which segments of lemon floated.

Gertrude Renfew regarded the sticky mauve-gray mass of poi and the delicate squid tentacles with equal horror. Lani, leaning across the table, advised, "Try the salmon and then the poi. It works. I'm becoming quite attached to poi myself, attached is the right word."

Frank Davidson sat by Muriel. It was very evident that he interested her, for she turned her back frankly on the plantation doctor on her left. Dr. Carver ate, resignedly. There was one appetite a healthy man could satisfy, and he was a philosopher. His wife was plain but he liked her. He breathed the perfume which, at thirty-five dollars an ounce, surrounded Mrs. Warren, and ate another chicken *laulau*.

Later a group of cowboys came up to the

house to sing and play. Frank Davidson, sitting beside Lani, asked, "Having fun?"

"Of course."

He said:

"Mrs. Warren's an interesting woman." His saturnine face was without expression. "She reminds me of someone I once knew." He added, throwing his cigarette in the fire, "My wife."

"Oh," said Lani, "I'm sorry."

"Why should you be?" he demanded savagely. "I'm not. Salt's supposed to be good for a wound." Regarding Muriel, standing by the fireplace, surrounded by men, he commented, "She shouldn't be dangerous, as she's so obvious. The unfortunate thing is that you don't realize it until too late. I wouldn't trust her as far as I could throw the *Queen Mary*." He grinned at Lani. "Apologies for my bad manners," he said.

A moment later he joined the group around Muriel, and Lani saw the lift of her broad white eyelids and the faint smile at the corners of her mouth.

Later, Lani wondered how many people had noticed that for more than an hour during the evening Davidson and Muriel Warren were absent from the room. They had left together, announcing that they were going for a walk. It must have been a long walk.

Lani found herself thinking, hot with disgust, If she can amuse herself with every man she meets, she has no right to refuse Dexter his freedom! But she had had prior knowledge of Muriel's predatory quality; Dexter himself had told her. Her thoughts checked, suddenly. It could mean nothing to her now, whether or not Muriel gave Dexter his freedom.

In the morning the Renfews and Wilkins left for Hilo where they would take the plane for Honolulu. Alison drove over with them, she had some shopping to attend to and a call to make. Helen was taking her own car and going to pay some calls on a forty-mile round. Jim would look after Lani.

Muriel Warren held out her hand to Lani and Lani took it, hating her, hating herself.

"It's been nice," said Muriel, "and we'll have to see a lot more of each other. I'll let you know when Dex joins me. You'll be in Honolulu again, won't you?"

Helen said quickly:

"We hope not, for a long time. We want her to stay with us."

"Oh, but it's less than two hours," Muriel reminded them, "and Dex will be so anxious to see her."

The car drove off, Alison waving from the driver's seat. Helen put her arm around Lani.

She said, "We aren't letting you go for ages."

Leaving, a little later, she cautioned Jim. She said, "You'll take care of her, won't you?"

"Feel like riding?" he asked Lani. "It's a grand day — we'll take a lunch. I know just the place."

"Were you there yesterday?" she asked.

He shook his head.

"Not me. Only special people get to see this place. Johnny and Alison took me there, years ago. It's very select. Take along a bathing suit — if you're bound by convention."

The horses were brought up presently and they rode away from the house, clattering over the cattle guards with sound and fury. The scattered cattle raised their heads to watch them pass. Jim said, "It's a small place, of course, compared with some . . . three thousand head registered and several thousand more not registered. Johnny's built it up from a pup, all forty thousand acres. He works hard, he gets results."

They left the main roads, and struck out into the hills, taking the narrow upward winding trails away from the grazing country, away from the desolation of lava which had flowed to the sea. Tall trees grew here, the round heads of monkeypods, in pink and white blossom, the koas, and there were flowers. Valleys and sheer rises, glimpses of the mauve and turquoise sea and more valleys . . .

Hidden in the forest, they came upon a clear small pool, fed by tumbling white water falling over sheer rocks. Wild ginger grew here, yellow and white, an unforgettable fragrance, and montbretia, the color of flame. A still, secret place with only the birds to break its silence, only the rushing, laughing sound of water.

Here they dismounted and Jim tethered their horses. They had come a long way and it was very warm. He said, "A swim before lunch? But not until you cool off, I think."

She said, "I'm starved. Jim, this has been too beautiful."

She accepted a cigarette, lay back against a tree trunk, her eyes on the waterfall and the pool below.

"It's deep," he said, "and very cold . . . think you'd like it?"

"I'd love it."

"The whole forest's your dressing room," he suggested.

He was standing by the pool when she came back from the green privacy of the trees. The brown trunks he wore were not much deeper in shade than his body. He looked up smiling as she came toward him in the brief, flower-printed suit.

"Last one in's a six-tailed toad," he said,

and dived, coming up gasping, shaking the water from his eyes, just in time to see her leave the rock on which she was standing.

Later they lay in the sun at the edge of the pool to dry. "I'm so hungry," Lani complained, "I could eat my horse and yours too."

"Johnny wouldn't like it," he said gravely.

He unpacked the lunch, brought towels from the saddlebags, tossed her one. "Gets cool early," he said, "drape that around you. What will you have in the way of a sandwich — beef, ham, chicken, cheese?"

"All of them," she said firmly.

After sandwiches, fruit, iced tea in the thermos, Lani smiled at him. She said, "Believe it or not, I'm going to sleep." And did so almost at once, lying full length on her side, her head pillowed on her arm.

He rose, to fetch his flannel shirt and put it over her bare legs. Looking down on her as Helen had done the night of their arrival, he experienced a protective tenderness. And then, with a shock as startling and unexpected as a tremendous blow, something more than tenderness. He sat down crosslegged beside her, snapped his lighter and set the little flame to his cigarette. There was no reason in it. He had seen her in Washington, liked and admired her. He had seen her again in Honolulu, liked her even more, been desperately

sorry for her. And when she came to Waipuhia his liking had increased, but no more.

And now —

She stirred, and woke. She said, "There's
something besides the ginger . . . something
fragrant. What is it?"

"Maile fern, I think," he told her. He rose,
looking down. "Had your cat-nap?" he inquired.

Lani sat up and shook her hair back from
her face. She said, "I'd like to stay here forever."

He asked gently, "Alone?" and held his
breath.

Chapter 11

Lani laughed. She said generously, "I don't mind you, you're a good provider. I meant, there's such certainty of peace here . . . " Her voice trailed off, she was frowning, unconsciously crushing the white bruised petals of the ginger between her fingers.

He said carefully:

"A girl of your age shouldn't be looking for peace, Lani."

"What has age to do with it?"

"Peace," said Jim, "that's for old people, when the blood runs slow, and you look back and not ahead."

"I don't look ahead," she admitted, in half a whisper, "and I don't want to look back. That's why I love it here, it's living in the moment, no past, no future. That's peace, isn't it?"

"I wouldn't say so," he told her. He stretched out beside her, his arms across his eyes and his voice came to her, muffled. "What are you running away from, Lani?"

His eyes were closed now but he could still see her, sitting there beside him, the white material of her bathing suit splashed with the gay flowers, the bend of her dark head, her gray eyes dreaming, the golden brand of the sun on her face.

She said, "The other night you asked me to tell you . . . I couldn't, not then. Lonely, dark, all those stars, and the hills . . . forever there, those hills. But this is different, with the sun shining and the water singing to itself. Shall I tell you?"

"Only if you wish," he said. He thought, *God, keep her from telling me.*

She said coolly:

"Last autumn I met Dexter Warren. I didn't know he was married, right away. I learned soon enough. I fell in love with him, and I thought he was in love with me. We drifted into it . . . he came to Washington often and we'd meet. Then I went to New York . . . " She paused and then said sharply, "I can't tell you about that."

"You needn't," he said.

"No, I've said this much," she said, as if to herself, "I have to go on. What he asked of me I couldn't give . . . I had my mother to consider. He — he said his wife wouldn't divorce him although he'd asked her to and that . . . we should take what we could, hurting no one. But there was my mother. I went back to Washington."

Jim was very still.

"Then my mother died," she went on, "and I was alone. I had no one to consider. I was independent. My only relatives were Helen Gaines, in Hawaii, whom I did not remember, and a cousin in Virginia. So I went to New York and saw Dexter again."

"Well?" asked Jim harshly.

"I had a choice to make, a decision. You understand? I couldn't make it. It wasn't that I was afraid. I can't explain." She spoke softly, as if to herself, arguing it out, forgetting her listener. "I was in love. I thought, Perhaps I should take the half loaf, the compromise — that is, if love mattered most to me. If it did, it wouldn't seem a half loaf, would it? Yet, I could not decide. I was held back, inhibited. Perhaps I'm not fully adult, after all. So I came out here, to make up my mind. . . ."

He did not want to ask, he did not want to know, and spoke without volition, hating himself and this lovely, still place and hating, with an insensate fury, a man he had never seen.

"And have you decided?"

"I thought I had, when I learned that Muriel Warren had come to the Islands. It was a shock, like cold water, it woke me out of a half-stupor, out of my drifting. I could face the issue then and I believed that I was strong enough to decide for — love. Then I met Muriel, and according to her I have been one of a procession. She told me all about her husband, his habits, his amusements. She even warned me. I did not believe her, I tried not to believe her. Now I don't know what to believe. Today I have thought, Is it fair to him, to me, not to give him a hearing, a chance to explain?"

Jim made an odd sound. He rolled over on his face and, when he righted himself, looked at her without expression. His sunburned hair was rumpled and bits of twigs and ferns were caught in it. He said:

"You're a damned little fool, Lani."

"I suppose so," she said, without rancor. "I've shocked you, of course."

"Sure," he agreed. "I can't fit you into the picture. Yes, I can," he amended slowly, thinking it out, "you're — honest, Lani. Your emotions are honest. And you've courage. And you've heard a lot of conversation about proving your courage. The — the way you had decided to take before you met Muriel seemed the hard way to you, but you were willing to take it. Yet the other way's harder — at least, I think it must be."

She said:

183

"I don't know why I've told you." She looked at him frankly. "I've wanted to tell someone. Your mother, perhaps, or Helen. But I couldn't. And besides, everything's changed in the last few hours, really. And you're detached . . . I'll even," she said, smiling, "try to listen to advice."

"You wouldn't take it," he said, "and I've none to offer. I wish you had told me this the other night, out on the steps."

"Why?" she asked. She reached out her hand, detached the twigs from his hair. "If you could see how you look!" she told him.

He tried not to jerk away from her touch. He said:

"I could — beat you, Lani, with pleasure. You see, the other night I wasn't in love with you. Or if so, I didn't know it. I am now and I know it too damned well. So, I can't advise you. I can't say, wait, listen to what he has to say, then make up your mind. I doubt if I could have said that even the other night. Because it would be such a waste, Lani — But my hands are tied now. I can't say anything, loving you — and hating Warren's guts."

She was scarlet. She spoke his name in distress, incredulously:

"Oh, Jim," she said. *"No!"*

"Never mind," he told her; "forget it. I

hadn't any intention of telling you, a few moments ago."

She was silent. There was nothing to say. The water chuckled over the rocks, the scent of ginger was sweet and heavy.

He asked:

"You're still in love with him?"

"I must be," she said forlornly. "I can't think straight about him, and I don't think much about anything else."

"Then you are," he said miserably. That was the way it seemed to him. He got to his feet and held out his hand. He said, "Well, that's that . . . thanks for telling me. Don't ever be sorry that you did."

"I won't be, Jim." She closed her hands on his, would not let him free her. She tried to smile. "Try to forgive me. If I'd known, I wouldn't have told you."

"I'm a dope," he said. "I didn't know, myself. So what? So I walk right into it. *Akamai* — clever, wasn't it?"

She said, deeply distressed:

"I like you better than anyone I ever knew. I'm — at home with you, Jim."

"Good old carpet slipper," he said. "All right, I'm around if you want me for anything."

Her hands loosened, he let them go and, turning, went away from the pool into the forest. She heard him cursing softly to himself, getting into his clothes.

Lani went to the edge of the pool and looked in. Still and cold and very deep. She shuddered back, and looked up at the clear and blazing sky. She was chilly, suddenly. She thought, I'd better dress.

A little later they rode away from the pool back through the forest, back along the trails to the open road. Nearing home some of the men from the Parker ranch passed them with leis of deep purple pansies around their hats. They called, smiled, waved their brown hands.

At the house, "Thanks," said Lani, "for everything."

"Cross-purposes, wasn't it?" he asked her. "A day or so ago I could have been fraternal, full of good works and better advice. Now I can't say anything, I don't dare. You'll forgive me?"

She went into the house, where Helen found her a moment later, still in her riding clothes, the gay aloha shirt, the slender breeches. Her head was bent, her coat over her arm.

"Good day?" asked Helen.

"It was wonderful," said Lani. "Alison home yet?"

"Not yet. I expect she'll be along presently.

Johnny came in half an hour ago. The Hereford's all right, everything's all right."

"Everything's all right," said Lani slowly.

Dressing, she tried to rationalize things. Jim wasn't really in love with her. Visiting fireman. Propinquity. She tried to explain it away. He'd get over it. Would he? She hadn't got over it. Of course, he would.

It alarmed her to become conscious of the fact that she was warming her uncertain heart at this new fire. It wasn't fair to Jim, she thought.

This was no way to bind up the wound Muriel had dealt her.

The rest of the time at the ranch passed quickly . . . Days of straight falling rain, with Johnny shouting his joy to heaven. Days of brilliant sunlight. Hours at the beach house, hours in the saddle . . . A day with Johnny following him on his rounds, getting to know the cowboys, pure Hawaiian, part Hawaiian, a few Japanese. Riding with Alison and Helen. Jim wasn't with them much, he seemed determined to spend most of his time with Johnny.

The clipper landed in Pearl Harbor and the following day Lani had a telephone call. She went to the instrument without much curiosity and with no premonition. People were always coming to Honolulu, it would be easy for anyone to find out where she was . . .

"Hello," she said.

"Hello," said Dexter Warren. "Surprised?"

She said, after a moment which seemed very long:

"No . . . Muriel told me you were coming."

He said lightly:

"Nice of her. Lani, when am I going to see you? When are you coming to Honolulu?"

"I'm not coming," she told him. "I'm staying with relatives, at the moment we're visiting here. We're returning to the plantation in a day or so."

He said, "You can't mean that. You can fly back . . . you must. Lord, what a heavenly place! I wish I were going to stay for months. I've rooms on the ocean."

"At the Renfews'?" she asked. She had to say something.

"At the Royal Hawaiian temporarily. Muriel's made plans and can't change them. She and the Renfews are booked for a visit on Maui. I'm not going. I'm going to lie on the beach in the sun or sit under a palm. I'm not going anywhere, unless it's with you."

"I can't," she said curtly, and replaced the telephone. She was shaking all over.

Jim had come in and was standing behind her. When she turned he saw her face.

"Bad news?" he asked, at once.

She said, "Perhaps. No, of course not . . . it wasn't anything, Jim."

"Warren's come," he deduced instantly.

Lani nodded. She said, "Please let me pass, Jim."

But he caught her wrists in his strong fingers. He said, "Look here, you aren't going to see him?"

"What if I am?" She was angry, her eyes darkened. "Will you let me pass?" she demanded.

He released her and she went on, back to her bedroom. He stood looking after her, in torment. He had seen her turn from the telephone sick and shaken, because she had heard Warren's voice. He swore to himself and went out to the dining room to mix himself a stiff drink. He needed one.

Lani sat down at the dressing table. She looked into the mirror but she did not see herself. She saw a crazy, unknown stranger, joy on her lips, delight in her eyes. Her heart was too big for her breast, she was wildly, sharply alive — as if she had awakened from the disturbed dreaming, as if she had recovered from a long illness.

There was no use telling herself, You mustn't see him, you don't dare. There was no use reminding herself of Muriel, a drawn sword, a warning, a mockery. He was here, in these islands, under this sky, under these stars. He was watching the surf roll in at Waikiki, he was standing on a balcony, looking *makai*, toward the sea. He was thinking of her. . . .

She could go to Honolulu, it would be very simple. When they left here, she could say to Helen that she'd like to fly over and see Betsy and Fred Bruce for a few days.

No one would know.

Jim would know.

She thought, What possessed me, why did I tell him?

It wouldn't have mattered so much, his knowing, if he hadn't been in love with her.

She would not go to Honolulu. Not that she cared what Jim thought, she told herself, what difference did that make? But she couldn't face the thought of Muriel, her laughter, perhaps her open comment. "So you wouldn't follow my advice?"

If she did go to Honolulu, what harm would there be? She need not see him alone.

You're a fool, her heart said. What sense is there in seeing him at all, if it isn't alone? And it isn't fair to him or to you to dismiss him without a hearing.

As Helen came in Lani threw her hairbrush across the room.

"For heaven's sake!" said Helen, startled.

Lani was flushed and her eyes were stormy. She said, "I — I thought I saw a mouse."

At breakfast next morning Jim had an announcement to make.

"I'm pulling up stakes."

Alison regarded him in dismay. She said, "But your holiday isn't over yet."

"Nope. I'll take the rest of it later. A weekend here or there, when I can be spared. I talked to Frank this morning. They've been having a spot of trouble. They're busier than hell too, so I'll be getting along," he said; "you gals can stay on."

Helen said, "If Lani doesn't mind, I think we'll go too. Or I will. I'm beginning to worry about my old man."

"Stay with us," Alison urged Lani, "there's no need for you to be dragged off."

Lani smiled at her. She said, "That's dear of you, I've loved it here. I'll come back, if I may . . . but now, no, as long as things have turned out this way, perhaps I'd better go with Helen and Jim. I've been thinking of flying to Honolulu for a couple of days. I don't quite know."

Jim pushed back his chair and left the room.

"What's the matter with him?" inquired Helen, bewildered. "He's been going around with a face like doom ever since yesterday. He nearly bit my head off last night about nothing at all. Did you have a fight or something?" she asked Lani.

Lani shook her head, hoping her denial would carry conviction.

"We had a wonderful day," she said.

"Well, he's never been moody before," said Helen in amazement, "and I don't believe there's any trouble at Waipuhia. He would have gone into details. I think it's an excuse."

Alison said, "Jim's like Johnny, like a lot of them. Thinks it will be heaven to get away from the job for a while and after a week or so is rarin' for the treadmill."

Jim drove them back that afternoon, after lunch. Johnny came back in time to see them go. Driving away, Lani looked back at the two of them standing on the steps, waving, Alison very small, her dungarees tucked into the high boots, Johnny big and protective beside her. The dogs were barking around the steps, the twins were in a huddle with them.

"If I've ever envied anyone . . ." Lani said.

"They're tops," said Helen. "Jim, I'm glad you suggested this. I was having a marvelous time but my conscience kept smiting me. Bill's been cheerful enough over the phone but I know he misses my fussing around him . . . although he usually curses it. Be honest, there isn't anything wrong, is there?"

"Slight accident at the mill," said Jim.

"Accident! Jim, no — tell me about it."

"It wasn't much, a man's hand caught, hurt . . . nothing serious," he finally admitted.

Lani said:

"The mill isn't your business."

"Anything's my business," he said.

Helen laughed.

"You were fed up," she said, "admit it."

"Perhaps," he said; "when you have a job it matters to you more than you think."

Get back to the job, busy yourself about something you understood, knew from the ground up. You knew the tasseled cane, silvery under the sun. You knew all about rainfall and lack of rainfall and supplementary irrigation methods. You knew all about getting up when the whistle blew and going out to see the men assemble for work. You knew about hand harvesting and machine harvesting and the new trucks that had turned out so well. You knew about the burning off of your fields and the harvesting afterwards and the progress of cane to mill. . . . You knew sugar. You didn't know anything about women. You didn't know anything at all about one woman, who could tell you that the man she loved was a heel, yet who'd turn faint at the sound of his God-damned voice and a few hours later announce blithely that she might be going to

Honolulu for a few days. To see him! With his wife standing by and letting it all happen under her eyes, until she was ready to call a halt.

Bill greeted the return of his family with raised eyebrows. Alison had telephoned him that they were coming. He said, "Couldn't stay away, could you?" and smacked his wife soundly on her thin haunches. Frank, coming up after dinner, reported, "Jim's a couple of tornadoes. You'd think the place had gone to pot in the time he's been away. What happened to him?" He looked at Lani and smiled. "It's pretty wonderful to have you back," he said.

Bill, getting ready for bed a little later, grunted to his wife:

"Who'd Frank meet at Johnny's?" he wanted to know.

"Frank? No one new, Alison had the gang over. Oh, yes, of course, the Renfews and their house guests, a slitherly young man and a Mrs. Warren."

"Good looking?" asked Bill. "Here, give me a hand will you?"

"I hope you never see her," said his wife promptly.

"That good looking? He's been getting phone calls from Honolulu, that's all. When he heard Jim was coming back he said he might have to fly over, he wanted to see his lawyer. I didn't know he had a lawyer, and if so, why?"

Helen's eyes were startled. She said:

"Muriel Warren! She wouldn't . . . " She was still for a moment, then she said, "Yes, she would. Any man. Even you, you idiot. But I can't imagine Frank — he's steered clear so long."

"It's pure speculation," said Bill. "Maybe he is going to see his lawyer. Maybe he wants to make a new will. Maybe he's — hell, what does it matter? It's nice to have you back, old girl. Place's been like a tomb."

Lani had not gone to bed. She was standing on the *lanai* and looking toward the sea. The stars were very bright, the sea was a dark moving mass. The color had drained from the fuchsia hedge near by, from cup of gold and torch ginger, from all the flowering bright things. But not the fragrance, potent under the spell of dew. Jim, coming out silently, startled her as she turned to find him beside her. He spoke abruptly:

"You meant what you said about going to Honolulu?"

"Why not?" she asked, her throat tight.

"Nothing. I understand why you want to go, naturally."

"It's none of your — " she began. Then she stopped. "I'm sorry," she said gently.

He said, "Well, I've no right to try to dissuade you. Less right than I had a little while ago. I could have talked to you then like a Dutch uncle, whatever that is. I can't now, and you know why. But for God's sake, Lani . . ."

She said, "I'm not going to do anything foolish."

"That isn't the point. You'll just be hurting yourself. And she'll be there."

She said incautiously, "She's at Maui."

"I see. But she'll be back. Did you know that she's been phoning to Frank Davidson? It's become a daily practice."

"Frank? Why?" asked Lani.

"Don't ask me. I don't know anything about her kind of woman, or any kind of woman for that matter."

The telephone rang sharply and Jim went inside to answer it. In his bedroom Bill was struggling out of bed, swearing loudly.

"Good Lord," said Jim, at the instrument. "No, we didn't feel it yesterday, we weren't here. Sure, I heard about it, but it was so slight. Boy, will that draw the tourists!"

He hung up as Lani came in, as Helen appeared with a robe thrown round her, as Bill stumped in on his crutches.

"Pele's doing her stuff," said Jim, with a rasp of excitement in his voice. "Kilauea's in eruption!"

Chapter 12

There was a moment of confusion, everyone talking at once. Jim snapped on the radio and the voice of the announcer at Hilo reached them, half strangled with excitement. "As soon as they can rig up their equipment," Jim told Lani, "they'll be putting on blow-by-blow — or explosion by explosion — descriptions."

Helen was crying, "Remember last time Mauna Loa erupted — weeks of it, with the flow threatening the Hilo water supply and finally the army bombers coming over?"

"Who'd forget?" said Bill. "Not likely. That was a sight!'"

The house servants were peering around the door, with their infallible sense of something happening. Bill beckoned them in and Kazue came, in her soft gray kimono, to stand beside Lani. The elderly Hawaiian woman who had been with Helen since her marriage stood over by the door, her head bent.

Helen went over and put her arm around

her. When, a little later, the servants had returned to their quarters, she told Lani:

"Poor old Makapua — she was praying, I think, to the old gods — which is fitting and proper. There's a belief that there's never an eruption without its warning ... for Pele, in the form of a tired old woman, or a lovely young girl, goes begging from house to house in the villages. When she is turned from the door, when she is treated unkindly, or refused food, she takes her revenge. So, you see, it doesn't happen often, for our people are generous ... they share with each other."

Frank Davidson came up to the house, half dressed. "This will bring the tourists in droves and flocks. There won't be space on an interisland plane or boat for weeks to come," he prophesied.

"We really should get on our clothes and go, tonight," said Helen.

Bill grunted.

"There'll be plenty of fireworks left tomorrow," he said, "you don't go gallivanting off now, my girl. This show will be continuous, it will keep."

"All right," Helen agreed, "but we can't see a volcano in action every day. I'll phone for rooms at Volcano House, right now. Lani and I'll go over tomorrow and stay a few days. You boys can drive up, evenings."

198

"I'll drive you," said Jim instantly.

"Thought your vacation was over," Frank said. "I could do with a drink, by the way."

"You know where to find it," Bill told him. "Me, I'm going to bed. The volcano will be functioning tomorrow. Lucky if you get a room, Helen; half of Hilo is probably up there already, and the other half camping out."

Helen was at the telephone, Bill was limping, yawning, back to his room, Frank went out on the *lanai*, his glass cradled in his hand, and stared out over the sea. Jim looked at Lani.

"This interferes with your plans?"

"Plans? I had none."

"I thought you were going to Honolulu . . . but, on the other hand, this may work out," he added, "as every tourist in the Islands will flock to Kilauea — you're bound to see him . . . a needle," he remarked, "in a smoke-stack, this time."

She asked, "You're being rather nasty, aren't you?"

"I don't mean to be." He came nearer, took her unresisting hand. He said, "But if I tell you I can't endure seeing you make an idiot of yourself, you'll set it down to purely personal motives."

She withdrew her hand, without answering.

"Sorry," he said, "my error."

Lani shrugged her shoulders. She said wearily:

"There's no use quarreling about it, is there? And I *was* an idiot to — "

"Stop!" he said violently. "You promised that you'd never regret telling me, and I — "

Helen turned from the telephone. She said:

"Well, they've a cubbyhole for us, Lani. I think we'd better make an early start tomorrow . . . of course, the time to see it is at night, but Jim can take us over right after breakfast."

Frank came in from the *lanai*. He was going home, he said, and turn in. He looked inquiringly at Jim and the two went out together. Helen put her arm around Lani. "Let's go," she said.

The mill whistle did not wake Lani on the following morning. She had fallen asleep barely an hour before it blew. How could she have been so mad, she had thought, how could she have entertained for a moment the lunatic idea of seeing Dexter Warren again, of her own volition? She thought wearily, if every time I hear his voice —

Could he persuade her, in that voice, that Muriel had lied?

They left early, driving the sixty-odd miles in good time although from Hilo onward the road was black with cars. The rain which they encountered for part of the way stopped before they reached the National Park; the red powder puff of lehua blossoms on the ohia trees glowed in the cool, sunny air.

Cars were parked in great numbers when they reached the Volcano House. Their occupants were mostly Hilo people, but every plane, every steamer would bring people in droves from the other islands. Walking with Jim and Helen over the difficult road of an old lava flow, some time later, Lani was terrified and fascinated by the stupendous spectacle: the great advancing wall of lava, moving very slowly but with a sort of predestined determination. She exclaimed, shouting above the noise. The heat was almost intolerable and great boulders splitting wide to show their white-hot, fire-red hearts, toppled down the moving wave. Fountain sprays of lava leaped into the air, died down, to leap again. Jim, lighting a cigarette on a boulder near by, gave it to Lani. "That's how close you can come," he told her.

Helen met any number of people whom she knew, Europeans, Hawaiians. At luncheon, Volcano House was crowded to capacity. Cars continued to come, to bring campers who, with rations and blankets, were prepared to stay the night, perhaps several days.

Jim left before luncheon, promising to return that evening with Frank and Bill. And when it was dusk, and the cool gray fog of the mountain drifted over the crater, tongues of flame shot upward, the mist was deep purple, brilliant rose, violet, and that night, with the darkness no longer darkness but a red glow, they looked into the molten lake, alive, vital, terrifying.

As days went on, the lava would cool and blacken, new flames would burst through the crust, the *aa* would give way to the liquid *pahoehoe* and the spectacle would continue until Pele tired of her dramatics.

The rangers were busy, keeping sightseers away from harm, herding them to safety. Thousands of people stood looking down into the crater, calling to one another above the constant roar. Flaming rocks, hurled by that gigantic force as if they were pebbles, lava fountains, tons of lava, crashing back into the pit, roaring, rebellious. Lani shivered, in the heat. But she had ceased to be afraid.

They stayed there three days and two nights, she and Helen. Later they would return again, and again, while the volcano remained active. The second night Bill did not join them nor Frank and Jim, but McDonald, the chemist at Waipuhia, and his wife were with them.

They were standing together watching the superb, everchanging display, when a man spoke to Lani.

"Absurd, to meet on the edge of a volcano, isn't it?" he asked quietly.

Her heart leaped convulsively, the palms of her hands were wet. She turned slowly, reluctantly, and he was there, smiling at her, not to be evaded. He was alone. She said, as evenly as she could:

"Hello, Dexter."

"Louder, please," he ordered, smiling. He held out his hand and after a perceptible hesitation she put her own in it. At his remembered touch her pulse went racing. Helen had turned, was looking at them. Lani moved closer to the older woman, presented Dexter. He shouted cheerfully, "This is quite a show, isn't it?"

Helen looked carefully away from Lani. She thought, You poor kid, if only you weren't so terribly young, if only your face wouldn't betray you.

She asked:

"Is Mrs. Warren with you?"

"No, I flew to Hilo late this afternoon in a chartered plane," he answered, "Muriel and the Renfews are still on Maui. I gather they were having too much fun for even a volcano to interest them." He looked out and away, frowning. "Scares you, a little," he decided.

He came nearer Lani and took her arm. He said, "It's weird — it's beautiful." He added, lower, yet she could hear, "You're beautiful too, Lani . . . even more than — "

She said to the others, abruptly, "Can't we get a little closer? Look, there are lots of people over there, on that sort of natural lookout."

She was shaking inside. She had to get away, from the pull of her senses toward him. The crazy light danced on her face, lit sparks in her eyes. Her skin was flushed with the heat. Yet when you moved back, the air was cold.

Later, somehow, she found herself at Volcano House with Dexter buying drinks for them all, laughing, talking, telling the little Scot about his trip to South America. "You should go there someday," he said, "Rio's a marvelous city."

He was sitting opposite Lani, as they crowded around a small table. His eyes were on her constantly, although he did not speak much to her directly. When he did so, he was gaily impersonal, talking of Washington, of their old friends, adding:

"Everyone asks for you; Washington is a desert without you. Ellie said she expected you back long before this. I thought perhaps

I'd miss you, that you'd be on your way home. I was delighted when Muriel told me you were still here."

For the audience, of course. As if his eyes were not speaking to her, saying, I had to come, forgive me, I couldn't go on without you any longer! A few weeks ago and she would have believed that. But Muriel had poisoned her belief.

She managed to answer, almost at random, and to ask him how he liked the long flight from the Coast. He shrugged his massive shoulders and smiled.

"Miraculous, of course, but monotonous. All that water . . . "

Lani said presently:

"Look, don't think me awfully rude, but I find I can't keep my eyes open. If you don't mind — " She looked at McDonald and his wife, who were planning to stay up all night, fortified by sandwiches and coffee.

Dexter asked, "Staying on for a while?" and Lani shook her head.

"No," she told him; "we're returning to Waipuhia tomorrow morning."

Helen said, "This lasts weeks, in varying degrees of activity. Or always has. We'll be back, of course; you can't stay away from it long. Is it true that they can see the red glow against the sky at Honolulu?"

"Perfectly." He added, "I'm staying, I promised the Renfews and Muriel I'd wait for them here. They may come tomorrow by plane. I wouldn't know. Muriel's a bit capricious, when it comes to plans. For instance, this was to be a short vacation trip for her. But now she's decided to take a house, in Honolulu, and stay for a time . . . for as long as it amuses her."

When they rose, he drew Lani aside. She could not demur without attracting attention. He said:

"Come back to Honolulu."

"No."

"What's happened?" he asked. "What's changed you? All these months, and no word. I've been nearly out of my mind. I had to come, Lani, you must realize that." He stopped and asked, "Or am I to understand that when I didn't hear from you, you'd made up your mind?"

"Dexter, I can't talk about it, not here, not now."

"Is it Muriel?" he said, quite loudly. "What's she said to you? You *have* changed, Lani."

"Please, Dexter, let me go," she said. She was fighting against him, her body tense, her mind taut. But her senses remembered.

"But we must talk," he said, "you owe it to

me, Lani. If Muriel's said anything . . . Why should you believe her?"

Helen was beside them, smiling at Dexter, putting her arm around Lani. She said:

"You do look tired, Lani. Suppose we turn in?"

Dexter said:

"If you're deserting me, perhaps I can persuade the McDonalds to let me camp out with them for the rest of the night." He walked back to the hotel with them, talking to Helen. Lani said nothing. She felt as if she had been drugged.

At the hotel he shook hands with Helen, touched Lani's shoulder briefly, "I'll see you soon," he promised, and turned and went away.

Lani stood looking after him and presently Helen spoke to her.

"Asleep on your feet?" she inquired. "Come on, let's go to bed."

From the windows of their room Lani could see the angry, illuminated sky, the mist wreaths, to which the colors of the bursting fires clung. She thought, I'm glad it didn't happen last night, when Jim was here. She resented Jim, sharply, definitely. Because he made her feel ashamed, uncertain. As she was.

Helen woke, some time later, to see Lani, a

dim shape across the room, huddled in a chair by the window. She wore a robe over her pajamas and had flung a blanket around her shoulders. She was smoking, her cigarette a little ember in the dark.

Helen asked, "Can't sleep, Lani?"

"No, I'm sorry. I was very quiet," said Lani remorsefully, "but I wakened you, I'm afraid. This chair creaks."

"How long have you been sitting there?" Helen demanded.

"Two hours, more or less. I don't know. I was — restless . . ."

Helen said, "We went to bed too early." She threw back the bedclothes. "What time is it?"

Lani glanced at the illuminated watch dial on her wrist.

"Nearly four-thirty."

"I always wake at four-thirty," said Helen, "force of habit." She yawned and stretched. "Let's dress and go out," she suggested. "We can come back for early coffee. Jim will be along for us about nine, I think. When we reach home you can take a nap."

"You go back to sleep," said Lani, "this instant."

"Never more wide awake." Helen rose and switched on the light. "Good Lord, where did I put my shoes? Not that they'll ever be good for anything," she said, "black as your hat and the soles a little scorched, believe it or not. I really want to go out, Lani."

"All right."

She had never been more grateful to anyone than to this spare, matter-of-fact woman. She had thought, lying wakeful, that if she could get out of bed, sit by the window and smoke she might bring some sort of order to her thoughts. But another twenty minutes of sitting there alone watching the incredible sky and she would have screamed aloud. She told herself, it was neurotic nonsense, she would return to bed, she would sleep as soon as her head touched the pillow. She knew that was nonsense too.

They dressed and went out quietly, leaving Volcano House, walking out into the chill, somber air, picking their way carefully. A ranger spoke to them and Lani jumped. He recognized Helen and smiled. He said:

"There are hundreds, camping out."

"We might find the McDonalds," Helen said later, "although heaven knows where they are."

"No," said Lani sharply, "no — please — "

She stopped, appalled.

Helen understood. She remembered Dexter Warren saying, "Mind if I join you and Mrs. McDonald?" and McDonald's hearty burr, "Not at all, we'd be glad to have you."

They walked on without speaking and drew close to a group of campers with coffee boiling on a Sterno, and blankets around them. Beyond them they heard the sound of chanting, eerie in the night, and Lani clutched at Helen's arm.

"What's that?"

"Hawaiians, keeping their vigil. Shall we go over, closer to them?"

Sitting there on ground that was warm to the touch, they listened to the deep grave voices. And after a while Lani said, low:

"Makes you feel pretty small — all this."

"Yes."

"As if your personal problems didn't matter."

"But they do," said Helen, "they must. I don't envy any person without problems. He's not really alive."

"I suppose so." Lani was silent a moment. Then she said, her eyes on a distant upward shooting flame, tremendous in its shattering release, "But sometimes I'd rather not be alive. In that sense, I mean. It's so hard having to fight yourself." She added, "Sometimes without much conviction. And there's no end to it."

"Nothing ends," said Helen gently; "everything goes on, in one form or another. It

210

depends on you just what form it takes."

"What do you mean?"

"I mean," said Helen firmly, "it's your conflict. No one can help you . . . whatever it is."

"You heard, at the Robertses'," said Lani, "you must have heard — you must have thought . . . and then, tonight — "

That didn't make sense, yet Helen made sense out of it. She said quickly:

"You'd better not tell me, Lani. You'll regret it. Whatever's wrong I can trust you to set it right. You're so very like your father."

"Tell me about him."

"When he was your age," said Helen, with half a sigh, "marvelous looking, grand company. Generous to a fault, always considering other people rather than himself. Impulsive, getting into jams. But basically sound. Then he met your mother . . . I never knew a happier couple, never. Bill and I are happy, but not like that. Alan and Mary were — it's a crazy word but it's true — were luminous with happiness. I never saw him touch her. I never heard him call her a caressing name. Yet when he looked at her, when he spoke to her, it was all there, in his eyes and voice. He settled down, and he had an immense capacity for work. He knew, after you were born, that Mary would never be very well and he protected her, he . . . " she added slowly, "he sublimated himself. Your mother spoke to me about it, once. We were very close friends."

One of the group of singers detached himself and came over to them, a big man, slow moving, slow speaking. Helen looked up at him and spoke.

"Maleko, isn't it? Your eyes are very sharp . . . it's still dark," she said, presenting him to Lani.

He sat down with them, saying, "I heard your voice. Where is Kimo?"

"At Waipuhia, he's coming for us tomorrow. What do you think of the volcano?"

Maleko shook his head. "I have seen this happen, many times," he told her. "It is always new."

While they talked Lani sat, half listening, half occupied with her own thoughts. She had been so ready to share them with Helen. But Helen had stopped her. She thought, She's right, I don't want advice or — pity. I have to think this out in my own way.

There was one way to think it out and that was to face it and see Dexter deliberately, listen to any explanation he might offer. Half of this inability to think clearly came from imagining, remembering. If she faced him she would face herself.

Maleko was going. He said something in Hawaiian and Helen answered. When he had gone, Lani asked:

"What's Kimo . . . or who? He kept repeating it."

"Jim. Maleko's very fond of him. Taught him to swim, and surf. In his day Maleko was a great swimmer — almost as good as Duke Kahanamoku."

"What did he say as he left?"

"That the dawn would soon come." Helen rose. "I'm cold," she said, "strange as it may seem, and stiff. Getting no younger, I imagine. Shall we go back to Volcano House? It's something of a walk and I imagine we'll be able to get coffee, someone will be up, I doubt if anyone slept much."

Lani rose and stretched. She caught Helen's hand in hers. She said penitently, "You've been so good to me, Helen, and very patient. I don't deserve it. If I do things that look a little insane, and if I don't explain them, will you try to understand? For that's all I'm trying to do too — to understand myself."

Helen said, "I'm betting on you, Lani."

She coughed, from the sting of the fumes. And Lani said quickly:

"Let's go back."

In the fire pit of Halemaumau, the crater within a crater, the live lava still flowed, the earth stirred uneasily in her long sleep, and Pele spoke in the thunder of crashing boulders.

213

Chapter 13

Several days later Helen, turning from the telephone, went in search of Lani, to find her stretched out on the grass in the garden, a book beside her. But she was not reading. She was lying on her back with her arms under her head, looking up at the blue above her, and through the delicate lace of the jacarandas to the snow on Mauna Kea.

Helen dropped down beside her. She announced, pulling a stem of grass between her fingers:

"We're to have a visiting fireman tomorrow."

"Who?" asked Lani lazily. She was accustomed now to the people who came and went at Waipuhia.

"Dexter Warren."

Lani stiffened, slightly. She said nothing. Helen looked over at the tangled mass that was the night-blooming cereus. The blossoms had been plentiful and magnificent since June and there were still a few opening their astonishing white petals to receive the darkness.

She said:

"It seems he has expressed an interest in our particular methods . . . there are, as you know, some unique features about Waipuhia . . . and so McDonald asked him to come over sometime for a day. It appears he's still at Volcano House where Mrs. Warren, the Renfews and What's-his-name joined him yesterday. Twenty minutes ago he telephoned McDonald and asked if he might drive over tomorrow, alone. Said he'd hired a car . . . Mrs. McDonald's not well — and so — "

Lani said, "And so he'll come to you for lunch!"

"Yes," said Helen, and waited. Lani said nothing. Helen, rising, said, "Well, that's that . . . I'm going calling: hospital . . . two new babies, a fractured arm, and a postoperative. Want to come along?"

Dexter arrived the following day before noon and drove straight to the manager's house. He said apologetically, to Helen:

"I give you my word I had no intention of forcing myself on you but Mr. McDonald was so kind — "

"We're delighted to have you," said Helen. "Have you been to the office . . . no? I'll call and tell Mac you're here."

He stood a moment later with Lani and

looked out over the sea. He said lightly, "Gorgeous place . . . no wonder you don't want to leave it. I suppose you could murder me for barging in like this. It was an excuse, of course."

She said, to his astonishment:

"Don't be silly. I'm glad you came." She smiled at him, the sunlight in her gray eyes.

"Good," he said, puzzled and relieved.

Excitement grew in him. If, during the lapse of time between Lani's sailing and his coming to Hawaii, he had forgotten — or almost forgotten — her in the interlude with Susan Tait, his interest in her had been forcibly roused when Susan gave him his congé. Up until then he had not thought of following Lani Aldrich to Honolulu. He had been so sure at first, certain that she would return to him. When time went by and she did not return, he hadn't cared, very much, except for the blow to his pride. There had been Susan. Then, suddenly, Susan was no longer in the picture.

It was perfectly clear to him what had happened. That chance unfortunate meeting with Muriel. Muriel had always known about Lani . . . she had a hundred ways of hearing. He knew that she had known but had seen no reason to disturb Lani by telling her. It was perfectly obvious that Muriel had succeeded in

216

alienating Lani. Yet today, she was no longer hostile, no longer withdrawn. And the change in her interested him, as the incalculable always interested him.

Helen came out. She said, "Drinks follow, long and cool. It's hot, isn't it? But we're ideally situated here, wind from the sea, wind from the mountain. Mac's ready to take you through the mill, Mr. Warren . . . and Jim Bruce will drive you around after lunch."

He said, "I hope Lani'll go too."

"I'd love it," Lani said.

Later she walked through the mill with Mac and Dexter, breathed its thick sweet odors, listened to the clatter of machinery, watched the cane traveling inexorably on the great belts, ascended and descended in the elevators, peered at the vats, and McDonald said, laughing:

"You know nearly as much as I do now, Miss Aldrich."

"I'd qualify as a Girl Guide any day," she agreed; "you forget I've been through a dozen times now."

They went to the store, and then to the hospital, and then to the office where they were to pick up Bill. Frank Davidson was there, sitting on the edge of Bill's desk, which was strewn with graphs. He rose when they came in and his eyes flickered from Lani to Warren.

After the presentations, "Davidson," repeated Dexter, smiling. "My wife's spoken of you."

Frank smiled slightly. He said:

"I'd hardly think she'd remember me . . . there were a good many of us at Wahi-O-Hoku that evening."

"She remembers you," said Dexter. Their glances crossed. Lani looked from one to the other, and Bill said, pushing back his chair and reaching for the one crutch which was still necessary:

"I'm starved. How about some lunch?"

They left Frank looking after them and went back to the house, where they lunched on the *lanai* on avocado, cold crab, cold meats, iced tea with long sweet pineapple "fingers" . . . "Highball for you, Warren? I don't indulge till sundown," Bill explained.

"This is the life," said Dexter, opening his cigarette case, when he had Helen's permission to smoke. "Half inclined to buy me a plantation — or a slice of one — and settle down."

"It isn't all lunching on a *lanai*," said Bill, "as others before you have found. It's work, and plenty of it. Obstacles, setbacks . . . take the original Jones Costigan Act, for instance. Or wouldn't you know about it?"

"Behold a completely ignorant man," said Dexter.

Helen caught Lani's eye. She said resignedly, "Suppose we leave them. You've heard all this many times before and as for me, since nineteen-thirty-four I've lived with it."

They went out to the garden, leaving the men alone. They could hear Bill saying, ". . . serious injustice to Hawaii . . ." Helen shook her head. "He's off," she said. She added, looking away, "You needn't bother girl guiding if you don't want to, Lani. I can find a hundred excuses."

Lani said, "I'd rather not have an excuse."

The men joined them a little later, Bill still explaining, heatedly:

". . . No reason in God's world why we shouldn't refine the sugar here," he was saying, "but no . . . we were to ship raw, in excess of three per cent of the quota tonnage . . . it took three years to get any modification of the act . . . and even now the restrictions — which don't apply to Cuba — say . . ."

Helen asked:

"For heaven's sake, Bill, must you bore all your guests? Suppose I show Mr. Warren the garden . . . there's no overproduction here, no quota."

Bill laughed.

"Sorry," he said, "your fault, you led me on . . . time I was getting back to the office anyway. Jim will be along for you later." He shook hands with Dexter, said, "Sorry you aren't staying on, hope you'll come again." Limping off toward the house he waved his work hat with its feather lei. "Aloha," he said.

His car came for him and he drove off. Helen said, looking after him, "He'll be rid of that crutch in another two weeks, the doctor thinks. It's been a long pull . . . he hates driving to the office . . . most of all he hates not being able to ride."

"I can well imagine it," Dexter told her; "he's so tremendously active."

Jim drove up in his small car and Helen walked over with Lani, and Dexter. Lani made the introductions, and Jim nodded. He asked, "All set?" and looked inquiringly at Lani. "Didn't know you were coming," he told her.

She said, "Take Dexter in front with you . . . I'll ride in the back."

Driving away she leaned back and looked at the two men in the front seat. Beside Dexter's greater height, Jim looked overbulky in the shoulders. He sat hunched over the wheel, explaining all they saw, in a completely controlled, almost expressionless voice. They stopped for a moment at the Welfare Center where the plantation babies were fed and weighed, where their mothers were instructed in their care, and where, under medical supervision, a nurse worked daily.

When they came out, Jim was doggedly quoting figures.

They inspected the camps, the rows of red-roofed cottages housing the workers, the bachelors' quarters, mess hall, the recreation equipment, gymnasium, ball field. They looked into the club at which the skilled workers gathered for parties, to dance or to swim in the pool, and they drove out through the fields of cane.

Jim's voice went on and on . . . seeding, ratoon crops . . . burning off . . . harvesting . . .

Dexter said, amused:

"You seem to be in love with your work."

Jim said, after a moment:

"If you're enough in love with it, it requites you. It's all I know, Mr. Warren; I was brought up in this job."

Lani said:

"He's supposed to be on vacation. But he couldn't stay away from work."

"I could," murmured Dexter, turning to face her.

When they returned Helen was waiting for them, with iced tea for Lani and highballs for Dexter. But Jim excused himself and went off. Helen said, "Not too sociable today, is he?" But Dexter answered, "I thought he was very sociable. A bit on the serious side perhaps. All work and no play . . ."

Lani said nothing. She had seen Jim's eyes, contemptuous, angry, but beneath the contempt and anger a deep unhappiness. She felt as if she had been picketed . . . Lani unfair to disorganized Jim . . . but she hadn't thought of him, she'd thought only of herself . . . and of Dexter, of forcing herself to face him.

He was saying:

"Lord, I almost forgot. I've a note for you, Lani, from Muriel."

She opened the envelope, looked for the first time on the big angular writing.

"Dear Lani," wrote Muriel, on Volcano House stationery.

"I'm returning to Honolulu today, so sorry I can't go with Dex to see you. Charlie and Gertrude have visitors booked and Howard's flying home, by clipper. I'm looking for a house for the balance of the summer. Dex has to go home soon, but he and I are going to Kona Inn, Friday . . . we'll stay a week or so . . . Can't you join us, during that time? It would be great fun . . . Sincerely — "

Lani folded the note and slipped it back in the envelope. She said:

"Thank her, won't you, Dexter . . . and I'd be glad to."

She saw the sudden triumph in his eyes, and was, for a moment, afraid. Then he said heartily:

"That's great. Shall we stop by for you Friday? I'm hopeless about direction but I assume you're on our route . . . " He turned to ask Helen, who nodded. But Lani said:

"Not Friday. There's a dance, Saturday. Besides," she said steadily, "you'll want to be alone for a little while, won't you, especially as you're leaving so soon. But if you stay on, I'll come, say Monday or Tuesday."

"Fine," he said. "Muriel will be delighted."

When Dexter had left Lani said, walking back through the living room:

"I suppose you think I'm crazy . . . accepting that invitation — but, in a way, it's a challenge, isn't it?"

Helen said, "I don't think you're crazy. And I thought we weren't going to bother about explanations."

The Gaineses gave a party before the dance Saturday night. Many people came, people from other plantations, and from Hilo. Johnny and Alison drove over, and Fred and Betsy Bruce flew over from Honolulu, with a stop to look at the volcano on the way. Much of everyone's conversation centered around the volcano.

Betsy drew Lani aside. She said, "Looking

a little fine-drawn, aren't you? I hadn't expected that, I thought you'd be fat and flourishing. You'd better come home, to us."

"That's what Kazue says," said Lani, laughing. "She's had to take in some waistbands for me, recently. I'm fine really, Aunt Betsy."

"We miss you. Fred's always growling . . . I want you to go with me to Kauai . . . there's a sugar place there on a little green river. You'll love it . . . and the people . . . I could kill Helen for making Waipuhia so attractive. What's the matter with Jim, didn't his holiday do him any good? He's got a face like doom," she remarked, looking after her son, who was dancing with one of the several beautiful Chinese-Hawaiian girls present.

"Jim? He's fine," said Lani.

She danced with him later. He held her close. He said:

"I hear you're going to Kona . . . with Dexter Warren."

"And his wife," she added. "News travels fast in the Islands. Yes, I'm going. Why?"

"Nothing. None of my business." He said grudgingly, "He's an interesting guy, Lani. I'll grant you that much."

"You don't have to grant me anything," she said.

He burst out uncontrollably:

"Can't you see that woman will just be watching every move you make — and laughing at you?"

Lani said furiously:

"People are looking at you. And I'm not making any moves."

"Waiting for him? I'm sorry," he said, and didn't sound it, "but I get so damned — "

She was sorry for him, suddenly. She had lived for a long time with pain, she knew what it could do to you. She said gently:

"Jim, forgive me. I hurt you so much, and so often. I don't mean to . . . if it will help any I will tell you that I have no intention of seeing Dexter alone. Not ever again. I can promise you that."

Johnny cut in. He said, "Can't monopolize her all evening." He smiled down at Lani. "How's tricks? And isn't this devotion? I'll be up long past my bedtime. But it isn't every day that Bill and Helen throw such a party."

"Alison looks — darling," said Lani, "you ought to show her off more often."

Johnny's glance followed hers. He said:

"She's good enough to eat. Far as that goes, she always is, where I'm concerned. Look, this isn't my business, but what are you going to do about Jim?"

"Jim?"

"Don't open your eyes at me that way, my

girl. Alison does, I know that trick. You're stalling." He swept her deftly around the room and out onto the *lanai*. Standing there at the railing, he offered her his cigarette case, and said soberly, "Old Jim's hard hit."

"Nonsense," she said, trying to laugh. "Visiting fireman. That's all. And, mind you, I don't even admit that much."

He said:

"Okay by me. Alison claims I lack the approach tactful. But you see, Jim and I have known each other since we were knee-high to bufos."

"Diminutive for buffaloes?"

"Frogs," said Johnny, "imported, big as the dickens. You've heard 'em. Sound like sawmills in operation. To get back . . . and don't think I don't know you're still stalling . . . we grew up together, and we know each other pretty well. He hasn't said a word — he wouldn't . . . but I'm on. I wouldn't like to see him hurt."

She asked:

"You're blaming me? I wish you wouldn't."

"I'm not blaming you, Lani. These things just happen. There's nothing the rest of us can do about it."

She said:

"You're practically asking me to go away."

Johnny turned.

"No," he denied. "You belong here . . . Oh, hell — " His cigarette described a small flaming arc as it fell to the ground below. "Forget what I said, will you? Jim would have my ears."

Frank came out and found them.

"How about a dance," he asked Lani, "or are you standing this one out?" He grinned at Johnny. "Alison's looking for you," he said. He took Lani's arm and they went back inside. The orchestra had warmed up, was in full swing. They were playing, "Sweet Leilani," the men were singing. Their good brown faces smiled, they showed their excellent teeth. One of them was performing miraculously on the steel guitar, drawing from it tones of indescribably melancholy sweetness. "Pity," said Frank, "to let that go to waste. This outfit's from Hilo, and they're pretty darned good."

He danced well, not so well as Jim, better than Johnny. He asked:

"Going to Kona, aren't you?"

She said, half exasperated:

"Monday, I think. I believe everyone knew it before I did!"

"Grapevine system," he said, "or comes in with the cane. Down the mountain on trolleys or across the gulleys in flumes. Well, you'll like it there. I have to go to Honolulu next week," he said, "on personal business. Can't be gone long . . . too much to do."

Always so much to do. Harvest field, plant field, the eternal round and the mill operating twenty-four hours a day for most of the year. Irrigation or partial irrigation unless, as on the wetter coasts, the rainfall took care of that. The laying down of portable tracks. The immense, constructive labor, continuous and unremitting.

Over in Honolulu on the beach at Waikiki the tourists oiled themselves against the sun, they could lie dreaming under the blue, they could rouse for sightseeing, for motor rides, for parties, and return to dream again . . . they could see Hawaii Nei — all Hawaii through a haze of languor, sweet with song, heavy with blossoms, vitalized by laughing, dancing girls. But those to whom Hawaii was home, people of sugar and pineapple plantations, of cattle ranches, of the great Agency companies, the business life of which the outward symbols were steamship lines or shops, tourist bureaus or hotels, were a million miles removed from the languid South Sea Island dweller of fiction.

He said, as he saw Perry, the social service director, coming across the floor with determination in his eye:

"About to be cut in upon. Hope you enjoy

Kona, I'd like to be there to see it through your eyes, for the first time . . . Helen going?"

She answered, "No; the Warrens have asked me to join them."

"Remember me to Mrs. Warren," he said, without expression; "a very charming woman."

Not until she was safely transferred to the large and emphatic arms of Mr. Perry did she remember the casual gossip about Frank Davidson and his telephone calls from Honolulu.

Chapter 14

One of the plantation store clerks drove Lani to Kilua, on the Kona coast, as he was going on for a brief visit to his mother who lived just beyond Kilua. It rained in torrents as far as Honokaa, and the waterfalls came hissing down the steep coast to the sea and the great flumes transporting the cane were filled with rushing water. The whole coast was a misty gray-green, like twilight in the fern crater. But beyond, on the road to Kamuela, it cleared and the sun shone, with the Kohala Mountains close on the right, trying to reach the sunny sky and farther over, on the left, Mauna Kea, seemingly succeeding, towering nearly fourteen thousand feet.

At Kamuela, they stopped at the Waimea for luncheon, where Alison met them. She was going on to Hilo to stop with friends and go to the volcano. She was waiting on the hotel porch when Lani's driver drew up with a flourish. He vanished presently, and Lani and Alison ate at a small table by the windows.

It was cool, at that elevation, there in the heart of the great Parker Ranch. Alison had a lei waiting for Lani, heavy purple pansies, dewy and wonderful. When she had put it around her throat Alison exclaimed:

"They make your eyes turn their color — "

"Purple?" said Lani, laughing. "Only girls in eighteen-ninety stories have purple eyes."

"Not purple, silly, sounds as if you'd taken a beating. Mauve, really," said Alison. "I don't know."

They parted a little later, and Lani went on, down the Mamalahoa Highway, past old lava flows, desolate and strange, past caves ... She sat in the front seat and talked to her companion, anxious not to be isolated with her thoughts:

"Do you know where there are burial caves?" she asked him.

He had a lean, dark face, and a pleasant smile. His smile faded and he answered cautiously:

"As a little boy I have found some."

She said quickly:

"I just wondered. I didn't want to be shown any ... it would seem desecration for a stranger to intrude."

He looked frankly relieved and presently she had him talking, of the burial caves, of the sacred *heiaus*, or temples, of his father, now dead, who had witnessed the lava flows of 1887 and 1901 . . . and how he himself had seen the 1919 flow go hissing like a vast serpent, into the sea. . . .

As he talked, telling her bits of history, legend and fantasy, she thought how much there was to learn, one could spend a lifetime at it, learning of the little men, the *menehune* people of Kauai, of the ghost army and its drums, of *kahunas*, and their magic. But now and then her undersurface preoccupation betrayed her and she grew panicky, on the verge of begging Mr. Kaaihue to turn, to take her back, at least as far as the Roberts ranch, that she had changed her mind, and did not want to go to Kona after all.

They came to forested ways, with the golden needles of the silver oak like petrified sunlight, and the silvery leaves of the sacred kukui trees. She saw monkeypods and mangoes, and jacarandas, tree on great tree. And presently Kona coffee growing and the sturdy little donkeys, passing with their burdens, the Kona nightingales which sang in their own extraordinary fashion to the horror of the hearer. And everywhere along the road were children who halted to salute and call "Aloha!" Japanese babies tumbling in the dust, women sitting outside their shacks weaving the lauhala — into baskets and hats and table mats.

This was a different coast, friendly, lazy, dreaming, as if time had stood still.

They came to the inn, with its wide welcoming doors, and great central lounge and rooms which opened on a long narrow *lanai*, to right and left of the lounge. A boy took her bags, the genial manager came forward to meet her, rising from his game of dominoes, and Dexter Warren came in from the wider *lanai*, which faced the sea.

He said, taking her hands:

"So you finally got here."

"Yes. Where's Muriel?"

"She'll be along — " He stopped, as one of the clerks hurried up.

"Your room is ready, Miss Aldrich," he told her. "Mrs. Gaines telephoned."

"Join me later," Dexter called, "for a drink. The planter's punch here is something very special."

Join *me*. Not, join us.

Panic overtook her again. She steadied herself walking down the *lanai*, past the tennis courts. Vines grew thickly here and the white and yellow ginger . . . you looked across the courts to the hills. It was raining high up but here the sun shone, drawing out the sweetness of the ginger.

They had given her the last room on the

corner. Cool and spacious, the simple furniture of beautiful wood and with beautiful lines. Lauhala mats on the floor, Venetian blinds at the great window back of the bed. A little bathroom with a shower, a screened *lanai*, below which there was a strip of grass and then the curious formation of black lava, carved by time and water into hollows. The tide would run in there and out again leaving shining pools filled with little fish and tiny crabs and *bêche-de-mer*.

She could see a beacon on a rocky point to her left as she stood there, a strip of beach and wharves.

When she had showered and changed, she went back along the *lanai* to the main lounge. There was no other way to get there unless you walked part way along the *lanai*, down steps, through a passage under the house to the front lawn. Dexter was waiting for her in the lounge and drew her outside, near the bar. He said, "I've ordered for you."

The lawn was green and lovely, tall palms leaned, the myna birds were quarreling. She could see a small grass shack and the hotel annex, the low sea wall and the swimming pool. The waves dashed up and showered into the pool. Half a dozen people were swimming there. But there was no beach, merely the black jagged rocks of lava.

Dexter followed her eyes.

"Easier on tenderfoot feet," he said, "the pool . . . but the natives skip around the lava barefoot. Look at that one."

A boy standing on the sea wall, fishing, naked except for the bright scarlet *malo,* the loincloth, his body dark and polished.

"Saturday night," said Dexter, "they put on a show for us . . . hulas and songs . . . in front of the grass shack. Footlights in a hollowed-out log, very effective. Did you notice the bar, an ancient and honorable canoe . . . what wood . . . and what a polish! Here come our drinks."

She had not heard a word. She asked directly:

"Where's Muriel?"

His eyelids flickered. He said:

"Her compliments. She was so sorry . . . but she returned to Hilo yesterday — to catch the plane. Urgent business in Honolulu, seems that they've found a house for her."

Lani was white. She said, "I can't believe — I — " She raised her heavy lids and looked at him. "But she *asked* me to come," she said blankly. She thought, I've broken my promise to Jim.

"Of course. And to stay. She'll be back the end of the week. We can all return together."

He fished in the pocket of his shirt and gave

her a note. On Kona Inn stationery this time.

"My dear," it read, "I'm desolate — rushing off like this. But I can't accept the agent's estimate of the house. I must see it myself. There's no one's judgment I can trust, least of all Gertrude's. Do stay on and amuse yourself . . . I'll be back as soon as I can . . . "

She signed herself and underneath the signature she had written, "I dare you — "

The glass of planter's punch was frosty in Lani's hand. She drank a little and set it down. Dexter asked:

"You're very angry?"

"No."

There was nothing she could say. Muriel had asked her to come, Muriel had departed before her arrival, leaving an excuse, very plausible. So, Muriel had come out on top. See, declaimed the latter, how tolerant, how magnanimous I am. How I trust you . . . if not my husband. Not that it matters. Have your little hour, amuse yourself. I'll be back. She'd always be back.

Lani said slowly:

"You planned this."

"Plan . . . with Muriel? My dear child, I haven't the slightest control over her."

"In the morning," Lani said, "I'll get a car and return to the plantation."

"Certainly, if you wish. I'd arranged a fish-

236

ing party, however . . . "

"You expect me to stay here — with you?"

"With me?" He raised an eyebrow. "The inn isn't very crowded at the moment but there are a dozen people here besides us. We're ably chaperoned. And you aren't a child, or are you? Lani, I must talk to you. As I told you at the volcano, you owe it to me . . . an explanation of your silence and also, as I have come thousands of miles to see you, of your attitude. The last time I saw you you told me that you were going away to come to a certain decision. An important decision — "

She said, knowing that the time had come for her to say it:

"You must know now what my decision is."

"You make it clear enough," he agreed. "All right, that's your privilege. But I have a right to know what brought you to it . . . "

She couldn't answer . . . Muriel . . . Muriel and Agnes Palmer and all the rest. She couldn't base it on — jealousy . . . or on her feeling of sick shame. Looking at him now, she thought again, Perhaps it isn't true, perhaps she lied. Why shouldn't she lie? She's like that.

The whole pattern was falling to pieces in her hands. She had thought this a problem which was solely hers and Dexter's. But according to Muriel, it wasn't.

She said firmly:

"Dexter, I — "

"Don't say it," he interrupted. "Give me my chance, first. Let us be together this little while. Have you forgotten that I love you? That you loved me — not so long ago?"

She drew her breath sharply.

He said:

"Darling, please . . . Drink your punch, and we'll go walking. The tide's out, I'll lift you over the sea wall and we'll explore. This is a wonderful place. The sort of place I've dreamed of being in, with you. Or don't you want to be with me . . . ever? Stay, for a few days, Lani. I'm leaving so soon. . . ."

She said slowly:

"I'll stay — if — "

"Conditions? Make them."

"If you don't make it difficult for me."

"Why should I? If you like we won't speak of what has happened. Of what hasn't happened . . . not until you are ready. We'll join forces like any other tourists, fish for blue marlin tomorrow, and next day take a picnic lunch to the City of Refuge . . . As if, say, we'd just met."

"All right," she said, after a moment.

After dinner they walked again by the sea wall and he said, as the moon rose and hung silver over the water:

"Time you went in. Up early tomorrow, you know."

He did not walk with her to her room but left her in the main lounge. After she had undressed, she sat for a long time on the *lanai*, a thin silk robe around her, looking out over the restless water, watching the punctual flash of the beacon. She thought, I will stay till Muriel comes, I will face this, and him.

How much easier it would have been, she thought forlornly, if this decision had come to her from her own innate conviction that the half-life he had offered her would not be good enough, would not be right in the larger sense. But to have to admit to him that Muriel had shattered an illusion, that she could not be one of many, that in order to justify herself and her love she had to be alone, set apart . . . She twisted her hands together. He would deny all Muriel had said, and perhaps she would believe his denial, wanting to believe it. For all evening she had been troubled by his nearness, helplessly troubled.

They spent most of the next day rocking over the waves in their extraordinarily sturdy fishing boat. They had luck, a number of hard-fighting game fish, but no marlin, so the flag was not hoisted nor the carrier pigeons released to take word of their catch back to the hills, whence it would be telephoned to the inn.

At dinner she was relaxed and drowsy, soaked through and through with sun and wind and salt. Once or twice Dexter caught her halfway through a yawn and raised his eyebrows.

"Company bore you?" he suggested.

"No, of course not. Only I'm so sleepy. There's something about the air here . . . I could fall apart and never know it."

He complained:

"We won't fish again. I haven't had a word with you?"

"Thousands of them."

"All about fish. Every time I wanted to say something important, you had a strike. Or I did. Or you were in conference with the guides. What did you find so interesting?"

"Lots. Fishing. Old legends of this coast. Did you know that if we'd caught a marlin and hadn't been able to land it alone, they'd much prefer to let it go than help? There's a sort of code that you give the fish his chance too. It's between you and the fish, and if you can't conquer him it isn't fair to howl for help. He can't."

"Sounds damned silly," he commented, "as the men are paid to see that you get a good catch, so if it takes two to land the brute . . . "

"They'd land it for you, all right," she said, "only you'd lose face."

He laughed. "That wouldn't worry me," he said. "Look here, I've had enough of fish for the time being. Tomorrow we'll picnic . . . I'll drive and we can be alone. . . ."

She said, "I think we'd better take a driver."

Dexter shrugged. He said:

"You're very cautious, suddenly. You didn't demand an academic chaperone the time we drove out to the old country inn. Or have you forgotten?"

"I haven't forgotten," she admitted, troubled.

He leaned back and looked at her, smiling. Very sure of her, very sure of himself. One of the boys came hurrying from the office to tell him that Honolulu was calling.

"Sorry," he said, rising, "I'll be right back."

Alone, she looked out over the lawns to the sea, hearing the wind in the palms. Far along, someone was torch fishing now that dark had fallen. She thought over her day with Dexter. Despite all that was as yet unspoken between them, she had loved being with him, under the blazing sky. There had not been opportunity for intimate discussion, argument or quarrel. And she had been glad.

A shadow crossed her face, recalling that Dexter hadn't come off very well during the day. He had been brusque with the men and the boat, and demanding . . . they were hired, as was the boat. He did not enter into any unnecessary conversation with them. There had been arrogance in his attitude. It wasn't that he was obviously rude, simply that he ignored the men except when he wanted something . . . nor was he open to advice. He'd lost one good fish that way. "My good man," he'd said, "I've fished the Florida coast and off Montauk and in a thousand other places. I can handle this."

She'd tried to make up for it. Not merely because of him, but because she had liked the two men, the old Hawaiian, with his lined face and laughing eyes, and the younger man, a lithe Portuguese-Hawaiian. They had much to teach her, she thought, and she wanted to learn.

The boy from the office came down the few steps from the front *lanai*. Mr. Warren asked if she would come, please, he said.

When she reached the office Dexter was behind the desk at the telephone. He beckoned her. "It's Muriel, she wants to speak to you," he reported.

Lani went behind the desk, and took the instrument from his hand. "Darling," said

Muriel, "how are you? Having fun? I'm so glad you decided to come; Dex tells me he had some difficulty in persuading you."

The malice was perfectly definite.

Lani said evenly:

"I'm sorry you're not here. When are you coming?"

"I've found my little house. It's divine . . . I can't wait for you to see it . . . "

Lani asked patiently:

"But are you coming to Kona or not, Muriel?"

"Tomorrow," said Muriel, "or next day . . . Wait for me. 'Bye, darling . . . tell Dex to behave."

The connection was broken. Lani went around the desk. She said abruptly:

"I don't believe she intends to come at all."

Dexter smiled. He said:

"I wouldn't let it worry you."

They went back to their table, for dessert and the strong, unusually flavored coffee of the Kona section. Stirring hers, Lani said quietly:

"I'm beginning to understand how much of an understanding you and Muriel have. I had a very different impression, at one time." She raised her eyes and looked at him. She was a different girl, cool eyes, bright lips without laughter, delicate and remote in her evening frock, from the girl who had been with him on the boat, in slacks and a gay shirt, her bare feet in canvas shoes.

"I'd never deny to you that we have an understanding — of sorts," he said.

"If I'd asked you, you mean? But you gave me no reason to ask you. Was she as complaisant about Agnes Palmer?"

"Who told you about Agnes?" he asked, off guard.

"I heard about her," Lani said, "before I left for the Coast. I didn't believe it, of course. But I've heard since . . . from Muriel."

"Skip it . . . there wasn't anything in it . . . it didn't mean a thing to me, Lani."

"Or to Miss Palmer?"

He said:

"I don't know why Muriel — " He broke off. He knew why perfectly well. He knew why Muriel discussed his past affairs with his current interests. He knew why she permitted, and often encouraged him in, such affairs. He knew, and loathed knowing. He couldn't if it had meant his life, lean across the table and explain to this grave girl, My wife is amused by my — excursions into romance. She had never objected, except once, on our honeymoon. Occasionally she deliberately throws someone my way. I met Agnes Palmer through Muriel. She said, "Just

244

your type darling." She was right. And she does it in order to protect herself . . . I can't reproach her, can I? I can't call the kettle black. She knows perfectly well that there are good and sufficient reasons why I do not want a divorce but she's fixed it so I can't divorce her if I did want to — yet so she could divorce me, if it pleased her. But she won't. I'm too useful to her. We are too useful to each other.

Lani said slowly:

"I am beginning to think that you and Muriel know each other — thoroughly. She told me about Susan Tait."

"Susan!"

She was startled to see him flush. He dropped his coffee spoon, picked it up, his hands uncertain. He said, with unnecessary vigor:

"That's pretty silly . . . a girl I met on a trip . . . I took her to lunch once or twice."

Susan, in South America, had given him to understand that when they returned to New York . . . When they did return to New York he had seen her, taken her to lunch, to dine, for cocktails, for long drives. But he didn't get anywhere. Not that Susan had any scruples, her reputation said she had none and no inhibitions either. She knew all the answers, she piqued his imagination, infuriated, interested him. Eventually she had yawned in his face. She had said:

"We're too much alike. You don't accelerate my metabolism by a faster pulse beat. It's a matter of fencing, it becomes monotonous. I know every trick in advance. There are no surprises. And the Casanova type doesn't really interest me. Always too anxious to prove himself, poor Casanova, because he isn't quite sure of his charm."

She had mentioned other things that the Casanovas weren't sure of — and Dexter hadn't forgotten. Returning to Lani would be like salve to his wounds, balm to his bruised ego, or so he had thought when he made his clipper reservations.

He said:

"Be honest with me, Lani. Did you make up your mind about — us — before you met Muriel?"

This was the hardest thing she had ever done. She raised her eyes to his and said gravely:

"Before I met Muriel I was going to cable you, Dexter, and tell you that I was coming home . . . on your terms."

"Damn Muriel," he said, white around the mouth. He leaned across the table. "You'd believe her," he said furiously, "all her nasty little lies, and you wouldn't believe me?"

"I don't know," she said wearily. "Dexter, I'm tired; I am, really. If you don't mind, I'll go to bed."

"I mind terribly," he said. "Listen, you must let me explain, must let me — "

She shook her head.

"Not now," she said.

She went, and he was left with the evening on his hands.

He swore, went off to the bar to sit and consume highballs. Palms, moonlight, a singing sea . . . the setting was magical. Much good it would do him.

Someone passed close under the private *lanai* off Lani's bedroom, three local girls laughing and talking. They could not see her beyond the closed blinds. Later, a man went by singing. And then everything was still again.

Long after she had gone to bed she was aroused from her first light sleep by someone calling beyond the *lanai*, speaking her name, urgently.

She rose and went out. The blinds were down to keep out the morning light. She leaned against the screening and asked drowsily:

"Who is it? What do you want?"

She knew before he answered. Dexter said, "It's I — don't tell me you were asleep, I don't

believe it. Come out, the night is too wonderful to waste."

"I'm going back to bed," said Lani. "I've
no intention of dressing and coming out."

He said urgently:

"Then let me come in. It's just a step
around the corner and you're quite alone at
this end of the house. No one will see or hear,
no one will be the wiser."

Chapter 15

Before dawn the myna birds were quarreling furiously in the palms. It seemed hours later that Lani heard another sound, like sudden thunder, and rose to go out on the *lanai*, open the blinds and see the ship which had just anchored, waiting there, the cowboys on the strip of beach to her left, the little dog which ran barking furiously into the water after the horses, the frightened cattle calling mournfully.

For a time she watched the activity, the steers swimming out to the longboat, where men caught them by their halters and held them, still valiantly swimming, beside the boat, until it reached the ship. She watched the belt drop down, catch a steer by his startled middle, lift him kicking or stiff-legged high in the air and lower him into the hold. At any other time this unique method of cattle shipping, complete with seagoing cowboys, would have held her fascinated attention but after a time it palled and she went back to her room to put on her bathing suit.

Alone, in the early morning, she went down the *lanai*, the steps, under the house, and out on the lawn. Around the big cement pool there was a strip of sand, chairs, tables, umbrellas. The blue water swayed in the pool and every now and then a wave crashed against the lava rocks beyond and fell over, and into the pool in a shower of diamonds.

No one was about, she saw no one stirring at the inn. She swam steadily for a time in the warm, refreshing water. She went to the deep end of the pool and clung to the ledge waiting until the water could come over and engulf her. A little wave, a shower . . . a big wave, and she swam away, gasping.

She was not afraid of meeting Dexter. He had been very drunk the night before. He had remained standing, under the *lanai*, for perhaps half an hour, pleading, threatening, arguing, by turns importunate or frankly ugly. Afterwards, he had stumbled away.

The summer sun was a glimmer of golden light, the wind cool in the palms, when she dressed and went to the lounge. The night clerk was startled when he saw her. He commented, "You're up early, Miss Aldrich."

"It's such a wonderful day."

"Did the cattle ship wake you when she anchored?"

"I didn't mind," she told him, "I've had a marvelous swim."

He said, "Breakfast isn't ready yet. But I'll take you to the kitchen, I'm sure Tony will give you coffee."

The pleasant informality of the Kona coast prevailed here in the hotel. Lani, suddenly conscious of emptiness, followed the clerk into the big kitchen. The staff was just reporting for duty and Tony, the cook, poured her a cup of steaming black coffee. She shook her head when he offered her cream. He offered eagerly, "I'll make you some toast," but Lani refused.

"Not now . . . later. I'm going for a walk," she said.

She went back to the lounge and out, away from the sea, and walked down the dusty road. The few houses were deserted. She passed the store with its ramshackle porch where, yesterday morning on the way to the wharf, she had seen a card game in progress . . . half a dozen men around a table, surrounded by onlookers, one, a big brown boy, with a baby on his shoulder. Dexter had said, "That game's been going on ever since I came here . . . it's interminable."

Bougainvillaea dripped from fence and trees, bignonia was pure orange-gold in the sunlight, hibiscus ran the gamut of shades

251

from red to flesh pink, and a variety strange to her, shaped like little tasseled lanterns, showered over a wall. She passed, unseeing, the ancient stone church, the beautiful Royal Palace.

Presently she stood by the sea wall and looked up, toward the beach and wharf, listened to the shouts of the cowboys, the barking of the self-important little dog, the lowing of the cattle. The sun grew higher and hotter. There was a mist over the hills. . . .

Presently she retraced her steps to the inn. There was every indication that breakfast was ready although only two lone fishermen, anxious to get away, were taking advantage of it. Lani sat down at the table she had shared with Dexter and ordered. She was absurdly hungry. This was a time to fast, not to feast, yet her healthy young body took no note of what was fitting. She ate her chilled golden papaia, marvelously sweet, and some of the hot black pepsin seeds. She poured fresh coffee and her waiter brought her a delicious piece of fish — "Opapapaka," he told her, beaming; "you call it big snapper, I think."

Toast and passion fruit jam . . . another cup of coffee. If Dexter came down the steps toward her, what would she say? She would say, easily, calmly, "Good morning." She would say, "I hadn't expected to see you again before I left."

When he exclaimed, as, of course, he would exclaim, she would lift an eyebrow and ask as coolly as Muriel had ever said anything. "You didn't believe I would stay, did you?"

She smoked a cigarette, sitting there, watching the sunlight dance on the sea. A young Hawaiian went across the lawn, a spear in one hand, a pair of water goggles dangling from the other. Her waiter came up to inquire if she lacked anything and to tell her that there was to be a big *hukilau* later in the day, at the next village. She let him explain the term to her, although she knew perfectly well that *hukilau* meant, "pull the leaf," and that leaves were attached to a great net, fluttering, to drive the fish into the net. And that whole families, whole villages, would go out and take part in the *hukilau* when the schools of fish were running.

She went back to her room and packed her bag. Afterward she sat for some time on the edge of her bed and looked down at the matting on the floor. Someone knocked and she jumped, her heart fainting, but it was only the pretty Hawaiian maid, Loika.

"I'm sorry," the girl apologized, "I thought you had gone to breakfast. The housekeeper saw you and told me I might do the room."

"Of course," said Lani, rising.

Loika saw the bags and looked at her. She said, "You aren't going away!"

Lani tried to smile. "I think so," she said.

"That is too bad," the girl said sincerely.

Lani tipped her, Loika smiled, murmured *"Mahalo,"* and busied herself with her work. Lani went out and to the desk in the lounge. The manager was not visible but the day clerk, a round-faced Japanese, came hurrying up to inquire what he could do for her.

"I wanted to ask about hiring a car and driver," she said, "to take me back to Waipuhia."

The clerk looked sad. He said:

"We hoped you would stay with us . . . I — "

"I find I must go back," she said, "and I do not want to ask Mrs. Gaines to send for me, it may not be convenient."

"Of course, it wouldn't be convenient," agreed Dexter, at her elbow. Under the regard of the clerk she was able to turn and look at him. His eyes were clear, he was laughing. He said, "You can't go, you know, with our picnic all planned."

"I'm sorry . . . " she began.

But he had tucked her arm under his, was leading her away from the desk. He said, over his shoulder to the clerk, "Miss Aldrich has changed her mind. You'll send word about the car, won't you, and order the hampers?"

He held Lani's arm closer to his side, walked her through the lounge and out on the front *lanai*. Not many people were lounging in the big wicker chairs as yet. A spectacled and severe woman studied a tourist guide, her sensible brogues planted on the cushions of the chaise longue in which she was lying. A middle-aged man was taking motion pictures from in front of the inn. A couple of teenage boys were running across the lawn toward the pool in brilliant trunks.

Lani said furiously:

"Let me go, Dexter."

"Certainly. Sit down a moment. I have something to say to you."

"Nothing," she retorted, "that I want to hear. Meantime as you must have understood from my abortive conversation with the clerk, I'm hiring a car and leaving here, as soon as possible."

"I'm afraid not," he said, smiling.

She stood by the broad steps and looked at him, directly.

"Exactly what does that mean?" she inquired.

He said:

"You're prettier than ever when you're angry. I've never seen you angry before, No, not angry," he repeated reflectively. "I have, I fear, only the foggiest remembrance of last night ... but, as I was saying, you can't go. You see, I telephoned Mrs. Gaines, this morning."

"You telephoned Helen!" she exclaimed, incredulous.

"Yes. I told her that Muriel had been called back to Honolulu — that's what you'd prefer me to tell her, isn't it, since you've developed such a passion for convention — and that, naturally, you thought of returning to the shelter of her roof. But it seemed a pity, we'd planned a pleasant day here — so I asked her if she and any of the others who could come would join us. Instead of a picnic luncheon at the City of Refuge we'd have an early picnic supper, with a little sightseeing thrown in first, for good measure."

"You dared do that?" she asked him, too stupefied for anger.

"That's bad theater," he said critically. "Mrs. Gaines didn't feel as you do. She thought me most considerate. She's accepted ... I suggested that she spend the night here, and take you back with her tomorrow. She thought it an excellent idea. She will lunch en route, and arrive in the early afternoon. . . . If you aren't tired of standing," he added, "I am."

Lani turned and walked mechanically to

one of the lounge chairs, sufficiently removed from the spectacled tourist to be out of earshot.

Dexter sat down on the foot of the chair.

"That's better," he said. "Please be reasonable."

She said slowly:

"So Helen assumes that Muriel left us here, this morning?"

"I hope so. It's what I indicated, in more or less plain English."

He lit a cigarette. His hand was not quite steady and the blazing morning light was not kind to him. His skin looked drawn, there were lines about his eyes and mouth which she had never before noticed.

"I'm supposed to endorse this lie?" she inquired.

"It would be awkward for you if you didn't," he said, smiling. "Wouldn't Mrs. Gaines think it odd that I had gone to all the trouble of telling her that Muriel left this morning, if you insist on telling her that Muriel left before you came and that, nevertheless, you stayed on until today?"

A pretty girl in blue linen shorts strolled out on the *lanai* and down the steps. Dexter's regard followed her with appreciation.

"Why did you do this?" Lani asked him after a moment.

He said lightly, "To protect you, naturally." And then, not so lightly, "Last night . . . Lani, I was very drunk. You left me, the bar offered the only consolation. I made a damned fool of myself. I don't often. I remember going along the lawn to stand under your *lanai* windows. I remember calling you."

"Is that all you remember?" she asked quietly.

"Later, I found myself back in my room," he said.

She said, with repressed rage:

"I don't believe you. You weren't that drunk, Dexter. To come like — like a prowling alley cat and — "

"Lani!" A vein sprang into prominence on his forehead. The cigarette, bitten through, fell to the cushion of the lounge chair. He picked it up, tossed it into an ash tray.

"Like what else?" she demanded. "Not a very pretty comparison. But the things you said, when I wouldn't let you in, weren't pretty either. About your wife. About — Susan Tait. I was to restore your self-respect," she said furiously, "which I gathered Susan had shattered. Self-respect! After listening to what you had to say last night, Dexter, I haven't a shred left of my own."

He said viciously:

"All right. She turned me down. What has

258

that to do with us?"

"Nothing, perhaps. I'll try to make you understand," she said slowly. "It won't be easy. I hardly understand myself."

He said:

"I'm wondering. How much of all this is an excuse? Young Bruce — for instance. I saw him look at you, the day on the Gaines plantation. Perhaps he is the reason — "

She said:

"Jim doesn't enter into this. I wish I could say he *were* the reason." She regarded him steadily. "I was terribly in love with you," she said, "I made all the familiar excuses, stupid, fallacious excuses, for us both. I believed in you, in your love for me. When, that first time in New York, I refused to go to your apartment with you, I actually thought I was being noble, self-sacrificing, because I knew that I must consider someone dearer to me even than you were, who mustn't be hurt. Then when she was past hurting and I came to New York and you planned our life together — our half-life — I was still sure, Dexter, of you, of myself . . . but it was such a big step to take, such a tremendous step, my whole world changed . . . I wasn't afraid, because I thought I loved you well enough to make up for everything else. I thought we could make our world. But I wanted to be fair, to us both.

So I came away to think things through. It wasn't easy . . . I'd been so tired, so unhappy, that for a while I couldn't think . . . I drifted, that was all. But gradually I began to believe that there was no life possible for me unless I went back to you, and when I heard that Muriel was in the Islands . . . " She paused and said thoughtfully, "You see, I believed too that I understood the situation between you and Muriel . . . " She found herself laughing at that, with genuine humor. "That was funny," she added, "that was really *funny.*"

"Sorry," he said, "if the humor escapes me."

"Never mind," she said, sobering. "When I heard she was here, I made up my mind. Nothing she could do would hurt us. I was going back — to you. I was still filled with the romantic ideology which I thought noble, and which was ignoble. Ready to sacrifice myself and not count it a sacrifice. Love, and the world well lost. And perhaps I thought Muriel would tire of trying to hold a man she didn't love, who didn't love her. When I met her — and she told me exactly where I stood — one of a troupe . . . one of a procession . . . "

He said sullenly, "If you believed her, you didn't love me very much, Lani."

"I didn't believe her," she said promptly,

"not wholly. I didn't know what to believe. When I met you again . . . oh, you could have persuaded me of anything, Dexter. I was fighting, not you, not loving you, but my pride, my jealousy. I was willing to let you convince me how wrong she was . . . until last night. Because last night you told me the truth . . . and I believed that. And this morning . . . " she looked at him, with sudden sorrow . . . "this morning, everything's changed. There's nothing to fight now, Dexter. I don't love you. I never did. I loved someone else, someone I thought you were. Muriel didn't shatter that illusion. You did."

"This is all very interesting," he said, after a moment.

"You can't hurt me now," she said quietly. "I was still in love with you that night at the volcano. I was still in love with you last night, until you came to my room. I'm not now. It's a horrible feeling, empty, lost. You're not to blame, really. You are as you are."

He had completely regained his poise. The wind stirred lazily in the palms, the summer sun blazed above them, they could hear faintly from the pool the shouts of the youngsters chasing one another like dolphins. A Hawaiian woman walked across the lawn, wearing a cotton *holoku* and a broad shade hat of lauhala. She carried an entirely naked

261

brown baby in her arms, and two stumbled along beside her, the boy in a wisp of a *malo*, the girl wearing a cotton frock as her only garment . . .

He said:

"I believe you're growing up, after all. I wish I'd met you later."

She said quite gently:

"I'm not angry now, Dexter. Talking like this, it's all gone, the anger. I'm only sorry — for us both."

"Sorry? My dear girl!"

"It was all such a stupid waste," she said, remembering what Jim had once said to her, "a waste of good honest emotion. Mine was honest, anyway. And I'm sorry for you, because of last night. The things you said, the things no one should ever have heard, for which, if you remember them, you'll hate me for hearing and yourself for betraying, someday. Because I know you now, the things you fear, the things you resent. It's always been Muriel, hasn't it? But something went wrong between you, a long while ago. So you had to prove yourself attractive to other women, because you no longer attracted her. You had to make money, lots of it, had to become necessary to her, in one way at least."

He said, a white line about his lips:

"You have it all figured out, haven't you?"

262

"I think so," she said steadily; "I tried to, last night, after you had come around the corner of the house, along the public *lanai* and knocked at my door . . . I tried, and I think I succeeded. And this morning's gesture — it was hardly chivalry, Dexter, nor remorse."

"What, then, in God's name?" he demanded.

The tourist shut her guidebook and rose with a heavy stamping of her sensible feet. She looked at them over her spectacles. She had not been able to overhear, to her sorrow, but she knew that the ugly, interesting-looking man and the quite lovely girl, obviously much his junior, were quarreling. The man's voice had been raised, just now. She sighed. Beneath an exterior as forbidding, and as little romantic, as the walls surrounding a prison, Miss Mellony had a heart of a frustrated Juliet. She yearned to implore them to kiss and make up . . . life, thought Miss Mellony, stumping off to her bedroom, to fetch a bottle of sun oil, was so pitifully brief.

Lani said:

"Please lower your voice . . . that woman — "

"What does she matter? Lani, listen to me!"

"Your turn to listen; you did the talking last night," she said inexorably. "No, neither chivalry nor remorse. A — form of revenge, I think. To implicate me in a lie . . . I can't tell Helen the truth now, nor anyone. Yet the truth wouldn't have hurt me and Helen would have understood it. But now — if it becomes apparent — "

He shrugged.

"I can't follow all this tortuous analysis," he said, "I'm not even trying. Why should it come out . . . and how? And if it did . . . so what?"

"Please," said Lani, "if you don't mind — I want to tell the clerk that I'm staying over and that Helen will join me."

He rose and stood aside. He said, walking with her to the door:

"You'll have to call a truce while she's here, Lani."

"That was clever of you too," she said, unmoved.

"I'm at your disposal," he suggested, "when you've finished your errand."

She said:

"I'll go for a walk, I think, possibly to the Palace Museum. I'll see you later, Dexter."

There was no use arguing. No use saying, "It's a free country, you can't stop me from walking with you." He didn't want to walk with her, anyway. He greatly regretted the impulse which had caused him to telephone Helen Gaines, which he had thought particularly brilliant at the time. Nothing left now but to go through with the whole stupid day. Yet, as he walked over toward the pool deftly, to achieve the acquaintance of the girl in the blue shorts, who was lying under the striped umbrella, her sun oil and glare goggles beside her, he reflected, with astonished bitterness, that within the last hour he had come closer to loving Lani Aldrich than at any time in their stormy, unsatisfactory relationship. And he conceded her a reluctant admiration for her divination of a fact, one that he always denied, even to himself, a fact, the roots of which were obscure — the fact that he was incapable of loving anyone completely except his wife . . . whom he hated.

He smiled down at the girl under the umbrella, an ash blonde with large, unintelligent blue eyes, her upper lip too short, her fingernails too long. He thought, before his first light word was spoken, that the bright blue water of the pool looked very inviting . . . and the girl might serve as a pleasant barrier between himself and Lani, at the luncheon table, a little later.

There are many substitutes for love. Or proxies.

Chapter 16

Dexter and Miss Tourist — he could never recall her name afterward — lunched together under the umbrella at the pool's edge after their swim. Lani had not appeared and when Dexter went to his usual table to announce that there would be a third at luncheon, his waiter informed him, with an innocent brown regard which concealed busy speculation, that Miss Aldrich was having a tray in her room.

Hence the tête-à-tête with Miss Tourist. By now Dexter had explored her mind, her past, most of her future, and certainly the majority of her possibilities. He was heartily fed up by the time she faced him across the table, with her hundredth reiteration of, "Oh, Mr. Dexter, isn't Hawaii too divine?" Now and then he looked openly at his watch, wondering how early a start Helen Gaines had made.

Lani was wondering too, eating her chop and grilled pineapple on her *lanai*. A tall frosted glass of iced tea, with a pineapple finger in it, stood on the tray. She was tired from her walk, from the hours preceding it.

She had gone into the dim cool Royal Palace set in palms and wandered through the great echoing rooms with their delightful guardian. She had admired the old tapa bedspreads, the polished poi bowls, the many material reminders of glories that were past. She had gone down to the wharf and sat there a long time, talking to the half-naked Hawaiian children who thronged there. She had wandered into a Chinese store and bought herself a lauhala hat, talking to the incredibly old woman behind the counter.

Across from the Hulihee Summer Palace the stone church stood, the first Christian church in the islands, Mokauekaua. Originally it, and the palace itself, had been of thatch. Now the cornerstones of the church were those King Umi had hewn for a *heiau* in the old days. Many of the old beams were still intact. A pearly golden light filtered in and she stood there, alone, feeling the silent presence of all the gods mankind had ever knelt to in humble worship. And the constriction at her heart and in her throat was loosened, and she could draw a deep breath again.

Leaving the church, she went back to the inn, and there, on the house phone in her room, ordered her luncheon tray and asked that the desk let her know when Mrs. Gaines arrived.

She would get through the rest of the day somehow. She had to, and she owed it to herself. She felt drained of all emotion except that of resentment — resentment that she had been involved in a stupid, unimportant lie — if a lie was ever unimportant . . . and one dictated, she was certain, by an incredible, inexplicable malice.

Around three o'clock she heard Helen's rapid step on the *lanai*, opened the door and stood smiling at her, waiting.

Helen came in, looked around, breathed a sigh.

"The room Bill and I always have," she said. "I adore it." She tipped the boy carrying her overnight bag, dismissed him, put her arm around Lani. She said, "Such unexpected fun . . . I hoped that Bill could come. But he couldn't. Frank's still away, you know. Jim drove me."

"Jim!" said Lani. She almost laughed. That was the final irony, she thought. Aloud she said, "But with Frank away and — "

"Bill told him to come. He rated a month's vacation, you know. You saw how much of it he took! He went out this morning with the men, came back in time to change and get going. We lunched at Kamuela. We'll stay part of tomorrow if you like, leave after lunch."

She unpacked briskly, a cold cream jar, her brush and comb, her night things. She asked:

"Had fun?"

"Lots. I love it here," Lani told her. "I saw the cattle shipping this morning, right out the windows."

"I'm so glad . . . not everyone has the opportunity. Kona's old Hawaii — doesn't it seem that way to you? An atmosphere all its own, as if you were swimming through a beneficent golden sea, warm and tideless. Bill and I come as often as we can. Too bad that Muriel Warren had to leave, but nice for us. I was amazed when Mr. Warren telephoned." She asked carelessly, "Is she — Mrs. Warren — more amusing — or less — on closer acquaintance?"

"Oh, more," answered Lani, almost instantly. It had begun, the silly tissue of lies, strong as a spiderweb yet as unsubstantial. She began to talk about the fishing trip.

Helen looked at her for a moment. What had happened? Lani talked too fast, too much, the words stumbled over each other. Had something gone wrong? Helen thought, Anything could with that woman around!

She said:

"I thought it rather nice of Mr. Warren to call me."

"Very considerate," said Lani. She laughed,

lit a cigarette, crushed it out again, and rose from the edge of her bed. She said, "I took the bed next to the *lanai*, I'm afraid."

"Suits me," said Helen; "grand beds. I understand we're driving to the City of Refuge and taking a supper. That's fun. I haven't picnicked there for — it must be five years, I think."

The house phone in the bedroom rang and Lani answered. Dexter said easily:

"Lani? Where have you been keeping yourself? Jim and I just had a quick one at the bar. I've persuaded him that he's done enough driving for today. We'll take along that pet Hawaiian of yours, the one with the tenor voice — Pelelika. I think if you and Mrs. Gaines are ready we might make a start."

Ten minutes later they were getting into the car, Pelelika, the Portuguese-Hawaiian driver, wreathed in smiles, the hamper stowed away carefully and most of the inn's staff at the door to wave good-bye. Dexter sat in front with the driver. He said:

"I'm leaving this jaunt to our friend here. It's all new to me and Lani." He added carefully, "Muriel was greatly distressed that she had to miss it. But as she's remaining in the Islands she will have other opportunities while I, alas, will not."

Jim grinned at Lani. He asked:

"Surprised to see me, aren't you?"

"A little. I thought you were wedded to your work."

"I got a divorce. I couldn't resist ... besides, Bill is anxious to prove that with me and Frank both away, Waipuhia functions as smoothly, if not more so. This is my last junket. Back to work in earnest day after tomorrow."

"How about the vacation?"

"I'm taking it out in rain checks, weekends. You're looking very fit, Lani."

She said, "Who wouldn't in this place? It irons out all the kinks."

"You must see more of it," said Helen lazily, "not just Kona, but more of this island. You've yet to see the black sands, and the villages, where the roads don't go and where outsiders don't go either. Bill and I saw them once, back of the beyond, on our honeymoon. We were curiosities then, we would be now. The old life goes on its even pace, it will persist, I think, as long as there is life at all. I like to think so."

The streets of Kailua curved and twisted, the old trees cast their shadows on the road, as they drove south to Napoopoo, on the shore of Kealakekua Bay. Standing on the beach by the monument to Henry Opukahaia, the Hawaiian boy who precipitated the American

271

missions to Hawaii and whose bones lie, incredibly, in New England soil, they looked across to the Cook Monument . . . Helen, her arm through Lani's, was pointing out the ruins of the ancient *heiaus*. "Across the bay," she said, "there are burial caves."

An outrigger canoe danced toward them, bringing visitors from the monument to the Napoopoo wharf.

A little later they drove to Keei, dreaming in the sun, nets drying on the coral and lava rocks. A man was standing on the reef of rock with a throw net, casting into the surf. There were stone walls, vine covered, lean poi dogs, and children playing under the palms.

"Here," said their driver, "Kamehameha landed, coming from Kohla in the great war canoes."

They retraced the short distance on the branch road which led over the old lava to the fishing village and went on to Honaunau, the City of Refuge. Here Pelelika unloaded the hamper and took it to the picnic tables under the royal palms. Sunlight filtered through, a checkered gold. The inevitable dog arrived to beg. Not far away the incurious Hawaiians lived their lives . . . fishing boats, outriggers, stood off near shore; a woman, mat weaving, looked up to smile . . . and Jim strolled away to talk to an enormous man who was carving a canoe made from a solid block of koa, shaping it with love and artistry, and an ancient adz.

Helen and Dexter walked away from the grove, and clambered over the stone platforms, within the walled enclosure. These walls still stood, colossal lava blocks. Here, in the troubled times of tribal wars, the women and children had fled, sheltered by this sanctuary of the priesthood.

Jim came up and caught Lani's hand in his. He said, "Moves your imagination, doesn't it?" He stooped to pick up some pebbles, perfectly round, black and white — and put them in her hands. "For luck," he said.

"What are they, Jim?" she asked.

He took her to a block of stone rudely cut with its crude, regular indentations. "A *koane* board," he said, "like checkers. If we could find some more stones we'd have a game."

They stood, one on each side of the great stone. He said suddenly, low:

"I owe you an apology. I don't expect you'll forgive me, Lani."

"Why?" she asked. Her breath was shortened, her heart quickened. The light touched his untidy sunburnt hair, dazzled his blue eyes.

"I thought — Oh, hell," he said, disgusted, "I didn't believe that Mrs. Warren was to be here . . . so . . ."

"Never mind," she said. "Please."

"You forgive me?" He jerked a shoulder. "He's not a bad chap," he said. "Sitting there at the bar today, I — I liked him, I almost understood." He smiled at her with pleading. "And of course, when he phoned Helen — " He broke off. "I won't ask you if you've come to any conclusion — "

"Please," she said again, "there's nothing to forgive. I suppose it was natural to think . . . "

She could not go on, she would have choked. The web was around her, intangible, stifling. She wanted to stretch out her arms, break it, cry, You were right, she wasn't here. I didn't know beforehand, truly I didn't. She never had any intention of being here!

Helen was calling to them and Jim took her arm to help her over the rough places. He said, "It wasn't natural. I was jealous as hell. I still am. I'll always be."

Later, the contents of the picnic hamper on the table under the palms, Pelelika produced his ukulele and sang . . . the old songs, because if Dexter and Lani were strangers, Helen and Jim were not. He nodded to Jim when, replete with sandwiches, cake and fruit, Jim pushed aside his paper plate and poured himself another cup of coffee from the thermos.

"This one — you sing with me, Kimo." He

274

struck a chord and waited.

Jim grinned.

"Ladies present," he reminded Pelelika.

An old song, very gay, entirely Hawaiian, and as full of double meanings as a fruit cake is full of raisins. Helen's mouth twitched, now and then she laughed, but Lani's face was blank. Dexter said:

"I take it — no translations?"

"Not for that one," said Jim, "it's a robust number. I like it." He glanced at Helen, and smiled. "Your Hawaiian's quite equal to it," he suggested.

"Not altogether," she said, "and perhaps it's just as well."

They stayed in the grove until sunset, walking out over the jagged lava to watch the light on the water, the clouds drifting high, rose and mauve, violet and gold. The fishing boats and outriggers were black, the figures in them silhouettes. The wind dropped and was still, the palms stood unstirring in the pause between sundown and night.

Pelelika was feeding the yellow-brown poi dog, from one of the fishermen's shacks, which was still sniffing around the table. And in a little while they had packed the remnants of their supper and returned to the car, and the inn.

The rest of the evening lay before them.

Lani shrugging herself out of her clothes, standing under the tingling shower, thought despondently, It's too early to go to bed. There'll be no break in the evening, we certainly can't eat a late dinner. She was relieved when Jim suggested, after she and Helen had joined him, that they drive to a near-by town and see a movie.

Dexter refused, gracefully. He must pack for an early start, he had a telephone call or two to make and some letters to write. "I'm certain that when I reach Honolulu I won't have time," he said. "You go along and enjoy yourselves." He stood on the steps and watched them go, an extraordinarily tall figure in the white mess jacket he wore very well.

"Fooled me," said Jim, as they drove away, "changed into fancy dress." He laughed. "How are you girls?" he inquired. "Enough room?"

They were sitting in the front seat, the three of them. The roads, winding enough by day, were corkscrews by night. Jim was talking of the hunting in the high hills and of the wild pigs which sometimes came out, a bit farther north, to lie on the road at night, seeking perhaps the warmth of asphalt still hot from the sun . . . "cause a lot of accidents," he said; "talk about road hogs!"

The little movie theater was brilliantly

lighted, many cars in varying degrees of dilapidation were parked around it, including the "banana," or station wagons from near-by plantations. They went in and found seats well in the rear and Lani viewed an assorted audience, adults, youngsters, babies in their mothers' arms, Orientals, Polynesians, Europeans, and admixtures. A cheerful, appreciative audience which clapped at the right time and hissed at the right time and sat forward breathless when evil was about to be done.

They secured their money's worth. A serial, a double feature, a travel short, a sport short, and a cartoon. When they left the theater they were dazed and blinking from hours of concentrating on the screen.

Jim had been sitting between Lani and Helen. When the lights were down, he took Lani's hand. He said, "Always hold hands in the movies. It's still fashionable. Besides, I'm a timid soul, I couldn't sit through a murder mystery without some sort of protection. Helen, give me your hand too."

They laughed about that, and again when Helen, withdrawing her hand, complained that it was too hot for sentiment. But Jim wouldn't release Lani's.

His hand spoke to her, through the darkness. Warm, firm and steady, it spoke, until she began to imagine crazily that she could feel the current of his blood, the message of the nerve fibers. It was as if his hand told her, You are safe, you are loved, you are desired.

Once, twice, she tried to pull away with an excuse as Helen had . . . it was too hot, her fingers were cramped. But he'd have none of it. He said, "See here, my girl, I won't be responsible for my blood pressure unless you hang on. Want me to make a scene, here and now?"

All the way back to the inn he sang, at the top of his pleasant baritone. He sang "Song of the Islands" and "Sweet Leilani" and "Little Grass Shack," and some purely Hawaiian songs which Lani did not know. But she recognized the song he and Pelelika had sung together.

"How about a translation now?" she suggested. She was sitting next to him, very close, her head near his shoulder. All evening she had put away her unhappy preoccupation with the situation in which she had found herself. For hours now she had almost forgotten it.

"Nothing doing," said Jim promptly. "You're too young. But I'll tell you what," he added in an exaggerated, carrying whisper, "I'll translate it for you after we're married."

Helen cried:

"Of all the nerve. Smack him, Lani. Or was

this a bona fide proposal?"

"It was," said Jim cheerfully, "I'm just in the mood. Summer night, starlight on the sea. And I always believe in witnesses. Remember, Helen, you were present the first time I told Lani she was going to marry me?"

"You told her," said Helen, with a slight snort. "Nice masculine idea. Don't ask, order!"

Lani said:

"He's safe, Helen. He knows I wouldn't take him up, even with a witness. He thinks there's safety in numbers."

"Numbers? Am I a bigamist?" asked Jim indignantly.

"Do slow down," said Helen; "this road scares me."

"Want to hold my hand?" he inquired.

When they reached the inn they found the manager hidden behind a large cigar concentrating on his dominoes. He rose to greet them and report that Mr. Warren had ordered a special little supper, out on the front *lanai*, and was waiting for them.

Lani said, "Supper . . . I couldn't . . . " Yet she was hungry, sandwiches and fruit do not stick to healthy young ribs, but she'd rather be hungry than . . . She said, "I think I'll go to bed. It's pretty late, isn't it?"

"Nonsense," said Jim, "I'm famished.

Let's find our host."

They found him outside sitting with Miss Tourist, who was diaphanous in white organdy and had reached the giggle stage. Glasses on the table beside them indicated that they had not waited for refreshment.

Dexter jumped to his feet. He commented: "Hello. You've been gone forever."

"Marvelous movies," said Jim, "all seven or eight of them. You missed a very large evening."

"Sorry," said Dexter. He made the introductions and had to be prompted. "Not Miss James," corrected the blond girl, with a snicker, "Miss Haynes . . . but just call me Kitty."

"Supper coming up," said Dexter, when the others had found chairs. "Drinks too. Name them."

Crab salad, bread and butter sandwiches, coffee, fruit, and planter's punch. Miss Haynes declared that things were not like this in Remington, North Dakota. She also declared to goodness that she'd never had such a wonderful time. She grew more and more southern, which puzzled her hearers considerably. A little careful research on Jim's part elicited the fact that she had read *Gone With the Wind*, spent two weeks in Florida, and knew a girl who came from Kentucky. Which might have accounted for the mounting you-alls.

She added that it was too marvelous of Dex — she meant Mr. Warren — to offer to drive her to Hilo tomorrow, she thought it would be ever so much more fun than making one of a tourist party as she had expected. And they were going to lunch, she confided to Lani, at some too-divine Japanese place where you saw the fish caught right before your eyes. Goldfish, she thought.

"Mullet," said Jim; "they're better eating."

"Oh, mullet?" She was terribly dumb, she said, apologetically.

No one agreed with her — aloud.

Helen broke up the party. She was dead, she announced, she'd driven considerable mileage that day. Miss Haynes — Kitty, to you — demurred. She cried, "But it's so silly to waste time sleepin' . . . don't you think so, Dex?"

He thought so.

He went with them as far as the entrance to the lounge. Kitty waited, humming, swinging a pretty leg and wondering if she hadn't better call a halt on the planter's punches. But, of course, the fascinating Mr. Warren was a gentleman, she decided, optimistically.

Just before Lani stepped into the lounge, Dexter halted her.

"One minute," he said.

"Yes?"

"This is good-bye . . . we'll be making an earlier start than you in the morning."

She said evenly, "Good-bye, Dexter."

"I'm forgiven? I should be. I sacrificed myself this evening to — "

"Not a difficult sacrifice, I should say," she remarked.

"My dear, how little you know me. I am bored to insanity."

"Even so," she suggested, "you must keep in practice."

"That isn't very kind. Haven't I made amends at all? Your mercurial boy friend has ceased to suspect me. You must admit he's rather a different young man from the statistic-quoting, hard-working guide who drove me around Waipuhia with utmost reluctance. I was amazed by him this afternoon . . . a very likable lad, complete with humor. The answer is perfectly obvious. He's in love with you. So I gave him his opportunity tonight — I even tried to persuade Mrs. Gaines to remain with me."

"Not very hard," said Lani, "and only in passing. After all, you had wires to send, or was it letters to write? And a phone call to make."

"I called Muriel," he said, "and couldn't find her. She wasn't anywhere. Not at Renfew's, not at the hotel . . . "

Lani said, "The others are waiting for me."

"I won't see you again," he said, "and there's no use trying to tell you I'm sorry?"

"None," said Lani.

She went into the lounge where Jim was talking to the manager. Helen, he reported, had gone on to bed.

He walked with her down the *lanai* to the corner room. He took her arm and demanded:

"What was Warren saying?"

"Good-bye," she answered; "he's leaving early."

"I'm glad," said Jim, "or don't you care? You see, Lani, I know you better than you think. You have made up your mind. You've sent Dexter away. I'm so happy I could yell, turn handsprings, make a general fool of myself. I know that it doesn't change things — between us. You're hurt, you're unhappy, I could kill him for that . . . but you're free. In one sense at least. And I can wait."

She said brokenly, "Jim — "

"It's all right, Lani, I'm not going to propose again, now. I suppose Helen gave me courage. I've imagined all sorts of things. We won't go into that, and I've already asked your forgiveness. But no matter what I imagined, I believe that you belong to me — or at any rate that I belong to you. So I can wait until you realize it too . . . someday. And if you never do — but you must."

They had stopped by the steps leading into the room. They could hear Helen moving around back of the closed door. And he said suddenly:

"And you'll forgive me for this, too, won't you — beforehand?"

His arms closed around her, his mouth brushed her cheek, as she turned her head away.

"Sometime," he said, "you won't evade me. Good night, my darling."

She watched him, a shadow in the darkness, going away from her. She heard his step on the wooden boards and stood there, frightened, scarcely breathing. Afraid of the response he had elicited, and fighting it. She told herself, It can't be like this, you don't fall out of love and in again so easily, you don't go from one man's arms to another's. It's just that I'm tired, it's a sort of lunatic reaction.

Helen called, "Is that you, Lani?"

"Coming," she said, opened the door and went in.

Chapter 17

Life at Waipuhia resumed its usual round.
Jim went back to work and Lani saw him only
during the late afternoon or evening. He made
no attempt to be alone with her, he said nothing that could not have been overheard by
anyone, but sometimes she saw his eyes, and
they were unguarded. She was touched, she
was troubled, she was unhappy for him. Yet
he did not seem unhappy. He was, she realized, an extraordinarily stubborn — or was it
patient? — young man. She and Helen made
a round of calls on the people near by. They
flew to Kauai to visit distant relatives of
Helen's and of herself. They stayed for several
days in the manager's house of one of the
smaller plantations, a pleasant place with gardens and great trees and a lazy green river a
stone's throw away. They went on excursions
to Waimea Canyon, to the Barking Sands, to
the superb peace of Hanalei, with the young
rice green under its blanket of clear water.
They swam at Waipahee Falls and spent the

day with friends of Helen's on a pineapple plantation, returning after a week of parties and sightseeing to Waipuhia.

Helen said:

"Fun, wasn't it? But it's nice to be home."

"Bill's an angel to let you trek around like this," said Lani gratefully.

"He doesn't mind. Someday he and I will do it together," said Helen wistfully, "when he has more time. Not that we haven't been on vacations and all that. But someday we'll take months . . . I'd like to go back to the mainland to visit too. But it's all in the future. And it's been a good holiday for me having you with me . . . There's still Maui, you know, and Molokai."

"They can wait," said Lani. "I've all the time in the world."

They were lunching alone. Bill had gone off to look at a new mechanical harvester on the other side of the island.

"Then you've made up your mind?" asked Helen.

"Just about. When I return to Honolulu I'll look for a house . . . it's nearly September . . . I didn't mean to become a permanent resident of Waipuhia."

"Jim means you to," said Helen.

Lani flushed.

"Nonsense," she said. "He's just being nice."

"Don't nonsense me. I've known him since he was born. And you too, for that matter," Helen added, "although there's been a gap in my knowledge of you. Jim's serious . . . Betsy writes me pages about it. Not that he's said anything to her. But she knows him too. She spoke to me after the dance here . . . she said, 'If Lani would only marry Jim I could die happy.'"

"Die?" asked Lani, in alarm.

"That's Betsy. She's strong as a horse, really. But she'd be delighted, and Fred too. I think he believes this is fate, you coming to the Islands, Jim's interest in you. His nephew, as close as a son to him, and Alan's girl. Can't you see what it would mean to him, Lani?"

"Perhaps," she admitted. "I like Jim . . . I have never liked anyone better — as much."

"It's a good beginning," said Helen quickly. "I've never believed that falling in love had to be preceded by antagonism."

"There's been a touch of that too," said Lani absently. "But liking . . . isn't enough."

"It's a start. Sometimes," said Helen, "you fall in love and then have to learn liking as well. You don't always. This way is better. I'm not counseling you. You'll go back to Honolulu, perhaps return to the mainland. You'll take your time. You may meet someone else." She added firmly, "Fond as I am of you, Lani, I don't want Jim to be on the receiving end of second best. He rates more than that."

"I know," said Lani, low. She added slowly, "How do you know? I mean you think you're in love. No, you don't think it, you know it. Then suddenly it's over, you look back and convince yourself it wasn't love at all. How do you know when anything's real?"

Helen said gently, "Perhaps it's real each time. The point is to know when it will endure — when it will stay real. Dreams are real while you're dreaming."

"That's just it," said Lani. "How do you convince yourself it will endure, what guarantee have you?"

"None," said Helen. "When I first set eyes on Bill I thought, *that's mine*. He was a shy creature, believe it or not. I went after him frankly, hammer and tongs. I was too busy trying to interest him to figure out whether it would last or not. But it has lasted. In books and plays something dramatic always wakes the heroine to the fact that she's been, let's say, in love with the wrong man and is now in love with the right one . . . danger, illness, a rescue, something big and important. I don't think things happen like that often, really. You just grow into a security of knowledge."

She looked at Lani and smiled, "You've time to grow."

Lani said, "It's nearly September, I can't believe it, Helen . . . it seems yesterday since March . . . and a lifetime away. I've settled down here as if I had never left."

"Next summer," said Helen, "we'll go on a holiday to Kokee . . . cool and high, we'll live in riding clothes, we'll hike, it will be wonderful. Bill will be all right by then. You used to go there summers, as a little thing, you know."

"Jim told me . . . he said he was there with us. I wish I could remember it."

"Perhaps you will when you return," said Helen.

When Jim came in late that afternoon he brought the mail. Mainland mail for Lani and a letter from Betsy, plaintive and insistent. "When I let you go to Helen's," she wrote, "I didn't expect you'd stay a year. Do come home. It isn't too hot, the shower trees are magnificent, and the poinsettias . . . Our night-blooming cereus is doing its stuff . . . and Fred's taken a beach house over on the windward side . . .

"And your friend, Mrs. Warren," she added, "has taken a house there too, next door to us. Her husband clippered back to the mainland some time ago. But I suppose you knew that."

Lani gave Helen the letter. She said:

"I must go back, really. It isn't fair to Aunt Betsy. And I have trespassed on your — "

"Shut up, do," said Helen, reading the letter. She said presently, "All right. But your room's ready for you here any time you wish to come. I'll be in Honolulu for an orgy of shopping in October . . . "

Jim said:

"If you think you're escaping me, Miss Aldrich . . . "

She thought, I can go back now. Dexter's gone . . . perhaps she'll follow him soon, she won't stay on all autumn surely, she'll tire. She thought further, She won't bother with me — now. I won't have to see her.

The night before Lani left for Honolulu Helen gave a dinner, for the plantation people and the Robertses. An early dinner, because tomorrow was another working day. Frank Davidson came, the McDonalds, others whom Lani had learned to know. Frank left early. He said, holding her hand, "Good luck — if you see Mrs. Warren, remember me to her." His eyes laughed but his mouth was controlled. "I saw her several times," he added carelessly, "when I was in Honolulu."

"Boasting," reproved Jim, appearing at his elbow, "you couldn't have . . . she was at Kona with Lani until the day Helen and I went over. And you came back right after that."

Frank's eyes flickered from one to the other. Lani said something, anything, and Frank broke in easily:

"Sure, I was boasting. Why not?"

"Wish fulfillment," suggested Jim, laughing. "See you later, Frank." He took Lani's arm and drew her out on the *lanai*. He said, "I'll miss you every minute, no matter what I'm doing. Getting up when the whistle blows, going out with the men, riding through the fields. I won't have the afternoons to look forward to, nor the evenings. I won't be able to think, In eight hours, in six hours, in two hours, I'll be with her again."

She said, as lightly as she could:

"Don't be so tragic, Jim. I'll be back, you'll be in Honolulu."

"Of course. Lani, have you been happy here?"

"I've loved it."

"Could you go on being happy here, for, perhaps, a long time?"

She said:

"Jim, you mustn't — "

"All right," he said quickly. "But I'd like you to think about that if you will . . . Sometime, back in Honolulu — when you're lying on the beach, or out on a surfboard, when you're dancing on the terrace at the Royal, when you're skimming around Pearl Harbor in Uncle Fred's boat, when you're riding or walking, or shopping for jade and sandalwood at Gump's, when you're eating coconut ice cream . . . or when you're falling asleep or just waking up, I want you to think about it, I want you to begin to wonder — Could I be happy at Waipuhia . . . for a very long time?"

He bent his head quickly, and kissed her before she could speak, or move . . . a competent kiss, not on her cheek this time but firmly on her mouth. Then he said, "Goodbye, Lani — *aloha nui* — " turned, and was gone.

Flying back from Hilo the next day she watched the moving shadow of the plane on the distant face of the water, the shadows cast by the clouds . . . shadows darkening the blue. She tried to think of Honolulu. She would stay at the Bruces'. Her trunks would follow by steamer. She would look for a house somewhere . . . would it be up in the hills, a little house on Tantalus, looking over the city to the sea, or would it be on the water, with a strip of grass, a strip of sand, and the waves nibbling at the edges? She tried to plan, she must replenish her wardrobe, which had had pretty hard wear. And she must do something about the bank statements, she had hardly looked at them all these months. She should put her affairs in order. Her lawyers wrote her plaintively and paternally. They would like to hear from her occasionally, they said. They wrote her regularly about such things as inheritance and income taxes. She acknowledged their letters and that was all. She thought, I should make a will, I suppose.

All that money — people with money always made wills.

She thought of the boats moving below her at, it seemed, a snail's pace. She talked to Kazue and to the little girl across the aisle who was going with her mother to Honolulu to shop, to inspect Punahou where presently she would go to school. She talked to the bride and groom, in the Islands on their honeymoon, and to the elderly couple who were returning by the next boat to the mainland and who hadn't been away from the Islands for twenty-two years. She talked to one of the pilots who came through, collecting cameras, offering gum, cotton. He squatted down beside her on his heels and they had quite a conversation.

Yet all the time she was remembering what Jim said. She was wondering, as he had asked her to wonder, if she could be happy at Waipuhia for a long time. Of course, she could be. Forever, if it came to that. But that wasn't what he had meant. He had meant, would she be happy at Waipuhia — or wherever he might be sent — with him?

She didn't want to think that out, she didn't want to think at all. She told herself impatiently, All you do is try not to think, all you've been doing for months is trying to acknowledge only the surface part of your mind.

The water below was a miracle, indigo, with frills of lace . . . and there in the shallows the apple green and far out the deep wine. She thought, Why can't people paint this just as it is?

They were on time, they landed, and Betsy and Fred were waiting. They held out their arms and she went into them, first Betsy's, then Fred's. She hugged them both. She cried, "I'm so glad to see you. I've missed you so much."

"Pity you wouldn't know it before. Let's look at you," said Betsy. "I haven't seen you since Helen's dance. You look all right. How's my mildly insane son?"

"Back in harness, working hard."

"Drive you to Hilo to the plane?"

"No, Helen did. Everyone's fine. And Kazue's enchanted to be back. I felt like a brute keeping her over there. But she said she loved it." Kazue, tiny and neat as a gray bird, nodded, her opaque eyes shining. "I didn't take her with me to Kona," Lani went on, as they walked toward the car, "she went on a round of visits instead."

"Liked Kona, did you?"

"Loved it."

"You didn't write me from there. Who was with you, Helen?"

Before she could stop she had said it.

"No, the Warrens at first . . . then when Mrs. Warren left, Helen and Jim came over."

"Mrs. Warren?" Betsy was looking at her, a little frown between her winglike brows. She said slowly, "I remember she said something about Kona, and hating to leave. I've seen her off and on, now that we have places next door."

Why did I have to say anything? Lani asked herself. I could have said, yes, Helen was with me and let it go at that. More lies. If Aunt Betsy has a memory for dates . . .

Evidently she had not or was no longer interested. Frederick Bruce was speaking . . . he was asking:

"Suppose you went back to the volcano after your first go at it?"

"Several times," she said, "each time more marvelous than the first."

"Not so much of a show as last time," he said, "but good enough. You missed some goings-on here. I suppose you got to the boat races in Hilo on July Fourth?"

"Yes," Lani told him, "it was fun."

"You'll see Regatta Day here, in late September," he told her. "Pete, drop me off at the office, will you? I'll be seeing you girls later."

They reached the house and went up to the remembered room. Lani took off the leis they had brought her, the leis she had been given on her departure from the Big Island. She tossed her brimmed hat on a couch and Kazue put it away.

"I've decided," Lani said. "Are you glad?"

"What?" demanded Betsy. "Not — "

Lani said hastily:

"House hunting. Will you go with me, Aunt Betsy? Kazue and I will find a place and then we'll give a party. Kazue, can you cook?"

Kazue said gravely:

"Not very well, Miss Lani, but my sister can."

"Good," said Lani.

"Not yet," Betsy implored; "stay with us, take your time looking."

"All right," Lani offered, and hugged her again. She added, "Jim sent you his love."

"He's a wretched correspondent," said his mother. She looked at Kazue, busy unpacking, and drew Lani out on the *lanai*. She said,

"I have news for you."

"What? You look all excited."

"I am. Fred said I might tell you. No one else knows yet, although of course in a lot of ways we aren't at all surprised," said Betsy.

"Darling, will you stop being mysterious? What in the world is it?"

"Fred had a long talk with Bill Gaines," said Betsy, "and, of course, with Frank Davidson resigning . . ."

"Resigning," repeated Lani. "Frank? But he didn't say . . . he hasn't . . ."

"He was here in Honolulu for a while," said Betsy. "It appears he's inherited some money. He told Fred about it then. After he returned to Waipuhia he wrote him. He's leaving, effective October first, to return to the mainland — says he's going to buy himself an orange grove in California."

"He hasn't even hinted . . . I don't believe Helen knows," said Lani thoughtfully.

"No. Bill does. Fred talked to him by telephone. It won't be announced for another week. Frank's leaving and Jim's assistant manager."

"But," cried Lani, "how marvelous!"

"I thought you'd be pleased," Betsy said. "Bill — well, the company was thinking of giving him an executive berth here in the office. He rates it. But he doesn't want it. He'll stay on at Waipuhia for a while. Another five years perhaps. By that time Jim should be ready . . . I don't know," she added, "even in five years he'd be very young for a manager."

"As if that made any difference!"

"It does," said Betsy; "you'd be surprised." She put her arm around Lani. "That's my news," she said, "I'm boiling with it. Jim doesn't know yet, Fred's phoning him today to come over the end of the week as he can't get away, there's a conference of sorts on . . . "

"I'm so happy for Jim," said Lani, "but I don't understand about Frank."

"No one does," said Betsy.

Until the weekend, Betsy and Lani were too busy to go to the beach house. People called. There was a party at the Royal. There was a party at the Governor's. Lani went shopping for sports things, for evening frocks. Standing to be fitted she thought of Jim. "When you're shopping, — when you're dancing . . . " he'd said.

She went to Gump's and bought a beautiful extravagance in jade for Helen who would have a birthday soon. Sliding the cool smoothness of the stones through her fingers, she thought, "When you're shopping for jade at Gump's . . . "

On Friday they packed night clothes and bathing suits, took Kazue and one of the houseboys, and drove over the Pali to the beach house near Punaluu. Palms and an old hau tree, a tangled, neglected garden, and a wide sweep of beach which the house fronted. *Lanai,* living room, simple bedrooms, showers . . . Lani went through, enchanted.

"It's just right," she told Betsy.

"We rented it furnished," Betsy said; "the owners have gone to Maui. I like it . . . it's quiet, and comfortable, without luxury. Not like the place next door."

The place next door was built of stone, and from where Lani stood she could see its tended formality. Betsy went on:

"That was built by the Richardsons, Chicago people, about five years ago. They haven't been here this year and Mrs. Warren took it . . . she isn't there, as yet, to stay. The servants came in last week. She told me she intended to move in this weekend. What's the matter?"

"Nothing," Lani said.

They bathed, sunned, rested, listened to the portable radio, ate satisfying, simple meals, went to bed early, rose late. On Saturday there was activity next door, cars drove up, people got out, and lying on the beach, her lauhala hat tilted over her eyes, Lani could hear Muriel Warren's voice. Apparently she had brought guests for the weekend.

She thought, She isn't on may-I-borrow-a-cup-of-sugar terms with Betsy, she doesn't know I'm here, perhaps we won't see her.

She moved herself, her cushions and her book farther along the beach, near the little summerhouse on the property. From there she could see the stream of people presently come out of the stone house and go into the sea. She could distinguish Muriel among them, her superb figure in a remarkably revealing black bathing suit. Later she saw them troop up the lawn, to sit under umbrellas with robes flung around them. Houseboys came out with trays of drinks.

After luncheon Lani went to her little bedroom and slept for a long time on the narrow white bed with the sea wind blowing the white curtains at the windows. When she woke she felt refreshed, and equal to anything, even Muriel Warren. Kazue brought her hot tea. "Cold tea is not good for you," said Kazue, "not too much of it."

She swam again with Betsy before dinner, and changed into her coolest linen dress. Betsy had said that morning, "If everything goes well, Jim and Fred will be down in time for dinner."

They came, shouting, hungry, demanding food and drink. Jim had a bottle of champagne under his arm . . . in an ice bucket. He gave it to Betsy, laughing. "Celebration," he said. "You've told Lani, I suppose."

"Naturally."

"Well," said Jim, "don't I get kissed or something?"

His mother kissed him and Lani smiled. She said:

"Congratulations . . . it's wonderful news."

"I'll say it is, I didn't expect anything like this for years and years." He lifted her off her feet exuberantly. Before he set her down he said softly, "Are you still wondering if you'd like it at Waipuhia?"

They had dined and were sitting on the *lanai* watching the darkness settle over the water when Jim heard the light step on the grass. As he rose, Muriel Warren said:

"May I come in?"

She came, in a long print dress with a tiny jacket, her blond hair in place. She said, after she had shaken hands with Frederick Bruce and greeted Betsy and Lani:

"Nice to be neighbors, isn't it? My gang just drove off a little while ago . . . only two are staying over with me . . . the Renfews, you remember them, Lani , . . they're dressing for dinner."

"You dine late," said Jim, smiling.

She smiled, and leaning forward spoke directly to Lani.

"I just ran over to tell you how sorry I am I couldn't be at Kona with you. Such a disappointment — having to leave before you arrived. I hope Dex explained to you and that you had fun — without me," she said.

Chapter 18

She spoke lightly, certain of her effect, watching the reaction of her audience with curiosity, Betsy's brows high with astonishment, Frederick's frank bewilderment, Lani's swift pallor. Jim spoke almost instantly, his face as blank as if it were shuttered. He said:

"We missed you, Mrs. Warren."

"You? But you weren't . . . "

He interrupted, with unnecessary vigor:

"Oh, but we were, Mrs. Gaines and myself. Didn't Mr. Warren tell you about our picnic at Honaunau?"

She said brightly:

"Of course. I'd forgotten. These Hawaiian names defeat me . . . I must run along . . . I just ran out on my guests to say hello."

She was gone, and a brief heavy silence followed. Frederick Bruce asked, after a moment:

"What in the world did that woman mean?"

Lani rose, and leaned against the *lanai* railing. She said:

"You needn't have bothered, Jim."

"What's it all about?" demanded Frederick. He knew of Lani's plans, her comings and goings, only vaguely. He hadn't heard this Kona trip discussed at all. His grave eyes went from her to his nephew. He recognized the warning signal of Jim's infrequent anger, the darkening face, quiet and watchful as an Indian's. He went on plaintively, "This has all the earmarks of a situation. No one ever tells me anything!"

Betsy laughed, an effort of valor. She said, "It isn't anything, Fred," and added; "that's a perfectly poisonous woman!"

"Wait a minute," said Lani. She turned and faced them, her chin lifted. "I think Jim at any rate is waiting for an explanation." She spoke slowly, deliberately, so that none could misunderstand. "When Dexter Warren came to Waipuhia for the day — the McDonalds had asked him — he brought a letter to me from his wife. You see, Uncle Fred, I knew Dexter in Washington, but met his wife for the first time at Johnny Roberts's ranch. Her letter said that she and Dexter were going to Kona and would I come along. I couldn't, as it happened, right then. Helen was giving the big party — the one you and Aunt Betsy flew over for, remember? But I did go the following Monday. When I reached the inn I found that Muriel had been called back to Honolulu. She left me a note, saying how sorry she was. Later I talked to her on the telephone. I considered returning to Waipuhia at once but it seemed pretty silly, as there was nothing unusual in my being alone at a hotel. And I wasn't Dexter's guest," she added. "It would all have been perfectly simple if he hadn't decided to complicate it, after I'd been there two days, by calling Helen, telling her that Muriel had had to leave and would she care to join me . . . I didn't know until after he'd phoned her, and then there seemed nothing I could do about it. I loathe lying," she concluded passionately, "and there I was, absurdly involved, for no reason . . ." Her voice faltered, ceased. It was, she knew, a very thin story, like the pattern for an embroidery before the threads have been filled in solid.

"I still don't see," began Fred helplessly. "What difference did it make if Mrs. Warren was or wasn't . . . and why would her husband . . .?" He shrugged, his bewildered eyes on his sister-in-law. Betsy said briskly:

"Don't try to make sense out of it, there isn't any. There was no reason why Lani shouldn't stay on at Kona if she wished, she's a perfectly free agent . . . and Mr. Warren's reasons for assembling an elaborate story will probably remain his own."

She rose and beckoned her brother-in-law. "Come in the house a moment, will you, I want to talk to you about Ah Hee," she said.

Ah Hee was the elderly Chinese cook, who kept a tight rein over the Honolulu kitchen of the Bruce menage.

"What's wrong with him?" demanded Fred, rising.

"I think he should go to Queens for examination," Betsy said, "he isn't well, and you know he abhors the very word 'doctor.' I've tried, heaven knows. But he won't listen to me. He will to you, he'll even go to the hospital willingly, if you say he must."

"Stubborn old . . ."

Their voices died away.

"Well," said Lani, "Aunt Betsy arranged that nicely. Please say whatever it is you want to say."

Jim crossed the *lanai* to stand beside her. He said:

"There isn't anything."

She had been angry, defiant, now she was near tears. She said:

"It's just as I told it. I believed Muriel Warren would be at Kona. She wasn't. I planned to return to Helen's at once. Then, it seemed silly — "

"No doubt," said Jim.

She said, "You don't — you can't trust me? Is that it?"

He said miserably:

"You told me you would not see him alone again. When you went to Kona you were as much in love with him as ever — you can't deny it."

"I don't deny it," she said. "That is, I mean — "

But he wouldn't let her finish. He said brusquely:

"Then what else is there to say?"

She couldn't say, "A great deal . . . I was in love with him then but I am no longer." She couldn't tell him, in the face of his quiet hostility, exactly what had happened that other starlit night. She said wearily:

"I don't understand why he telephoned Helen, made her believe Muriel had just left. He said it was to protect me."

"Well, wasn't it? And to protect himself?" he asked.

"No. It was . . . " How could she explain, a form of revenge, a fit of malice, a delight in involving her in a silly tissue of lies? She shrugged her shoulders. "You wouldn't understand," she said hopelessly.

"Frank was right," he said abruptly, "he was seeing Muriel Warren at the time she was supposed to be with you at Kona. He must

307

have been very much amused."

"Please Jim," she said "if you'd listen to me. It wasn't as you think."

"What does it matter what I think?" he asked violently.

"All right," she said, and like sudden fever anger rose to burn away her unhappiness. It made her feel better, the anger, stronger, alive, uncaring.

He said something under his breath, turned and went into the house.

Lani walked down the steps and out under the twisted old hau tree. She looked across the water, the dark shapes of rocks, the faint glimmer of starlight on the surf. She stood there for a long time and then went in, slowly, with reluctance. But there was no one visible, and she could go directly to her room.

She was standing at the mirror half undressed when Betsy knocked.

"May I come in?" she asked.

"Of course."

Betsy closed the door, carefully. She wore her gayest kimono but her small brown face was grave above the frivolity of cherry blossoms.

"Jim's gone back to Honolulu," she said.

"I thought so," said Lani evenly; "I heard a car drive away."

"Fred," said Betsy, "is in a swivet. Tell me,

308

what's come over you two infant idiots?"

"Nothing," answered Lani dully, "except that he doesn't believe me."

"Jim? He's a born fool, where women are concerned," his mother said vigorously. "I used to be delighted. I'm not any more. Nor am I trying to pry, Lani. I don't want you to tell me anything that you don't want me to know. But I thought I might help. You see, Jim's very much in love with you . . . I don't know how you feel toward him — "

"I don't either," said Lani honestly. "One moment I think . . . like tonight when he came down and I saw him again. I'd missed him so much. And then the next — "

"Sit down," said Betsy, and patted the smooth white bed.

Lani laid aside her hairbrush. She looked very young, almost childish in her negligible garments, her brushed dark hair cloudy about her face, and her unhappy gray eyes. She sat down beside the older woman. She said after a moment:

"I'd like to tell you. I wanted to tell Helen but she wouldn't let me. Not chapter and verse. She guessed, of course."

"Start at the beginning," suggested Betsy.

"There's nothing you can do," said Lani. "Promise me you won't try to influence Jim in any way . . . even if you do understand?"

"I promise," said Betsy. "It has to be of his own accord, doesn't it? Jim's like his father," she added, "stubborn, idealistic."

Lani said steadily:

"Almost a year ago in Washington I fell in love with Dexter Warren. When I met him I didn't know that he was married. I learned it, within a few hours, however."

She went on steadily . . . the whole unhappy story, sparing neither herself nor Dexter. When she reached the events of the night at Kona, her voice was uneven.

"I can't tell you what he said," she admitted, "it was — pretty degrading."

"Don't try," said Betsy, holding her hand tightly.

"Whatever he said, it was enough. I understood him then, and Muriel too and all the whole sordid business. And when in the morning he found me at the desk arranging for a car to take me back to Waipuhia, he told me he had telephoned Helen asking her to come down . . . under the impression that Muriel had only just left."

Betsy said slowly:

"That's what I still don't understand. Why would he do such a thing? It's utterly irrational."

Lani said:

"He wanted to involve me in a lie. He knew

310

it would be found out. He wanted to involve me further in a lot of explanations, each one sounding more ridiculous. If he hadn't called Helen, I would have gone back to Waipuhia and told Helen — and Jim too — that when I reached Kona I found Muriel wasn't there, so I stayed on a little while, and then decided to come home. Helen wouldn't have thought anything of it . . . even knowing what she did. And possibly I would have told her — everything that had happened, anyway. I don't suppose I would have told Jim," she said frankly.

Betsy was scowling. She said, "I could kill that man. And, of course, Jim would have." She looked up, tried to laugh. "I don't mean," she said, "that he would have killed him, but he certainly would have wanted to and who could blame him!"

She released Lani's hand, and put her arm around her.

"You know we love you?" she asked.

Lani said thoughtfully:

"Men are odd, aren't they? Jim loves me — so he doesn't trust me. Are they all like that?"

"I wouldn't know," said Betsy, "but you're both pretty young." She added, "I could straighten this out, I think . . . if you'd let me."

Lani shook her head.

"I'd rather you didn't. I — I don't know how I feel myself — it's all pretty mixed up. If you asked me — again — am I in love with Jim, I couldn't tell you. I thought I was at Kona, for a moment . . . once at the inn, once in a stuffy, crowded movie house — at Wai-puhia, before I left, and tonight, when he came down. I was — frightened. I didn't really believe it. I was even a little horrified, off with the old love, on with the new — but now I don't know at all. At the moment I don't even *like* him," she ended furiously.

"It's always like that, I think," said Betsy thoughtfully. "When you read about it, it's clear-cut enough . . . she loves me, she loves me not. Nothing in between, no doubts, no misgivings, no sudden hostility, enmity even. I was terribly in love with Jim's father. But I was in love with Fred first."

"Uncle Fred?"

Betsy nodded.

"He wouldn't look at me," she said rue-fully. "I thought I was the most miserable, the most misused . . . I'd grown up with them both; Fred was the younger brother. I was visiting here in Honolulu and he wouldn't even ask me for a dance. I wasn't much to look at," she admitted. "I never was. Then Fred went away to the mainland, and Big Jim came home, after his graduation from college.

I never thought of Fred again. It was just as well, because he was so hopelessly in love with your mother."

"My mother!" gasped Lani.

"Yes. Didn't you know? From the very first moment he saw her. She must have known, although I'd stake my life that he never told her. You see what a burden he's had to carry all these years," she added gently.

"Poor darling," said Lani slowly. The tears she hadn't been able to cry for herself were bright now in her eyes for Frederick Bruce.

"Yes. What was I saying? Oh, about Big Jim. I adored him, I would have let him walk on me, yet a week before our wedding I blew cold, I blew hot, I wasn't in love, I was in love, I didn't want to marry him, nothing could prevent me! I was at home at the time, at our old place in Maui . . . sometime you must go there with me . . . and when Jim had arrived for the wedding I was ready to run away. I did, three hours before the ceremony. I was supposed to be resting. But I sneaked away from the house, persuaded a startled stableman to saddle my horse, and rode into the hills. And there Jim was — running away too. I remember how we got off our horses, sat down and looked out over a green valley and told each other how scared we were. Then he began to laugh, and I stopped crying. And we rode down the trail quite openly, to the horror of my mother and the guests, and I whisked upstairs and into a tub and my wedding dress."

"And — lived happily forever after?"

"Forever after. Only forever wasn't long. When Big Jim died, Fred asked me to stay with him. You see, when Jim was transferred to the office here, we came to live with Fred. So I stayed on although there were a few good people who were a little shocked, and more who expected us to marry, eventually. But neither of us ever had any idea of that, Lani."

Lani said, "You're trying to tell me that everyone goes through these doubts and — "

"I wouldn't wonder," said Betsy. "Not your mother, not Alan. They were — different from most of us, I guess."

Lani said uneasily:

"But I was so *sure*, the first time."

"Too sure perhaps." Betsy rose. She ordered, "Get some sleep. And don't worry about Jim. I'll keep my hands off if you say so although I'm itching to get them on him and shake some kind of sense into him." She bent to kiss Lani. "It will come right, for both of you, one way or another. You'll see. If it was meant to be, it will be . . . if it wasn't, then you're well off, if he is my son and I adore him, and if you are close as a daughter to me,

314

Lani. I don't want either of you to have second best."

"Helen said that too, about Jim," murmured Lani, "and Johnny said something a little like it."

"They love him too," said his mother. "I hear Fred prowling around. He's frantic because Jim suddenly decided he had to get back to Honolulu, wouldn't stay over, must take the early plane tomorrow morning. Fred thinks he's crazy. I'll have to — "

"What?" asked Lani.

Betsy said:

"I'll tell him you've quarreled . . . he'll understand that much. He's practically forgotten the arrival of Mrs. Warren this evening. You see, it didn't mean anything to him . . . and even your explanation appeared unnecessary. I mean, Fred wouldn't need an explanation from you. You can do no wrong . . . you're Mary to him, and Alan . . . but you must understand that now."

Lani said:

"Jim — "

"Let him stew," said his mother, "as long as you've made up your mind that I'm not to interfere."

"You're dear," began Lani. To her horror her voice broke in a small, forlorn sob.

Betsy came back to her. She put her arms

around her swiftly. She said, "Cry if you want to — it can be a great help."

"I won't cry," said Lani fiercely, "I don't want to, it makes me feel awful. But you see, Aunt Betsy, he doesn't trust me, he's caught me in one lie — or at least subscribing to it, and he'll never trust me again."

"Then," said Jim's mother briskly, "he's more of a fool than I think he is." She patted Lani's shoulder with her small brown hand, very hard, very efficient. She said, "I hear Kazue outside. I'll tell her you've put yourself to bed. Try to sleep. There are some harmless tablets in the bathroom. Bromides. They wouldn't hurt you."

She pattered into the bathroom, brought water and the tablets, stood over Lani while she took them. She added, "Our friends next door are making the night hideous with revelry. Lucky you're on this side of the house."

The bedroom door closed after her and Lani went back to her mirror to finish brushing her hair. By the time she was ready for bed she was sleepy. She lay quiet, relaxing, listening to the sound of surf on beach and rocks, to the murmur of the wind. She tried to think, to be angry and frightened and unhappy and miserable all at once. But she was only drowsy. And after a while she slept.

Chapter 19

Whatever explanation Betsy offered her brother-in-law of Jim's unusual conduct and, the next morning, of Lani's shadowed eyes, it was sufficient. Frederick Bruce was the most incurious and least analytical of men. For many years his chief interest had lain in his work. Betsy Bruce and her husband fearing, after Alan Aldrich's death, that Frederick would isolate himself from companionship, had managed, deliberately, to keep his house full and to force him, by degrees, into some social activity. After Big Jim's death Betsy had set her little jaw and persisted in the same way of life, afraid that with his brother, as well as his closest friend, gone Frederick would evolve into a routine that would allow him little time for relaxation. It would have been easier for her, during the first years of her widowhood, to shut herself away from her friends, gregarious as she was by nature. But for Frederick's sake she did not.

He was unconscious of being managed. He

was a considerate, charming host, a courteous, welcome guest, and a loyal friend. His own rigid integrity set high standards but he was a singularly unsuspicious man and, except in business, accepted people at their face value. His few affections were deeply rooted, he was devoted to his brother's wife, and had Jim been his own son he could not have loved him more. And ever since he had first seen her in Washington, Lani had taken her place in his heart. He had loved her as a child, it was not difficult to go on loving her as if the years between had never been.

He abhorred matchmaking — meddling, he called it — but when Betsy had drawn his attention to Jim's obvious interest in Lani he had been delighted. He'd said, "It's too soon," and "It may not mean a thing," he'd cautioned Betsy not to interfere . . . and added, "Even if Jim is in love with her it doesn't mean that Lani gives a hoot for him."

He was being cautious from pure supersitition. It wasn't wise to want anything too much, he thought, so when Betsy offered her explanation of last night's events he was secretly pleased. A quarrel of such proportions that Jim rushed off without so much as by your leave, and Lani looking, next day, as if she'd been put through a wringer was a good sign, he believed. That the explanation was thin to transparency, once you brushed aside Betsy's covering blanket of words, didn't occur to him; he accepted it and that was all.

September was a superb month. The Hawaiian language has no word for weather. Now and then there was a Kona wind, the south wind, bringing rain, but it didn't last; there were always light rains on the mountains, but you'd ride into and out of them again, and you could always find a rainbow.

People came and went on the big white ships, hardly a boat day came that did not bring someone Lani knew, for a brief or a longer stay. Regatta Day arrived, the harbor was brilliant with activity, and Frederick grumbled because Jim hadn't managed to come over. He had not been in Honolulu since that night at the beach house. He had an excellent excuse, with Frank leaving.

Frank came, and stayed two days with the Bruces before he sailed. He took Frederick, Betsy and Lani to the Royal for dinner, and Lani was astonished at the change in him. His saturnine face was more open, more friendly than she had ever seen it, his whole attitude seemed altered.

Betsy had a headache and Frederick took her home. "You kids stay on and dance," he suggested. "Pete will come back and wait for you. Take your time."

The moon was slanting silver on the surf, and the palms sighing in the wind. They danced on the terrace, and presently went back to their table and watched the others. Frank said, "I'll miss it . . . I was thinking at the Waialae club last night; I'll be homesick a thousand times for the music and these special stars and the something you can't put into words no matter how you try, the something which means the Islands."

She asked, "Why are you leaving, then?"

"It's never been my place," he said; "I don't belong. There's something in me that fights it. It's no place for bitterness and resentment and distrust of oneself . . . at least not for me."

"Frank, what will you do?"

"What I never expected to be able to do," he answered: "buy a little place, work it, settle down with half a dozen dogs and as many ponies, catch up on my reading, vegetate. You see, Lani, while I've drawn a good salary for a number of years, I haven't bothered to save. There didn't seem much sense in it. Then a stupid old cousin dies, a man I haven't seen in twenty years, and they discover that I'm his only living relative. Funny, isn't it? If it had happened years ago it might have rescued — I don't know," he said, "perhaps I'm wrong."

She knew what he meant. She said:

"A marriage saved by money — perhaps it wasn't worth saving."

He said, "You're very young. It would have been good enough for me."

"You'll be lonely," she said, "on the mainland."

"I'm used to loneliness. This will be a different kind. Perhaps I won't always be," he said, smiling, "perhaps I'll find some pleasant, companionable woman, not too hard on the eyes, who won't mind pipe smoke, who likes dogs and oranges. I wish," he added suddenly, "that it might have been you."

Lani smiled. She said, "That's nice of you, Frank."

"I mean it. I have something to offer a woman now . . . or have I? Something material, at any rate. But it could never have been you. You look especially delectable tonight, I like that dress — what color is it?"

"Aquamarine."

"That's the name of the stones in your earrings and necklace, isn't it? The water you see looking down into the coral gardens looks that color. And your skin looks like the pikake lei you're wearing, if it had been dipped in gold dust."

She said:

"That's a very pretty speech."

"You weren't for me," he said, "and I wasn't for you. You attracted me violently, you'd attract any man, but I liked you well enough not to —" He broke off. "Maybe there'll be a woman sometime who will understand that I can give her what is probably the best any man can offer — security, companionship, laughter, affection — yet can't give her what she really wants. The capacity left me long ago."

"I'm sorry, Frank," she said gently.

"So am I. Perhaps there's a young widow somewhere," he said, trying to smile, "who'd be willing to take — and give — second best. Lani, I haven't spoken of this to anyone . . . but you will understand, I think . . . I learned shortly before the word of the legacy reached me that my wife is dead. She left a child, a boy. I hadn't told you that."

"Oh, Frank," she said pitifully.

"Funny, isn't it?" he demanded. "I always wanted children. But she didn't. When I reach the mainland I'm going to see the boy, see if he'll come with me."

"But his father," said Lani, appalled. "You can't take the child from his father, you have no claim."

"He didn't marry her after I divorced her," said Frank stonily. "I've never spoken of that either. The people here — who didn't know

322

us — didn't learn that, and there was no point in telling them. He deserted her, after a year and a half. She wrote, asking me to take her back. The letter was a long time in reaching me. When it did I answered, I said, 'Not if you come crawling to me on your hands and knees' . . . I suppose you blame me, Lani."

She said, troubled:

"How can I? Most men would have done just as you did. It would take a big man, a man head and shoulders above the common herd to — "

"Sure. And I wasn't . . . lost, bitter, ingrown. Well, that's that. She went to Canada, where she had relatives. The boy was assumed to be mine. That's why I know I'll have no difficulty claiming him. She left enough money to look after him, since her death. The relatives were willing to keep him for a consideration. They wanted, of course, to ship him right out here . . . but I said that wouldn't be feasible. When the word of the legacy came I started negotiations with them through my lawyer, here."

She said, after a moment:

"You're being very generous."

"No. You see, I've been kidding myself, all along. No matter what people here have told you, it was my fault. We won't go into that, it isn't a very pretty story. When she wrote me,

I had my chance . . . and I wanted her so much. But I couldn't lose face, I thought, I couldn't forget my mean little revenge, and I wasn't sure of myself, whether or not I could endure getting up and lying down with a ghost."

"Things will work out for you," she said, after a moment, "I'm sure of it."

"Your eyes shine," he said absently. "You have the strangest eyes. Lani, what are you going to do about Jim?"

The slow color rose, and for a moment she could not speak. So many people had asked her that. Helen, Johnny, Betsy . . .

He added, "It's not just curiosity. We've had our battles, Jim and I, but I speak with authority when I say he's one of the best."

She said:

"We've had a misunderstanding."

"I know."

Her eyes widened. She said, faltering:

"Has Jim — ?"

"Of course not. How little you know him, after all! I'm to blame, in a way. I've done you a bad turn, Lani. I didn't mean to, I never thought — "

"Done me a bad turn?" she repeated, puzzled.

"Muriel Warren. I told you she was like my wife, remember? She is, superficially. She looks very like her, she is very like the woman my wife probably would have become if . . . if he had stayed with her, perhaps, if he had married her. He was not unlike Muriel Warren's husband, Lani."

"What happened to him?" she asked, diverted from her own problem.

Frank shrugged.

"God knows. I had years of imagining how it would be when I met him again, what I would do. Now, it doesn't seem to matter so much. Whatever I could do wouldn't undo all the old misery. But that's beside the point. What matters is the fact that the women I've known — since — they've been a form of revenge too. Most of them were the type that could take it, so I have no great remorse. There was an edge of irony in my meeting Muriel Warren. She is a perfectly worthy opponent, I might add; no one need ever be sorry for her."

Lani said:

"You shouldn't tell me this, Frank."

"No. But, then, I haven't any standards," he reminded her. "Muriel left Kona to meet me in Honolulu. I knew that she hadn't been there with you. I said nothing. I figured, possibly, I had done you a favor, as you were in love with her husband. I assumed that, by the way. Muriel talks too much."

Lani said after a moment:

"I was in love with him, Frank. I thought I'd never get over it — when I saw him again I was sure I never would. But at Kona — "

"You changed your mind? Then perhaps," he said, smiling, "I did do you a favor, after all, no matter what misunderstandings arose from the situation. They can be cleared away."

"How?"

He said gently:

"If you'll forget your pride. That's part of it, isn't it? Two stubborn kids, burdened with something they call pride."

She said involuntarily:

"How can I? Jim thinks — "

"Nonsense!" said Frank shortly. "He hasn't that sort of mind. He thinks you lied to him. That's what sticks. He doesn't think beyond that. I would, in his place. I'm not like Jim. None of this has been discussed between us but you'll remember that when I said I'd seen Muriel in Honolulu, he jumped me immediately and said she'd been with you at Kona. I can put two and two together. So, he thinks you lied, he thinks you're still in love with Warren and that's all there is to it. It shouldn't be hard to convince him that he's wrong."

She said, "I'll try."

"Good. I wonder if you really — " He leaned across the table and looked at her. He smiled. "You do," he said, "but you're afraid of it, afraid to admit it even to yourself."

"Perhaps."

"Get over it," he advised. "I wish I'd known enough to, years ago." He looked over the terrace to the sea. "Music's stopped," he said, "time to go. This town clings to early closing. Must have seemed odd to you at first."

"I liked it," she said, smiling.

He said, beckoning their waiter:

"Think Pete can see you safely home?"

"Well, of course," she answered. "Aren't you coming?"

"Later. Mrs. Bruce kindly provided me with a key. I've a date," he explained calmly. "Rude of me, isn't it?"

"Very, but you're like that." She rose and stood there a moment, looking at him. "Frank," she said, "you're not seeing Muriel Warren tonight in order to — ?"

"Don't worry," he told her instantly, "if I'm seeing her, it is with no charitable motive." He grinned, without humor.

She said, "But she's at her beach house."

"That's right," he agreed. "I've a car, waiting. Tomorrow I sail. Shall we say that I am paying farewell calls tonight?"

They walked up the steps and through the lounge, where the ancient Chinese familiar to most of Honolulu was emptying ash trays. They went to the lobby, past the flower stand, the magazine stand, the shops, the piles of coconuts, and out to the driveway. Pete was waiting first in line and drew up with a flourish and a broad, white-toothed smile.

A carful of Navy officers had just pulled away, a pretty girl and a good-looking boy sat on a bench near by waiting for their car. Somewhere in the grounds someone was playing a ukulele and singing.

"I'll miss it," said Frank; "and damn it, I don't want to."

He put Lani in the car. "Good night," he said; "see you tomorrow."

He stood watching her drive away, spoke to Joe, the big doorman, and waited for his car, his hands in his pockets, staring absently across the driveway. The pretty girl nudged her escort.

"Fascinating-looking man," she said, in a perfectly audible voice.

"Probably a heel," remarked her companion glumly. Tomorrow he would sail for the mainland, his brief holiday over. This girl, whom he had met on the boat, was staying until the next cruise ship — she would go to New Zealand and Australia, forget all about him.

"I don't care," she said stoutly, "I like disagreeable, bored-looking men, they're so romantic."

She was seventeen.

Frank heard and grinned, dourly. A romantic heel, eh? Well, possibly.

His car came, he drove away, in the direction of the Pali and the Warren beach house.

He had plenty of time to think during the long drive. He thought, I must be going soft — adopting a kid who isn't mine.

He wasn't sure. That was the irony of the situation. The woman who had been his wife wasn't sure either, or so she had sworn, in the desperate and frantic letter she had written him after her lover had left her. The little boy had been born eight months after she had run away from Frank Davidson, in an impersonal hospital in a city strange to her. She was "Mrs. Lenord" on the hospital records, the devoted Mr. Lenord had come to see her every day and paid her bills punctually. Lenord wasn't the man's name, never had been. Yet as Mr. and Mrs. Lenord they had lived in the bleak northern city until the day he failed to come home. By that time the divorce had gone through, and she was waiting to go away with him, and the baby. He had promised to marry her, to take her to Europe, to live with her there happily forever after.

Frank Davidson was thinking of this as he drove over the dark, wind-swept Pali and looked across the green plains and gardens, clothed in night, to the mobile sea. The blond girl he had married, with the narrow brown eyes and the trick of sudden husky laughter, hadn't been very brave . . . afraid of the simplest things, snakes and mice, sudden shadows on the ceiling, and dark streets. She must have known many dark streets before she reached the darkest of them all, the one on which she could never retrace her steps.

The man had given her money . . . to see her and the boy through. He had even written, "Perhaps Davidson will take you back, he was always besotted about you. And the boy's no problem, you can tell him he is his — Myself, I've never been sure!"

She'd written all that to Frank, she had sent him the other man's letter.

He'd heard again, after her death. The Canadian relatives were distant, almost unknown to her. They had accepted her explanation, an unhappy marriage, a divorce before the birth of her son. They had taken her in and she had paid her way. A short way, when you considered everything.

He thought, If the boy is mine . . .

What difference did it make? The boy was hers, at all events, growing up all these years, in alien surroundings, with people only distantly of his blood. Did it matter whose child? A *child*, that was all. A child who needed the important, intangible things ... not just a decent bed, three meals a day, and schooling.

Frank unclenched his hands, they were stiff and ached. He thought, Can I give him what he needs, can I make it up to him?

Chapter 20

The car stopped at Muriel's beach house. Frank told the driver to wait and went to the door. Muriel opened it and he looked at her coolly.

Velvet slacks, a lace blouse ruffled at throat and wrists like a chevalier's. Her figure was beautiful, her fair hair, softly curled, flattered her enormously. Her eyes were bright and her lips a soft carmine. She cried, "I've been waiting and waiting!"

She drew him into the house and shut the door. Beyond the enormous living room was a great *lanai*, with hurricane candles shielded by etched-glass shades and a number of deep chairs and couches, facing the sea. She murmured:

"I sent the servants away."

He sat down, lit a cigarette, reached for the decanter near by, dropped squares of ice in a glass.

"You were sure I'd come?"

"Of course. Frank, must you leave the Islands?"

"Tomorrow, my dear."

He raised his glass and smiled at her over it. Her breath caught. She was alive, as she had not been for years. All the years, all the men — she could not recall them, their faces, even their names, but this was the first man to puzzle her, hold her interest. That night at the Roberts ranch when she had first seen him, his cold curious eyes on her, she had known. A brutal, casual man who made no pretense, who did not say the usual things, false or true, who made her remember again the uncertainty, the unhappiness of youth.

"Frank?"

Her hand was on his arm. He looked at it with detachment. A lovely hand, quite useless.

She said:

"You could stay — "

"My dear girl, not a minute longer. I've earned my freedom."

"Have you decided where you are going?"

"Southern California . . . I think."

She said thoughtfully:

"I can break this lease . . . in a month, two months. Perhaps if I spent next winter in Pasadena . . .?"

He said carelessly:

"That would be nice. By then I'll have a place, you must come see us."

"Us?"

"My son and me."

Muriel's eyes widened.

"A son?" she said incredulously.

"Why not? He remained with my wife, of course, but she died not long ago. It did not seem feasible to have him join me, but now I am free to join him."

Muriel began to laugh.

"It's crazy," she said, "to think of you as a family man."

"Yes, isn't it?" he agreed, smiling. He looked at her then gravely. She was so like the woman he had loved, the woman whose memory he still loved. Hair and eyes, figure, short upper lip. Yet very unlike. She was saying:

"You've never told me about your wife."

"There's nothing to tell," he said harshly.

Nothing. The Renfews had heard nothing about her, nor had Muriel Warren.

He added:

"I haven't long, Muriel. And there's something I want to ask you."

"You haven't long?" she repeated. "But — "

"You didn't expect that I'd stay here, did you?"

Her lips tightened, the color rose under her fair skin. She said:

"Why the sudden scruples?"

"Never mind." He leaned back, laughed a little. He said curiously, "You and Warren understand each other don't you? Have you ever considered divorcing him?"

She was very close to him, he had but to reach out his hand.

"No," she said, "never. Or, not until now . . . if . . . I have a good deal of money, Frank. We could be happy, I think."

He said, "He could divorce you a hundred times over."

"That's not a very gallant speech," she retorted. "Well — so what? He doesn't want to — he's secure this way."

"Quite. Am I to understand you would consider divorcing him — for me?"

She said quickly, "It wouldn't be difficult — especially now."

"For me?" he repeated. "Nothing to offer: neither money, as you count money, nor position. An orange grove in California . . . a hard-working man, and a little boy. I doubt it, Muriel, very much."

She argued, "But that's nonsense. Why — an orange grove? We could travel, the boy would be in school."

He said, almost gently:

"I think you would regret it. You would be giving up too much."

She said unhappily:

"I'm in love with you, Frank."

He hadn't meant that to happen. He hadn't

thought that it would happen. He'd met a woman who reminded him of someone else and his impulse had been to strike out, to hurt her as he himself had been hurt. He'd met a man who had reminded him of another man and his impulse had been to hurt him too. Now that was over.

He said, "I sail tomorrow. I'll let you know where I am. You must take time to think, to make up your mind. It might be all right at first. But you'd tire very soon. Because I meant that about the orange grove and the work, and the boy will remain with me, Muriel."

The slow, unusual tears slid down her face. This frightened her, for she never cried, she hadn't in years. Tears were fatal to her skin, this disrupting emotion was fatal also.

She said, "You don't understand. I've had such a rotten time. I was so much in love with him, you see, but from the moment we were married, almost — " She took the handkerchief Davidson gave her. "After a while I grew hardened, I no longer cared. It was almost worse than caring," she said.

"Yes, I know," he told her.

He was unaccountably sorry for her. But he could not take her in his arms, make promises he would not keep. He did not love her, and never would. She was not the woman for him, the companionable woman who might exist somewhere, who would heal his hurts and make a human being of him again, who would hold out her arms to another woman's son.

And there was something he must do, he reminded himself, even if it meant lying a little longer.

He said:

"Don't cry — please. Time will pass, quickly. I'll write you, and then, next winter . . . "

She nodded, trying to smile.

"Will you do something for me?" he asked her.

"Of course," she said, "anything. You know that."

"It's about Lani Aldrich."

"Lani? But — "

He said, "You probably meant no harm. This Kona business. But, you see, she's in love, Muriel."

"Of course. With Dex." Muriel shrugged her shoulders. "I wonder if he'll marry her . . . after . . . I don't think so. She's young, inexperienced, she could never hold him." She thought, If I couldn't, how could she?

"She's not in love with Warren," he said quietly, "but with Jim Bruce. They're nice kids. He has the wrong idea about that little episode at Kona. You can set it straight."

"Wrong idea?" demanded Muriel, astonished. "But the other night Jim Bruce told me that he and Mrs. Gaines had been there with Lani . . . I didn't know what it was all about. I talked to Lani and Dex by telephone while they were there and they never mentioned anyone else."

He explained briefly. When he had finished, he said, "You see? There was no reason for Warren to call Mrs. Gaines or to tell her that you had only just left the inn. No one would look below the surface situation — until it became complicated by a lie, which was certain to be found out. Oh, I've no doubt that Jim would have been properly jealous — But he knows Lani . . . and she could have explained. Not, however, after your astonishing husband had amused himself at her expense."

Muriel said, "That's very like Dex."

"You're to blame too," he told her; "you asked the girl to join you there, you left deliberately."

"To see you," she reminded him.

"Perhaps. But I doubt if you had any intention of staying."

"I thought I was doing her a kindness," she murmured.

"You thought nothing of the kind. I like those kids, Muriel. I feel implicated, myself. You can set it straight."

"How?" she demanded.

"You can sit down at your desk and write me a letter. You can tell me you are sorry I'm leaving. You can thank me for the flowers I didn't send you. Any excuse. You can say that you've heard that there has been some gossip about your trip to Kona. And that you want my advice as you'd like to clear things up. You can explain that you asked Lani to go with you or to join you there, but you were called back to Honolulu before her arrival and that, for reasons which you do not understand, your husband made an elaborate and unnecessary effort to convince Mrs. Gaines that you'd been there all along."

She said:

"But the other night, at their beach house, I saw Jim Bruce and his people and Lani. I said then I was sorry I hadn't been able to stay on while Lani was at Kona."

"Why?"

"No reason," she said uncomfortably. "I didn't dream that Dex had — "

"Don't lie," he said. "You knew exactly what Warren said and did. You did it deliberately."

She said sullenly, "It was amusing. I hadn't the slightest idea that Lani and Jim Bruce — I wanted to pay her back."

"For what?"

She was silent.

He said, after a moment, "All right. You can say in the letter that when you talked to Lani the other night you had no idea that your husband had invented the story . . . and you can add that it was probably pique on his part because he and Lani had quarreled."

She cried, "Who'd believe all that?"

"I don't know," said Frank. "What matters is that Jim should know that Lani had no part in that idiotic deception but was forced into the situation and that her interest in Warren, whatever it once was, amounts to double zero at the moment . . . and if you're thinking of using her as a lever for this contemplated divorce, forget it . . . and me along with it."

She said, after a moment:

"You make a compelling champion. Do you really mean that she's no longer interested in Dex?"

"She's in love with Jim Bruce, I tell you."

Muriel shook her head.

"It's beyond me," she said. "That kid! After Dex." She laughed shortly. She said, "Well, never mind, there have been other women."

He said, appalled, forgetting that he had ever been sorry for her:

"So, it *was* deliberate. You thought, if you

divorced Warren you could name — ?"

She said:

"What of it? I was going to Honolulu to meet you. It's always well to have a weapon in case — "

"In case you're found out?"

"Why not?" she asked. "This is all ridiculous, but since you've set your heart on it — "

She rose and went indoors to the desk. Frank stood beside her, smoking, dictating. She filled the pages with her angular writing, blotted and gave them to him. He read, smiling. He said, "This is a very nice apology for a wandering husband who has had his comeuppance."

"Satisfied?" she said. "I can't imagine you in the role of the dove of peace."

He looked much more like a bird of prey. He said, putting the letter in his pocket:

"Thanks. And now I must get back to Honolulu."

She went with him to the door, and put her arms around his neck and clung to him. She said, "I'll see you soon?"

He kissed her. "Of course," he promised.

He waved from the car and she waved back, standing there, looking small, somehow, and forlorn. He told himself as the car dove away and back to Honolulu, That's over.

He would never see her again. He doubted

that she would suffer long, if at all. His appeal for her had been his indifference, and such women were not important.

Just before he sailed he posted Muriel's letter to Jim, with a covering scrawl. He wrote, "Good-bye, old-timer . . . we've had some very fine days together, in peace and war. I was never a gentleman, as you know, so I've no hesitation in sending you a letter I recently received from a lady. I wish you'd read it. And don't be more of a damned fool than you can help."

Frederick Bruce was at the boat to say good-bye, with Betsy, Lani, and a dozen more. They were all crowded into the room, laughing and talking, when the door opened and Jim Bruce looked in. "Hello, gang," he said cheerfully.

Betsy's little jaw dropped. Frederick rose to smite his nephew on the shoulder. Lani, standing by one of the portholes, paled a little. Jim did not look at her. He said:

"Couldn't let you go without a send-off, Frank. Drove to Hilo this morning, after talking to Owen Mackaye. He'd hired a plane to fly over and see his brother off, so he took me along. He'll come in presently."

Frank said, "I sent you a letter this morning . . . it's rather important."

"Brought you something," said Jim, paying

342

no attention. He opened the door and shouted. A steward staggered in with an enormous basket of mangoes, pineapples, papaias, flowers, macadamia nuts, candy. . . .

"You'll have to get rid of the fruit before you land," said Jim, grinning, "there's a bottle of champagne in there somewhere."

Everyone was talking at once, again. Jim went over to stand by Lani. He said quietly:

"It was an excuse, of course. First I've something to do for Bill. I'll be up at the house tonight. I want to talk to you."

She nodded, her heart pounding so that she could not trust herself to speak.

The bugle blew. "All ashore that's going ashore! All ashore — "

Presently they were going down the gangplank, and standing on the dock, looking up. The bright confetti ribbons streamed down the white flanks of the ship, the band was playing. Frank leaned over the railing of A Deck, waving to them. He shouted, "Jim!"

"What?"

"Don't forget my letter."

"Let's not wait till it sails," said Betsy; "makes me feel blue. Jim, where are you off to now?"

"Business. Office with Uncle Fred. Errands for Bill." He explained with his arms around her that he had to drive out to one of

343

the big Oahu plantations to look at an innovation in the mill. He'd be back.

He reached the Bruce house in time to change for dinner. His mother knocked on his door and came in.

Jim, with a towel around him, protested, "Hey, woman, I'm not decent."

"Skip it," said his mother. "Fred's going out to dinner . . . did he tell you?"

"Sure, why?"

Betsy grinned at him. She said, "I think I feel another headache coming on — or would you rather I didn't?"

He hugged her. "Could you discover it, right after dinner? Otherwise . . . Well, it isn't easy to make idle conversation over the table — is it? — in the circumstances."

Betsy made the conversation. Lani said little, ate less. Jim talked in violent spurts or lapsed into silence. After coffee, Betsy said faintly that she felt one of her headaches was coming on, no, there's nothing Lani could do — and departed, with a histrionic hand to her temple.

The table was cleared, the servants had gone. Jim rose and went to sit beside Lani in the big canvas swing. He said:

"I didn't come to see Frank off."

"No?"

"I came to see you. Lani, can you forgive me?"

She said, low, "I'm not angry, Jim, any more."

He said, "I've had time to think . . . I'm the damnedest fool. There's just one thing I'm going to ask you and you needn't answer if you don't want to. I asked you once before, remember? Are you — still in love with Warren?"

"No," she said. "I tried to tell you the other night."

"That's all I want to know. Lani, can we begin again?"

She said, "If you hadn't come, Jim, I was going to go to Waipuhia and make you listen. I haven't any pride now. I want things to be — clear between us, always."

He said, "I know. Nothing you've done, or haven't done, matters. Nothing matters but you. I love you so much, darling. I'm not asking you to consider that. I know it's too soon."

She said, after a moment:

"If it hadn't been for that stupid lie — "

Jim said, "I had no excuse whatever. No matter what was said, no matter what anyone else might think, I should have had ordinary common sense. Because I love you, because I know you, and knowing you I shouldn't have had one moment of doubt. I should have tried to be of some small help to you instead."

She said, "Let me tell you just what happened at Kona. I can now."

He was very quiet while she told him, sparing neither Dexter nor Muriel nor, least of all, herself. She told it baldly, almost brutally. When she had finished he said slowly:

"It's a good thing he's back on the mainland."

She said:

"It was all very silly. Nothing — big or important. Just a stupid girl trying to grope her way out of the dark, a drunken man, a malicious woman and a lie."

He said:

"I'm glad — on my knees — that you don't love him, Lani. But even if you did, I could go on waiting."

She said, "I'll always love you for saying that."

He put out his arms and she went into them with a troubled sigh, as if she had come home the long way. He kissed her gently, with deep tenderness. He wanted no more, no less, at that moment. Nor did she. This was peace, and not passion. There would be time for the fire and the dream, the flame and the blinding rapture . . . but not now.

She said, after a while:

"Next week I was going house hunting with Aunt Betsy. I wanted a little house, in the hills, with Kazue to look after me."

He asked:

"I'm to wait?"

"I'd like it that way," she told him. "You'd be in Honolulu occasionally, I'd go to stay with Helen . . . and we'd both be sure."

He said, half ruefully:

"All the way over I planned that if, by some wild, wonderful miracle you loved me, after all, I'd make you marry me — tomorrow . . . next week."

She said gently:

"I want the conventional things: a ring, Jim, and a notice in the paper, in the spring, when the shower trees are just coming out, a wedding, here in Uncle Fred's garden . . . I want time to think and be grateful, time to write you silly little letters by every air mail, time to be myself again, before I can be yours. I wonder if you understand that?"

He said, "I understand," and kissed her. This time she drew away, with her breathing disturbed and her eyes shining. He said, after a moment, "I can wait."

She touched his hard brown cheek. "And I'll be happy at Waipuhia — forever, if you're there, Jim."

He drew her to her feet, held her close for a moment.

"Let's run upstairs and bang down Betsy's

door and tell her. She won't hear of any house in the hills now. You'll have to stay here and take her shopping. She'll want to come to Waipuhia with you and look over the house. As Frank was a bachelor, he and I shared one. It isn't a bad house, and perhaps the company would lift its face for us . . . commensurately with the importance of the assistant manager and his beautiful wife."

"Aunt Betsy has a headache," began Lani doubtfully, "I hate to — "

"Nonsense. She had an attack of tact, that was all. And we'll all wait up till Uncle Fred comes home. I've got to get back tomorrow, darling, the early plane."

She asked, "You'll write?"

"Every day."

They were going up the stairs, hand in hand, they had reached the turn, and he stopped there to take her in his arms again. She said, half laughing, "Look out, Jim, for heaven's sake, we'll break our necks."

"Speaking of letters," he said, as they went on and stopped by Betsy's door, "funny, Frank writing me. I wonder what was on his mind?"

"I can't imagine." She sighed. "I like him, Jim . . . and I'm so sorry for him."

"Sorry for Frank? We'll discuss that later. Whatever it is," he added, "in the letter, I mean, it couldn't have been very important, it will keep."

He bent to kiss her cheek lightly, and then battered violently on the door.

"Let us in, Betsy," he demanded, "we're practically inarticulate with tidings."

The door opened and Betsy, looking from one to the other, held out her arms to them both. The door closed, and the hall was empty. A gardenia, fallen from Lani's hair, lay on the stair, at the turn.

Later they stood together on the *lanai* opening from Betsy's bedroom. A destroyer was standing out to sea, and from its decks the men must be looking at Diamond Head, crouching and watchful, her feet in the enchanted surf, her protective bulk massive in the night, signifying her eternal vigil.

Betsy said softly:

"Look — a ship, on the horizon."

Lani put her arm through Jim's, a quick, close gesture. She could hear singing, far away, she could smell flowers and warm earth . . . the melody that is Hawaii, the fragrance that is hers alone. She asked, looking up to the dark velvet sky:

"Do you remember, Jim, at Johnny's ranch? We were out on the steps and you quoted Rupert Brooke . . ."

" 'And new stars burn,' " he said.

"New stars," said Lani. . . .

THORNDIKE-MAGNA hopes you have enjoyed this Large Print book. All our Large Print titles are designed for easy reading, and all our books are made to last. Other Thorndike Press or Magna Print books are available at your library, through selected bookstores, or directly from the publishers. For more information about current and upcoming titles, please call or mail your name and address to:

THORNDIKE PRESS
P.O. Box 159
Thorndike, Maine 04986
(800) 223-6121
(207) 948-2962 (in Maine and Canada call collect)

or in the United Kingdom:

MAGNA PRINT BOOKS
Long Preston, Near Skipton
North Yorkshire,
England BD23 4ND
(07294) 225

There is no obligation, of course.